STUMPTOWN SPIRITS

LEGEND TRIPPING, BOOK ONE

E.J. RUSSELL

Stumptown Spirits

Cover art: Natasha Snow Designs, https://natashasnow.com
Edited by Carole-ann Galloway and Meg DesCamp

ISBN: 978-1-947033-53-5

First edition
May, 2016
Second edition
March, 2023

Contact information:
ejr@ejrussell.com

STUMPTOWN SPIRITS

LEGEND TRIPPING, BOOK ONE

E.J. RUSSELL

For Jim, Hana, Ross, and Nick.

Because.

Legend tripping definition:

"… to go or participate on a quest or adventure for something which has defined a mystery or legend… not verified or explained by science. These legends are cryptids… the paranormal… extraterrestrials… and lost treasures and places of wonder."
—Robert Robinson
http://legendtrippersofamerica.blogspot.com

"… an organized journey to an isolated area to test the bravery of the group when faced with supernatural phenomena. The trip experience involves the telling of appropriate legends… Sites include cemeteries, tunnels, deserted and "haunted" houses, and remote lanes and bridges."
—Gail De Vos
Tales, Rumors, and Gossip

CHAPTER ONE

The lobby of Portland's Vaughn Street Hotel seethed like a skirmish between rival armies: the hotel staff versus the invading Hollywood barbarians. Judging by the glassy stares of Team Hotel, the TV production crew was winning this round.

"Coming through."

"Sorry." Riley Morrel dodged one of the other production assistants barreling through the doors with a giant box of cables in her arms, and glanced down at his own empty hands. *Everyone knows what to do except me.*

Sure, Riley wore the show uniform—a black North Face jacket with the *Haunted to the Max* logo blazoned across the back in jagged neon-green letters—but he secretly identified more with the beleaguered hotel employees. Ever since his best friend, Julie, the show's unit production manager, had browbeaten him onto the crew, he'd been in a perpetual state of *WTF.*

Today, though, was a triple-header of *F.* The equivalent of Cerberus simultaneously slobbering down his neck, growling in his ear, and nipping at his ass. Because after almost five months on staff, today marked his first time on location with the show, the first time the showrunner had agreed to film one of his story treatments, and his first time back in Oregon since Julie had rescued him from his spectacular crash and burn.

At the moment, Julie was standing at the concierge's desk, scowling at her cell phone, the thwack of her ever-present clipboard against her thigh audible from across the lobby.

She met Riley's gaze through the shifting chaos of *HttM* staff jockeying overladen luggage carts, hand trucks stacked with production equipment, and armfuls of carryout Thai food, and her eyes narrowed.

Uh-oh. *Cue the emergency broadcast alarms.* Riley knew that look, although in the ten-plus years of their friendship, it had never been directed at him before. He ran a quick conscience check, but couldn't come up with any reason he'd be on her shit-radar. Nevertheless, he needed a diversion, or failing that, a barricade. *Empty hands won't cut it.*

He intercepted one of the grips passing with a luggage cart stacked with black nylon company duffels. "Hey, Wes. I've got this. Why don't you take a break?"

Wes grinned and wiped the sweat off his forehead with his bandana. "Appreciate it, man. Pad Thai and microbrew are calling my name."

Riley angled the cart until it blocked him from his dearest friend in the world, now charging toward him like a Valkyrie on meth.

Julie executed a neat end run around his luggage fortress and backed him into a corner between a faux-marble column and an aquarium with a single morose betta.

"Logan."

Riley blinked, gaping as if he belonged in the water alongside the fish. "What?" Julie never mentioned his ex-boyfriend's name without adding at least a pair of profane epithets.

"Logan, that dickhead douche-rocket. He's from Portland."

"So are a lot of people. Nearly three-quarters of a million within the city limits. Two and a half million if you count the surrounding counties that are part of the designated metro area and if you include—"

"Don't try to blind me with statistics. Explain this."

She thrust her cell phone at his face, so close that Riley had to rear back and adjust his glasses in order to focus on the screen. His heart dive-bombed the floor. Logan, behind a bar, silhouetted against shelves of liquor. In the harsh downlight, his forearms, decorated with Celtic ink, looked exactly as sculpted as Riley remembered, and his tight white T-shirt seemed to glow.

Riley swallowed against the sneaker wave of want and loss. "He's a bartender. So?"

"I know that, doofus. But this particular bar is here." She sliced the air with her cell phone as if it were a battle ax. "In Portland. This picture was taken last night."

His heart leaped and dropped again. God, in his determination to put Logan out of his mind, he'd missed the obvious. Logan was a native Portlander. Most of the people he knew were here, so it was natural he'd return. But when they'd met, Logan had been heading south, away from Portland, and Riley had assumed he'd continued in the same direction after his bolt.

"How did you find him?"

"Do *not* doubt my superpowers. Remember I herd Max Stone for a living." She whirled and pointed at two of the hotel's bellhops who were unwisely approaching the abandoned luggage cart. "Don't touch that," she barked, and they bounded away like frightened deer.

Okay. Wrong question. "Jules, why did you bother to look?" Although Riley had been tempted, he'd never given in.

Her forehead bunched, brows drawing together. "Somebody has to watch out for you."

"I can take care of myself." He didn't need Julie monitoring his emotional temperature 24-7. Edging past her, he grabbed the cart and pushed it behind a pair of couches, out of the main flow of traffic.

She dogged his heels. "Right. You were doing so well."

He scowled at his feet and kicked the cart's wheel. "You invented this job for me, didn't you? Out of pity."

"No, doofus." She blocked his second kick with the toe of her Doc Martens. "I got you the job out of self-interest. Having a real folklorist on the crew, vetting the stories, is bound to jack up our credibility."

He slanted a glance at her from under his bangs. "Not to mention the ratings."

"Why else would we *need* credibility?"

"Maybe you should shanghai a real folklorist, then."

"You're real. You're realer than anyone I know."

"No official credentials though." Riley ducked his head and pretended to steady the teetering mound of duffels, the hollow yawning in his belly as sharp and fresh as it had been five months ago when Logan had split with no explanation.

"If you hadn't withdrawn from school—" She slapped her clipboard against her leg. "I will *never* forgive that shithead dick-weasel. He couldn't wait one more week to punch his asshole card? One final. That's all you had left."

"Don't forget the thesis. They kind of insist on that before they'll give you a master's." He shrugged. "No degree, no authority."

"Bullshit. Close enough for Hollywood." Her lips firmed into a hard line, and in the draft from the open lobby doors, tendrils of blond hair that had escaped from her ponytail writhed like Medusa's unfortunate hairdo. "Damn it. Now I'm sorry I mentioned the fuck-bucket—"

"Jules." He caught her wrist. "Enough."

"Oh, fine." He let go, and she took a deep breath. "Promise me you'll stay away from him?"

Until that instant, Riley would have claimed nothing could force him to face Logan again, to set himself up for another emotional maelstrom when he hadn't climbed out of the first one yet. But as if Julie's words had lit a fire in his belly, he knew he had to do it. *It's your chance to find out* why.

"I—"

"Hey, Julie." Scott, their showrunner, beckoned to Julie from the registration desk. "Can you sort out my reservation? They've got me in a single, not a suite."

"Be right there." She pointed one long finger at Riley's nose. "We're not done." She zoomed off.

Riley sank down on the back of a sofa. He'd tricked himself into not thinking about the night before Logan disappeared by focusing on the hurt and anger he'd felt afterward. Hurt and anger were easier to handle than the memory of how ridiculously happy he'd been.

When he'd come in from teaching his last TA session, Riley had seen the DVD of *Help!* sitting on top of the TV, and he'd been sure this would be The Night. Not only was the movie one of his favorites, but it had a theme.

A ring. The perfect lead-in to a proposal.

He'd expected the two white-gold bands he'd spotted a couple of weeks earlier while rummaging in Logan's T-shirt drawer to make an appearance, maybe over dessert. He'd already planned how he'd say yes—using only words with no Rs in them, because nothing derailed his years of speech therapy like overloaded emotions—before he'd drag Logan to bed and show him exactly how much he loved him. Twice.

Instead, Logan had bailed before his last bite of crème brûlée, claiming an emergency late-night bartending shift. The next day, he'd vanished in a cloud of motorcycle exhaust, along with the rings and all of Riley's stupid happiness.

Yeah, someday Riley would get over that. Probably the same day the gates of Faerie opened in the back room of the Escondido Walmart.

Julie plowed across the lobby toward him, stopping midway to direct a gaggle of PAs who were transporting the show's precious night-vision cameras. "Those go in the equipment suite. And be careful."

Time to come clean. Or at least cleaner. He stood and clutched the cool metal handle of the cart. "Look. I didn't know he was here. Honest."

"You knew it was a possibility, though, didn't you?" She tapped her clipboard with the edge of her phone. "Why else would you propose a location shoot here?"

"Because Portland is supposedly the most haunted city in the Pacific Northwest?" He offered up a conciliatory smile, but she squinted at him, lips pursed.

"Right."

"If you didn't trust my motives, why did you approve the shoot?"

"I didn't approve it. Scott approved it."

"Since when does Scott do anything other than sign off on your recommendations and call his agent to pitch another show?"

She scowled at her clipboard and tugged her ponytail with the hand that still held her cell phone, her trademark *God-this-budget-is-out-of-control* tell. "I knew we should have gone for that poltergeist story."

He held up his hands. "Be reasonable, Jules. The alleged poltergeist moved a hairbrush a quarter of an inch on a slick countertop. The guy lives under a freeway overpass. His paranormal manifestation was probably nothing more than a passing beer truck."

"Maybe. But for that shoot, we wouldn't have had to leave LA. No travel. No hotel." She poked him in the chest with her phone. "No sixteen hours in the equipment van with Zack's lousy ska mix."

He captured her hand before the phone could become embedded in his sternum. "The fact that I heard about this story from Logan first doesn't matter. It's different, Jules. It could be the one that keeps the show from jumping the shark." Or hauls it out of the tank of circling great whites where it had struggled almost from season one. "It's all good. I promise."

"It better be. Because if I can't even manage a third-rate cable show, you think anybody else in Hollywood will hire me? God." She shoved her phone in her jacket pocket and scrubbed a hand over her face. "Tell me the truth. Did you originally pitch this story because of jackass dick-bag Logan?"

"In a way, yeah."

"Riley." Julie's voice dropped into her lowest register, the one the crew guys called the Linda Blair special.

What you can't deny, avoid like hell. "Not because I was looking for him. Swear. But he told me this story the night we met." Riley had been drawn to the tale of the Witch's Castle ghost war because it had all the earmarks of a classic mythic cycle: Romeo and Juliet on the frontier, with hints of a feud that lasted beyond the grave. It hadn't hurt that the guy telling the story had been hotter than dragon fire. "His grandfather claimed to have seen the manifestation back in the early fifties. So when you asked me to prep a story for you to pitch..."

He'd thought of this one, first thing. Despite months of nothing—no phone call, no email, not even a freaking text—his brain still launched every new search with a Logan-filter.

God, somehow that needed to stop. As much as he cringed at the notion of giving Logan another chance to trash his heart, maybe facing him was the answer. Riley needed to take this as serendipity. The gods throwing him a bone, or Cerberus taking firm hold of his ass with all three sets of jaws and giving a swift virtual shake. *Man up or shut up.*

"Shit, Riley. The look on your face," Julie muttered. She tossed her clipboard on the cart, and morphed back into his best friend as if the special effects team had given her an instant CGI makeover. "I'm sorry. But I want you to be over him. That bastard shit-heel cheated on you."

"Allegedly."

"Why do you have a different set of standards for him than you do for your work? You're the king of source-material documentation. You check every tiny fact twice, yet you insist on ignoring the steaming shit-pile of evidence he left behind. I *saw* it." Her voice rose above the chatter of the crew and the eighties mix wafting from the hotel's sound system. "There was enough foil condom confetti on your bedroom floor to set off the metal detectors at the Portland airport, and we were in fricking Eugene."

Riley winced and gestured for her to keep her voice down. "I know." Yet he could have sworn on a stack of holy books from six different religions that Logan would never cheat on anybody, even someone as nerdy as Riley.

The man was too forthright. He'd never pulled punches. Had always said what he thought. If he'd grown tired of Riley—and who could blame him?—he'd have said so. No drama. No nonsense. No arguments. Just boom: *It's over. I've found someone else.*

But to stage a scene like that and disappear? It was so out of character. As if Sir Galahad had suddenly turned as devious and cruel as Mordred.

"Don't get me wrong," Julie said. "If I didn't hate his guts, I'd probably fall at his feet and thank him. If it weren't for that douche bag, you'd be ass-deep in the Balkans by now and I'd be stuck excavating my career from under Max Stone all by myself."

"Speaking of our star," Riley muttered, "he's arrived."

"Fabulous." Julie retrieved her clipboard and hugged it to her chest like an acrylic breastplate. "I'd planned on at least two stiff drinks before I had to face him."

"It's your own fault. *Never* say his name. It conjures him. He's like a malevolent djinn."

She shifted to face Riley, her back to the entrance and the approaching show host. "Listen, Rile, I know he's a total asshat, but please—"

"I know, I know. The star is always right." He patted her arm. "Don't worry, Jules. I won't blow your gig."

Max Stone sauntered to the center of the hotel lobby, directly in the path of the grips wheeling crates full of equipment, and struck a pose, the same one he used before the first commercial break in every *Haunted to the Max* episode.

None of the crew paid any attention; they just navigated around him.

Totally business as usual.

Without the attention of an adoring audience, though, Max had an unfortunate habit of zeroing in on the nearest flunky to torment. Too often, Riley was the flunky du jour—his title might be runner/researcher, but he might as well have *Production Bitch* tattooed on his butt.

"Well, if it isn't Wiley." Max always made a point of mocking Riley's R-W lisp. He held a finger in front of his lips. "Sssshhh. Be vewwy, vewwy quiet. We'w hunting wabbits."

Yeah, like that never *gets old.* Riley felt the telltale heat in his cheeks. He drew a breath to retort—with words containing no *R*s whatsoever—when he caught Julie's pleading look. Right. Placate the star. He settled for a teeth-gritted smile instead. "Hello, Max."

Julie mouthed, *Thank you,* then pasted on a giant fake grin and faced Max. "Welcome to Portland. Is there something you need?"

"Yeah. I need you to book an episode in someplace less goddamn boring. What about Vegas? Miami? New York? Do ghosts only haunt the sticks?"

"Portland isn't exactly the sticks." Julie's knuckles whitened on the edges of her clipboard. "Its population is nearly three-quarters of a million in the city alone."

"It doesn't matter how big the population is," Max boomed, "if they're all losers."

Mr. Tact, that was Max. The woman behind the concierge desk glowered at them, and the bellhops stationed by the front door gave them the side-eye. Riley caught Julie's gaze and jerked his head at the PR disaster in the making.

"It's a natural for you, Max," she said, with a subtle jab in Riley's ribs. "The most haunted city in the Pacific Northwest."

"Yeah? Next time, book us a gig in the most haunted city in Monaco. Because this place sucks." Max heaved his own duffel —leather, with his name and *HttM* monogrammed on both sides in gold—onto the overfull cart, triggering an avalanche of luggage onto the tile at Riley's feet, then swaggered off to the elevators.

Julie sighed and pretended to tick something off the list on her clipboard with a flourish. "Max's first tantrum. Check."

"Does this happen at every shoot?"

"Of course it does. I think it might be in his contract."

Riley heaved the bags back onto the cart. "In that case, I'm glad I've never rated a location assignment before."

"Never mind, Max. You've got to admit this is more interesting than being stuck in the office on phone duty."

"If you say so."

"I know so." She squeezed his arm. "And I've got a surprise for you.

He eyed her warily. "You know I hate those."

"Don't be like that. This is a good thing. Scott wants you to do the briefing at the production meeting tomorrow morning."

Suddenly Cerberus grew a fourth head and chomped down hard on Riley's middle. "This can't be Scott's idea. He doesn't even know my name."

"Exactly. And he never will if you don't speak up. This is the perfect opportunity to show him what an asset you are to the show."

Riley hugged the last duffel to his chest. Once upon a time, he could face anyone. He'd had the regard of his advisor, the offhand respect of the students in his TA sessions, and against all odds, the hottest boyfriend in the Western hemisphere. While he didn't exactly *lose* the first two, getting dumped by Logan had stolen Riley's self-confidence as surely as if Logan had packed it on the back of his motorcycle.

Riley had no desire to alter the *HttM* status quo. Production Bitch might not be a glamorous gig, but at least it was low-profile.

"There's no point, Jules."

"There is too. It's your story, doofus. You deserve the kudos."

Riley fumbled the bag and knocked two others off the cart.

She stared at him, and he saw the instant when the penny dropped. "Shit, Riley. Are you afraid of them?"

He shoved his hands in the pockets of his jacket and stared down at the toes of his black high-tops. "I'm not exactly Hollywood material, Jules."

"Bullshit. Besides, you used to lecture to an auditorium full of clueless newbies three times a week. This should be a piece of cake."

Not the same thing. Not even close. In the lecture hall, he'd been secure in the knowledge that no matter how the students felt about the class, they needed it—and needed him to get through it, because the professor was freaking scary.

It was his turf, and he'd ruled it. The classroom. The library. The internet.

The insanity of a Hollywood production company? Not so much. These guys valued sensationalism, not scholarship. Ratings, not research. Riley's ability to remember their arcane coffee preferences was more valuable to them than his folklore chops.

"I'd really rather not."

"Too bad." She whacked him on the arm with her clipboard. "It's time. I refuse to let you hide your brilliance anymore. Now let's grab some dinner. I have a meeting with Scott at seven, but we've got a couple of hours."

"Are you kidding?" His voice squeaked on the last word. "If I've got to prep a presentation, I need to crack the laptop and assemble my notes." And he would—eventually. But he'd never be able to concentrate with the Logan elephant lurking in the room, shorting out his brain. It was like his thesis implosion all over again.

So before he got started—and despite Julie's undoubted disapproval—he intended to finally force a closure conversation with Logan. And if getting the man to talk required a nail gun applied to his damn motorcycle boots? Riley was totally on board with that.

"I'll pick up a sandwich and eat in my room." He avoided her gaze and replaced the fallen luggage, expecting her to activate her best-friend ESP and scream *Liar!* at any minute. But when he dared a glance, she was staring at her clipboard, chewing on the end of her ponytail.

Guilt wormed its way into his belly. *Wake up, you jerk. You're not the only one with a stake here.* This job was important to her, and whatever happened with Logan, she was still his best friend. He needed to hold it together, for her sake as well as his own.

"Jules." He put an arm across her shoulder. "What's wrong? What's got you so stressed?"

"Oh, you know. The usual suspects." She shrugged, but the worry wrinkle between her brows didn't disappear. "The budget. Max. The lack of any on-camera proof of paranormal activity in any of our episodes ever."

"Trust me. This is a good story." He grinned at her, feigning confidence, and gave her a squeeze. "Look at it this way. If nothing manifests, it won't be any different than any other *HttM* episode, and if you're lucky, that haunted hairbrush will be just as lively when we get back to LA."

CHAPTER TWO

Logan Conner wheeled another stack of Widmer IPA cases through the back door of Stumptown Spirits. Of all the shit jobs in the bar, inventory control—schlepping booze around the dank stockroom, checking deliveries against the shipping manifest—was in his bottom five.

Which was why he always volunteered to do it, along with every weeknight bartending shift, when the patrons drank for vocation not recreation, and the tips were lousy.

He didn't need tips. In little more than a week, he'd never need money again.

He tossed the packing list on the shelf next to the stacks of snowy bar towels, ready to spend one of his last nights on earth working for his old neighbor and childhood nemesis, who was more than happy to employ Logan—for half what he paid the other bartenders.

Perfect.

Heather, one of the servers, stopped in the doorway, tying the strings of her black apron around her waist. "Hey, Logan. Good thing you're on tonight."

"Why's that?" Unfortunately, he liked Heather, so he always tried to dodge her, but she was remarkably persistent. He picked up a bundle of towels. "The boss in a mood?"

She snorted and tucked a pencil behind her ear. "When is Bert not in a mood? No, there's *the* cutest guy sitting at the end of the bar. You should check him out." She sing-songed the last word, waggling her eyebrows.

"Stop trying to set me up, woman." He shooed her through the door. "You know nothing about what I look for in a man."

She fell into step beside him in the narrow hallway. "That's what you think. I notice who you notice, and this guy is totally your type."

"I don't have a type."

"Ha!"

Shit. Guess he didn't have as good a poker face as he'd hoped. He couldn't deny it—as his personal Judgment Day approached, he definitely had Riley Morrel on the brain. Anyone who bore the slightest resemblance to his ex-lover caught his attention with a stomach-churning swirl of desperate hope and complete terror. Didn't mean he had to admit it.

"You're hallucinating, Heather. Have you been breathing the fumes from that leaky keg?"

She grabbed his arm, and he fumbled the bale of towels, dropping it right in the perpetual puddle that had seeped into the hallway from that same leak.

"Damn it." He kneeled down and blotted the beer with the towels. "Can you hand me the wrench from under the end of the bar?"

"Since when do we have a wrench?"

"It's mine." He'd relocated it from his bike saddlebag because the boss was too cheap to spring for his own fricking tools, let alone replace the keg. "If I tighten the hose connector—"

"Oh, leave it, Logan. It'll just leak again in half an hour anyway." She shoved his shoulder when he tried to stand. "Stay down there. It's only another foot to the end of the hall, and you'll be less obvious if you scope out the guy from floor level."

"I don't want to scope anyone— Ow!" He rubbed the back of his head where she'd smacked him.

"Just look, you big baby. Twenty bucks says I'm right."

Logan heaved an exaggerated sigh. "Fine. Easiest twenty I ever made." He'd tuck it into her tip jar at the end of her shift.

He crawled forward, avoiding the remains of the beer leak, Heather shuffling along at his hip. A bar patron snickered as he passed them on the way to the john, but Logan ignored him. Five months ago, he'd never have been caught dead in such a ridiculous position. Now, he didn't give a shit how stupid he appeared.

When he reached the corner, Heather held up two fingers in a peace sign, pointed at her eyes and then at the bar. He mouthed, *Bitch*, and she grinned.

He rocked forward until he had a clear view of the far end of the bar. A bolt of fire shot from his throat to his balls.

Riley.

He scrambled back and fell onto his ass in the remaining beer puddle. God and the devil take it, what was Riley doing here?

"Logan?" Heather hunkered down in front of him. "What's the matter? You look like you've seen a ghost."

A ghost. What a joke. Logan was doing his best to face up to becoming a ghost himself, and the only man in the world who could shake his resolve sat less than twenty feet away. He heaved himself to his feet, snatching a marginally dry towel from the sodden pile to blot his jeans.

Heather propped her chin on his shoulder. "So. Do I win?"

"Yeah. No. I... need air. Taking a break." He retreated down the hallway, tossing the towel into the hamper inside the stockroom door as he passed. "Tell Jase I'll take over behind the bar in—" Jesus. How could he work his shift tonight?

He fumbled with the panic bar of the back door and escaped into the alley, drawing in deep breaths of air tainted with stale beer, urine, and garbage.

How the fuck was this possible? Riley was supposed to be hacking around Europe on that folklore grant with his freshly minted master's degree, not hanging out in Portland, and in Stumptown Spirits, of all the bad fucking luck.

Luck? Who was he kidding? Luck and Riley didn't coexist on the same planet, at least not where Logan was concerned.

He crept down the alley and emerged on the sidewalk in front of the bar. The October chill hadn't reduced traffic on the sidewalks of Old Town, but Logan didn't spare a glance at anyone. He sidled up to the tinted window, glad for once that Bert refused to invest in any window coverings, and peered inside. Riley was still sitting at the end of the bar, his profile illuminated by the pierced copper lantern overhead.

The downlight burnished his hair to a glow like polished mahogany. It highlighted the slope of his turned-up nose. Caught the upper curve of his ear where it protruded from the shaggy haircut he'd always insisted on because he was self-conscious about what he called "these open car doors on either side of my head."

Heather emerged from the hallway with her hands full of burger platters, and Riley tracked her, his head panning toward the window.

Shit. Logan jerked back, chest heaving, and leaned against the rough brick wall. Had Riley seen him? He didn't think so, although it would be hard to miss him once he started his shift. He'd be trapped behind the bar until midnight with Riley practically in his lap.

No fucking way.

He hunched below the window and duck-walked a couple of feet down the sidewalk before inching up to peek through the glass again.

Riley wasn't staring at the window, thank God. His head was bent, one fist clutching the hair above his forehead, which always made it stick up like a kid's who'd just awoken from a nap. He was scribbling notes on a legal pad, probably in that crazy shorthand he'd invented for himself. The bar in front of him held a scatter of papers topped by a fat paperback.

When Riley's glasses slid down his nose and he pushed them up with the eraser end of his pencil, Logan nearly sprinted into the bar to rip the thing from his hand. Christ, did he want to poke himself in the eye? Riley wasn't the most coordinated of men. Half the time he managed to fall *up* the stairs, for Chrissake.

Someone nudged Logan in the ribs, and he glanced irritably to his left. A hefty twentysomething guy with a tribal neck tattoo and a leather jacket chinking with more chains than the average bike shop crouched next to him, breathing alcohol fumes in Logan's face, his eyes avid.

"What's the show? Some chick with her tits hanging out?"

Another guy, this one in fashionably ripped denim and a backward black ball cap, jostled him from the other side. Logan scowled at them and pulled his elbows in tight.

"Don't be greedy, man. Share."

They matched his stance and peered through the window.

"I don't see nothing," Leather-guy said.

Jesus. Logan ducked and flipped around, his back to the wall and his ass on the less-than-pristine sidewalk. Between the dirt and the beer soaking the seat of his jeans, he'd smell like the back alley by the end of the night, but he couldn't bring himself to care.

Denim-boy stood up. "Place is a dump. Nothing but guys." He looked down at Logan, the whites showing around his faded blue irises. "This ain't one of them homo havens, is it?"

"Christ," Logan muttered, and levered himself to his feet and moved away from them, keeping low until he'd cleared the window.

"Hey!" Leather followed him. "He asked you a question."

"Back off."

"You gonna make us?" Leather-guy shoved Logan's shoulder, the jut of the idiot's chin begging for a swift uppercut. *Posers.* Logan's least favorite demographic.

When Logan didn't respond, Denim-boy strutted over but stayed safely behind Leather, out of first-strike range. "Like to see you try."

Posers *and* cowards. Perfect. Logan should spend the evening with these assholes, to remind himself why he wouldn't miss his life.

Except that Riley Morrel was within his reach, separated from him by one measly brick wall, rumpled and intent and infuriatingly oblivious.

In other words, totally fricking adorable.

So Logan did the right thing. He ran, the guffaws of Leather and Denim chasing him down the alley.

He'd forced himself to leave Riley once. He could do it again, although the tension snarling his belly called bullshit to that, mocking him more successfully than the laughter of the losers on the sidewalk. *You're not as strong as you pretend.*

Five months. Five months of self-denial hell down the tubes. Five months since he'd touched Riley's skin. Seen his eyes light up at some arcane mythological reference he'd managed to trace through the centuries.

Five months since Logan had staged that callous scene and bailed like a coward before he lost his resolve. He'd thought he'd been cauterizing the Riley-wound in his soul while he'd marked time here, waiting for the end. But one glimpse of him and Logan was as raw as he'd been that day in Eugene.

Goddamn it all to hell and back. It was way easier to get over the death of someone you hated than someone you loved. Logan knew that from experience. His cousin's first serious boyfriend had died in a car crash when the two of them were only nineteen. In her mind, he was still perfect, and as far as she was concerned, nobody could ever measure up. She hadn't even tried to get over the loss. Twelve years later, she still hadn't moved on.

He didn't want that for Riley, so he'd done his damnedest to make himself unworthy of devotion. Why couldn't the man take the fucking hint that Logan had scattered all over their bedroom floor?

Logan stormed down the hallway to the office. Bert Johnson, his short-term boss, sat at his desk, scowling at his dinosaur of a computer monitor and poking at the keyboard with both index fingers.

Logan took an unsteady breath and grabbed a discarded bar towel from the back of a chair to hide his trembling hands. "You'd finish that a lot quicker if you learned how to type."

"Bah." Bert didn't bother to glance up. "Bunch of nonsense. Pen and paper were just fine in my day."

"Hate to tell you this, but it's still your day." But it wouldn't be Logan's day. Not for much longer. He had to remember that. Had to resist the temptation sitting at the end of the bar, an impossible feat if he got within touching distance of Riley. "How about this? You take my bar shift tonight, and I'll finish the bookkeeping."

Bert raised a shaggy eyebrow, his long face and narrow chin making him look like a Victorian pen-and-ink illustration of Marley's ghost. "You don't get tips from bookkeeping."

"I know." It didn't matter. He'd have given the money away anyway. "Come on. You know you'd rather pour beer than inventory it."

Bert pushed himself out of his chair and stalked to the door. "Your funeral."

Logan dropped onto the unforgiving wooden seat. "It's my butt's funeral in this chair. Christ, Bert. Get a pad, for God's sake."

He snorted. "Young folks. So soft. In my day, we knew how to make do."

"Yeah, yeah. Big talk. Go on. You've got a bar full of thirsty people."

Bert disappeared down the hall with another snort, as close as he ever came to laughter, and Logan settled into the hard chair. Maybe the discomfort would keep his mind off the fact that Riley was bare yards away.

Nope. Nope. Nope. Thinking about Riley and *bare* in the same sentence was a recipe for disaster—or at least the call for a looser pair of pants.

CHAPTER THREE

Perched on a barstool at the short arm of the L-shaped bar in Stumptown Spirits, Riley tried to focus on the notes he was compiling for his unwanted starring role at tomorrow's production meeting. His heels bounced on the brass foot rail in time with the tap of his pencil on his legal pad, and his attention was hopelessly split between his work and the mouth of the hall where Logan should appear within—Riley checked his watch—seven minutes.

Whenever someone emerged from the hallway, his stomach leaped for his rib cage. Whenever it wasn't Logan, his stupid non-aerodynamic stomach went into free fall. By the time Logan actually showed up, Riley would probably be ready to puke on his shoes.

Not the reunion he had in mind.

He smiled at the friendly waitress who'd greeted him when he came in, and let his gaze wander around the room. Sheesh. Talk about your no-frills bars.

Tucked into Portland's Old Town with an emphasis on the *old*, the place was... plain. No neon beer logos in the windows. No big-screen TVs blaring sportscasts. Nothing on any of the bare plank tables that might be mistaken as decorative, although the rough-paneled walls sported a few faded sepia photographs of early Portland, back in the days when it had deserved its "Stumptown" nickname.

The booths along the side walls were flanked by rustic settles rather than upholstered benches, and the chairs grouped around the tables were a mishmash of styles, from cane-bottomed bentwood to rough-hewn wooden stools.

The bar was only two steps removed from dive status, and that confused him. He knew he was in the right spot. After all, research was his middle name, although Max would no doubt mock him by calling it *wesearch*. But why would Logan, with his love of elegant buildings and classic design, settle for a job somewhere so relentlessly... unlovely? In Eugene, he'd worked in a place noted for its architectural charm and historical significance, even though it had been packed to the rafters with half-drunk college kids six days out of seven.

Yet Logan had left that job, left their funky apartment, left Riley, for this. *Why?*

His whole life, whenever he'd been faced with a mystery or conundrum, Riley became obsessed with understanding *why*. It was the reason he'd gravitated to folklore in the first place. All the stories, from the grand mythic cycles to the smallest homely tales, were human attempts to make sense of their world. To understand why something happened the way it did. Why a person behaved one way and not another.

This was his chance to demand his own personal *why* from Logan. How could he refuse The Call? No hero in any of the tales, great or small, let this kind of opening pass. The upshot of second chances wasn't always positive—just ask Orpheus—but no hero worth their journey ever backed down from this perfect an opportunity.

He'd take Logan's dismissal, if that's what was coming. But he refused to let the man sidestep the conversation. Who knew? Maybe he'd manage to land a few jabs of his own, make Logan feel a fraction of the hurt he'd inflicted on Riley. Did that make him a bad person? Perhaps. But damn it, he couldn't move on until he knew *why*.

The bartender who'd served Riley his Coke waved at the waitress and disappeared down the hallway at the open end of the bar. Riley tensed, his fingers tightening around his pencil. His breath sped up. He brushed salt and pretzel crumbs off the front of his sweater, fighting the urge to smooth down his hair. Should he push his notes aside and sip his Coke, try to appear casual and unconcerned? Or should he pretend to be busy, important, just here by accident? So overcome by some brilliant insight that he'd had to duck into the nearest convenient watering hole to capture his thoughts?

Riiiight. Nobody, not even *HttM*'s gullible dwindling audience, would buy that one.

He took a gulp of his Coke, wishing he'd ordered a beer after all. Judging by his skittering nerves, caffeine had clearly been the wrong choice. God, he probably looked as panicked as a *wabbit* in the crosshairs. *Get your game face on. This is a confrontation, damn it.* He ought to scowl, look tough—or at least as tough as he could manage.

But he didn't have to bother because the guy who emerged from the hallway wasn't Logan. Not even close.

Instead of six foot three of broad-shouldered, square-jawed, tight-muscled man candy, the man who shuffled behind the bar could have modeled for Munch's *The Scream*.

Riley ducked his head, thumbing through his notes, trying not to let his disappointment show. He'd triple-checked the schedule he'd conned out of a harried server, while attempting to convince himself he wasn't turning into a creepy stalker ex. So where was Logan? Could his research be that faulty?

Suddenly, a narrow shadow fell over his legal pad. Every hair on the back of his neck sprang to attention, and a chill crept between his shoulder blades. He glanced up, directly into the eyes of the cadaverous bartender.

The man loomed over him and sniffed as if he were tracking down a nasty odor, the nostrils on his beak of a nose flaring. His brows pinched together over deep-set eyes colder than a frost giant's balls. "Bitch." The voice matched the face, grim and unforgiving.

Sure, Riley wasn't the butchest of guys, but he didn't exactly flame either. Yeah, he'd worn his best sweater, a cashmere V-neck that had cost nearly as much as his second-hand laptop, but it was burgundy, not pink or lavender. It matched his shoes —was that a giveaway? But the bartender couldn't see his shoes, and when strangers decided to hassle him, they usually passed through a rainbow of other gay slurs—queer, faggot, pansy, homo—before they hit on the b-word. And they certainly had never *smelled* him first.

"I, um, Excuse me?"

"We don't serve your kind here," he growled.

Riley shifted on the unyielding wooden stool and glanced around at the other people in the bar. It was about half-full, mostly men, but a few women too. He'd bet his prized autographed copy of *The Hero's Journey* that some of those men —and maybe some of the women for all he knew—were gay. Why single him out?

"I don't want any twouble." He winced. *"Trouble.* I'm just here enjoying your local dw—draft soft drinks." He lifted his Coke, his shaking hand sending the half-melted ice cubes into a chittering mambo.

"Get out."

Riley stalled with the glass halfway to his mouth. "What?" he croaked.

"You heard me. This is my place, and I have the right to refuse service."

"But I'm not doing anything."

The other men sitting at the bar eased away, drifting to empty tables to distance themselves from angry-bartender fallout. Riley wished he could do the same, or maybe disappear through a convenient inter-dimensional portal.

"You disgust me. That's something. Get out. Now."

Riley's hand jerked, and he lost his grip on the glass. It toppled over, and as the spreading brown puddle seeped onto his notes, his face heated until he felt as if he could barbecue on his forehead. Portland was supposed to be such a liberal city. He'd never imagined he'd get hit with homophobic crap here. He scrabbled the soggy papers together and shoved them in his messenger bag along with his tattered copy of *The Golden Bough*.

God, how could Logan work for this guy? Although Logan could pass for straight in any lineup, he'd never suffered bigots gladly—or at all.

Clutching his bag against his chest, Riley slid off the barstool and did his best to make an unobtrusive exit. Before he could slink out the door, the server caught up with him and tapped his arm.

"Listen. I'm sorry about..." she jerked her head at the guy behind the bar, who was attacking Riley's spilled Coke as if it was hazardous waste "...you know. The boss. I'm not sure what his deal is. He's never thrown anyone out before. Come back tomorrow, okay? He won't be here." She shot a nervous glance over her shoulder. "Our regular bartender is much nicer, believe me, and I really think you should meet him."

Yeah. I do too. "I'll try."

She scurried off, and Riley wrestled the heavy wooden door open. Outside, as the crisp night air cooled his face, he slumped against the wall, chin to his chest, and tried to collect his shot-to-hell wits.

"Nice bag, faggot."

Riley's head jerked up. Two guys in standard street-punk gear stood by the curb, sneering at him. *Seriously? Twice in one night?* So far, Portland wasn't thrilling him with its stellar hospitality. The sooner he got back to his room, the better.

But when the two of them flanked him, blocking his path down the sidewalk in either direction, he gulped around a lump the size of his heart. *Shit. Classic Riley Morrel tactical error.* How many times had Logan ragged on him for not paying enough attention to his surroundings? Maybe he should have taken the warnings more to heart.

He edged along the wall, the rough bricks catching the back of his sweater. "Hey, guys. Not looking for a hassle."

The bigger one grinned, the chains on his leather jacket chinking as he hemmed Riley in. "Too bad." He yanked the bag out of Riley's hands and tossed it to his buddy, who rooted through it and dropped a fistful of Coke-infused notes onto the sidewalk with a sodden *plop*.

Riley lunged for the soggy papers. The bag these goons could keep. But his research? His notes? Those he'd fight for.

But the big leather-jacketed guy blocked him and shoved him toward the street. As Riley stumbled over the curb and into a puddle of icy water that soaked through his high-tops and socks, he remembered the crucial thing about the stages of the Hero's Journey.

Most of them really freaking sucked.

Logan hunched over the keyboard, shifting from one numb butt cheek to the other, clammy damp denim making the hard chair a double torture. The window beyond the monitor framed a slice of the sidewalk at the end of the alley, where Leather-dude and Denim-boy still loitered. If they were hoping for another chance to strut their lame macho bullshit with Logan, they'd be waiting a long time.

Logan had more important battles to fight. With himself.

Damn it. He'd known Riley—who never quit until he ferreted out the answer to any question—would locate Logan someday if he wanted to. So Logan had done everything he could to make Riley *not* want to find him, because he didn't have a choice, and Riley made him *want* a choice.

He reached under the collar of his Henley and pulled out the chain he'd worn since the night he'd left, the one that held the rings he'd bought when he'd decided to give up his quest. He unhooked the clasp and coiled the whole gleaming mess in his palm.

Riley had tempted Logan to violate his own sense of right and wrong—no, screw tempted. He'd succeeded. Logan had been ready to ignore the debt he'd left behind him in Forest Park that night seven years ago when his own idiocy and carelessness had consigned another man to hell.

In the beginning, Riley had been his last-ditch effort to find the answer to his impossible riddle. But that had been when he'd thought Riley was just a resource like all the others before him, someone to pump for information and move on. Logan had kept their first conversation casual, like he always did— general Witch's Castle lore, nothing about his own experience or his grandfather's, not yet. Sure, the kid was cute, but a killer ass didn't translate into the expertise Logan needed, and he'd never entrusted the whole sorry story to anyone.

Then, on the night he'd watched Riley stand up to a bar full of drunken assholes, earnestly defending folklore as a way of life, he'd been intrigued enough to offer Riley a ride home. A guy with that kind of passion, that unshakeable confidence in his own knowledge and abilities, was worth a second shot.

The instant Riley's hard-on had snugged against Logan's ass, he'd decided to postpone sharing the unbelievable—and mortifying—personal revelations until after a little recreational sex, because after all, nothing would manifest at that damn fork in the path for another eleven months.

But something had changed that night, the first time he'd kissed Riley, the first time they'd lain skin to skin, the first time he'd heard Riley gasp and moan with Logan's dick buried in that perfect ass. He'd drowned in the look in Riley's dark eyes, the look that proclaimed Logan as some kind of superhero.

He couldn't bear to watch that adulation vanish into contempt, or disgust, or worst of all pity. So he'd hedged. He'd told Riley about the night his grandfather had witnessed the ghost war, but not about what happened to him afterward—the accusations, the arrest, the delusions, the disgrace. What sane man would want to hook up with a guy from that train wreck of a family?

He hadn't told Riley about his own experience either. About Trent. Because the shame of what he'd done, his failure, his guilt —well, that made him look like a full-time loser too. And after that first night, it had become vitally important that Riley think well of him. Respect him. Love him.

Riley had listened with flattering attention as Logan related the redacted version, but had said he wasn't really an expert on ghosts. Logan had been relieved. Used that as an excuse. *I've done everything I can and nothing worked. Nobody can expect anything more of me, right?* It hadn't stopped him from making excuses to Riley the night of October seventeenth and taking one last trip to Forest Park. When midnight came and went, once again with no sign of the ghosts, he'd said his last apologies, his final farewell.

He'd returned to Eugene and had dived into the happiest seven months of his life.

In his years on the road after Trent's disappearance, searching for an answer to something he was starting to disbelieve himself, Logan had learned to travel light. With Riley, though, he'd let himself get sloppy. Domestic. They'd acquired dishes. A dining table. Matching towels, for God's sake.

A bed.

He'd been *content*, for Chrissake, comforting himself with the delusion that he'd given Trent his best shot. He still couldn't believe he'd been that selfish, that complacent, nearly forgetting his best friend, who had no means of rescue, no one to depend on but Logan. But he had. Riley had almost made him forget.

Ironically, Riley had also made him remember, and unwittingly shown him what he had to do. Once he'd had the answer, the way to end Trent's torment, he'd been forced to make a choice: stay, saddling his lover with a man who was little better than a murderer, or go, and prove himself the kind of man Riley deserved by accepting his own responsibilities.

When he'd finally manned up to his obligations and bailed, leaving Riley had nearly gutted him. Tears that had nothing to do with the wind in his face had blurred his eyes as he sped north on his bike, every signpost on the highway another spike in his heart.

Abandoning the possessions, though, the evidence of those months of self-indulgence—that had been a fucking piece of cake. He'd left them all behind and gladly.

Except the rings. Those he'd never give up.

"Hey, Logan." Heather's low voice from the doorway interrupted his brooding.

He shoved the rings in the front pocket of his jeans and swiveled the chair to face her. "Hey. Sorry I bailed on you. Bert giving you his usual grief?"

"Not me." She bit her lip and glanced over her shoulder. "That cute guy. Bert just kicked him out of the bar."

Logan's caveman instincts roused with a roar, his belly burning with the need to clock his boss in the face. He unclenched his jaw. "You're kidding. Bouncing isn't in his job description." Bert always delegated that task, another on Logan's list of least favorite and therefore most sought-after duties.

"He made an exception this time." She wrapped her arms across her belly. "I felt so bad for him. The guy. Not Bert."

"I get it."

God, poor Riley. He hated confrontational shit, which was the prime reason Logan had opted for the coward's way out. Sure, he could have staged the bogus breakup scene in the bar where he'd worked, or at one of the nonstop pre-graduation parties that had been going on for over a week, ensuring that he'd never come within fifty feet of Logan again. But Logan hadn't been able to bring himself to do it. He'd hurt Riley, but at least he'd done it in private.

Yeah, you're a fucking hero, Conner. So afraid you'd lose your nerve that you bolted first chance.

"I've known Bert since I was a kid, and if there's one thing you can count on with him, it's his bad temper." He offered her his best imitation of a reassuring smile. "Believe it or not, he's mellowed in his old age. He used to be worse."

As he'd hoped, she eased her death grip on herself. "Bert was young once?"

Logan tilted the chair back on its creaking gimbals. "He's always looked the same to me, but adults always look old to little kids."

She nodded, shoulders sagging. "Too bad you won't have a chance to chat that guy up tonight after all."

"That was never going to happen, girl."

"No?" Her voice rose in her usual chirp. "I still say it's too bad. You're a good guy, Logan. You deserve some fun now and then."

No. I don't. And next week, he'd finally get his true deserts. He couldn't let anything or anyone—including Riley Morrel—divert him from his obligation.

Now that Riley was gone, though, he could take his regular bar shift and keep Bert from terrorizing all the other patrons. Logan may not need the money, but Heather and the rest of the staff did, since Bert was notoriously cheap. Logan wasn't the only one whose hourly wage verged on criminal.

"I'll finish this crap and take over from Bert. Hang tight for a few?"

Pressing her hand to her chest, she heaved an exaggerated sigh. "Thank the lord. See you out there." She disappeared with a finger-wiggle wave.

Logan turned back to the computer, glancing out the window to see if his fan club still lurked on the street.

His vision narrowed on the scene, and he clenched the chair's wobbly armrests. The two assholes weren't alone anymore. They had Riley trapped between them.

Fuck no.

Logan leaped up and barreled down the hall, exploding out the back door in a crash of metal against brick. He sprinted down the alley and onto the sidewalk.

"Hey! I told you guys to back off."

Riley's coffee-dark eyes, visible over Leather's beefy shoulder, widened, and he tried to sidestep the burly idiot again.

Leather grabbed Riley's arm and swung him off-balance. "So? What do you gotta say about it? You're the guy who ran."

But not for the reason you think, asshole. First order of business: get Riley out of the blast zone. Logan paced around Leather, forcing him to turn if he wanted to keep Logan in his sights. Unfortunately, he dragged Riley along with him. "You weren't worth my time. But now, you've pissed me off. Let him go."

Leather got up in Logan's face, almost chest to chest. "Make me."

Jerking his thumb at the bar entrance, Logan grinned. "Boss doesn't like it when I punch out douche bags *inside* the bar. But out here? Threatening his customers? That shit's bad for business. I get a free pass on assholes who threaten his bottom line." Weight balanced on the balls of his feet, Logan was ready to make a move if Leather so much as twitched in Riley's direction. "Trust me. You don't want to give me a reason to cash in on that. Let. Him. Go."

"Hey, Ace?" Denim's voice quavered. Out of the corner of his eye, Logan saw the guy drop Riley's bag. "There's two of 'em now. You can't get in another fight. You promised your mom—"

"Shut up, Tyler!" Red washed up Leather's neck.

Logan buried his urge to laugh. If it had only been him against the two of them, he'd have gone for it. He would have welcomed a throw-down with these guys, just to release the dual tensions of Riley's presence and his own approaching checkout. But when Riley could be collateral damage?

No fucking way.

And a sure-fire way to push a poser into blind idiocy was to call him on his pose. So he shut the fuck up and didn't bait Leather about his momma. Just stood there, staring the guy down.

Leather's chest heaved, and Logan prayed Riley wouldn't decide to distract the guy by struggling or, God forbid, talking. But Riley stayed still and silent.

A beat. Two. Three, and Leather's gaze finally dropped. He released Riley with a shove, although Riley managed to keep his balance.

"Come on, Tyler. This shit ain't worth our time."

The idiots swaggered away, leaving a trail of undervoiced profanities, and Logan was left face-to-face with Riley. Well, face-to-top-of-head. Riley's attention was on the water pooled around his shoes and the soaked hems of his skinny jeans.

Skinny jeans. Logan's mouth went dry. He knew what Riley's ass looked like in those jeans. Furthermore, he knew what Riley's ass looked like *out* of those jeans.

His cock punched at his fly. He wanted nothing more than to take Riley in his arms. Take him back to his own shitty apartment. Take him, period. *Christ, no. Don't let him get close. Do what's right. Be an asshole, damn it.*

Riley glanced up through the fringe of his bangs. "Thanks. I think I could have handled it myself, but thanks." He bent to pick up the yellow wad of paper on the sidewalk at his feet, giving Logan a perfect ass-shot.

Fuck.

He gritted his teeth, widening his stance to give his erection and tightening balls some desperately needed room, and grasped one wrist in front of his groin, fist clenched. "Where are you staying?" He'd intended to keep his voice neutral, but it came out rough, bordering on threatening. *Better.*

But when Riley stood, shoving the paper back into his bag, his eyes shone in the sulfurous light of the streetlamp and his mouth softened in a hopeful, heartbreaking smile. "Vaughn Street Hotel. You want to—"

Logan forced a harsh guffaw, although he'd never felt less like laughing. "You and me? No. I thought you got that memo five months ago."

He extracted a twenty from his wallet and held it between two fingers. When Riley didn't take it, just stared at it as his lips pinched together, shoulders hunched, Logan pitched it onto the sidewalk.

"There. Pick it up or not, your choice. But take a cab back to your hotel, and for God's sake, don't wander around on your own. You have no fucking clue about urban survival."

Logan yanked the bar door open and stalked inside, shutting Riley out of his sight. Christ, whoever had come up with the saying "Out of sight, out of mind" was either a fucking idiot, delusional, or had never met Riley Morrel.

CHAPTER FOUR

The crew of *Haunted to the Max* filled Scott's hotel suite to its fake-paneled walls, entertaining themselves until Scott and Julie got back from their daily power breakfast to start the production meeting. Riley kicked himself for forgetting to bring his headphones so he could settle his nerves before his presentation. Too much auditory input always shorted out his brain, and between the crew's banter, good-natured and otherwise, the music blaring over the sound system, and the rerun of *Sharknado* gibbering on the flat-screen TV, his sensory overload was approaching terminal.

Focus, damn it, focus. This was his first official presentation of something other than beverage-of-choice to the whole staff. His first chance to prove he was someone other than Julie's awkward sidekick. Someone worthy of respect in his own right.

He couldn't exactly claim his pride was at stake. He was fresh out of that, since he'd sacrificed its pathetic remnants on the altar of Logan last night at Stumptown Spirits. But his credibility—and by extension the credibility of folklore as valid source material for the show—was on trial today.

So he'd better not freaking blow it.

Scott strode into the room, followed by Julie, who gave Riley a tiny nod of encouragement.

"Settle down, people." Scott's raised voice added to the din. He pointed at the sound guy. "Chris, kill the music. Wes, turn off the TV." He looked around the room. "Where's Max?"

Max sauntered in and posed with one hand on the top of the door. "Here."

Scott scowled, but didn't give Max shit about being late, as he would have with anyone else. *Placate the star.* It was the official party line. "All right, then." He pointed at Riley. "You. You're up. Brief us on the ghost crap."

Oh God. *Showtime.* Riley wove his way to the front of the room through an obstacle course of outstretched legs, his finely tuned flight reflex continually recalculating the best path of escape. He fumbled with the projector cable, taking two tries to get it hooked to his laptop. When a smatter of laughter broke out, he made the mistake of glancing up. Max mimed a pistol with his finger and thumb, and mouthed *Wabbits.*

Fabulous.

He faced the crew. There couldn't be twice as many as usual, could there? *Just pretend they're a class of first-year business majors filling a humanities requirement.* A wad of paper sailed through the air and hit him square in the crotch. Someone snickered.

Okay, make that a study hall full of seventh graders cruising toward detention.

Nevertheless, for Julie's sake as well as his own self-respect, he could do this. He grabbed his laser pointer, his palm so damp it nearly slid from his grasp. "We're investigating an incident at a site called the Witch's Castle." He pulled up the PowerPoint slides. "It's a derelict stone building in Forest Park, next to Balch Creek."

"So it's haunted?" Scott asked.

Riley nodded. "According to local legend. Some of the sightings are just the usual clouds and inexplicable mist on photogw—" He cleared his throat. "*Photographs* that should have shown clean."

Max groaned and slid down in his chair—the biggest one in the room—tilting his ever-present fedora over his face. A cache of crumpled paper lay half-concealed next to his hip. *Great. More ammunition.*

"Um… I…" Riley's mouth was suddenly dry. Julie, her best-friend ESP obviously back online today, handed him a water bottle, and he took a grateful swig. *Ignore the idiot star. You know what you're talking about.*

Zack, one of the camera operators, leaned forward, elbows on his knees. "So, the witch who lived in the castle. She one of the ghosts?"

Gratified that someone other than Julie appeared to be listening, Riley smiled and shook his head. "'Witch's Castle' is only a spooky name. There never was a witch, and it's not really a castle. Some w—*rumors* claim the place was a trading post in the 1600s."

Max pushed his hat up his forehead with one finger. "Now you're talking. We could do a whole costume reenactment. I'd look great in buckskins, right, Charmaine?"

Charmaine, the wardrobe coordinator, shot Julie a panicked look. "Uh…"

Riley gave her a reassuring smile. "Those rumors are just that. And mistaken to boot."

"If there's no ghost," Scott said, without raising his gaze from his cell phone screen, "why are we here?"

"I didn't say there were no ghosts. Only that Witch's Castle wasn't a trading post. The building was constructed by the WPA in the mid-1930s. It was a restroom."

"This is your big story?" Max scoffed. "A haunted john? Jesus, Wiley."

The rest of the crew laughed, and heat crept up Riley's neck. Were they siding with Max's mockery or amused by the idea of a haunted toilet? He took a gulp of water and tightened his grip on the laser pointer. "It's not the building that's haunted. It's the location. We have multiple weports…" He took a deep breath.

Slow down. Don't let them rattle you. "*Reports* of partially corporeal spirit sightings connected with a local legend. It's a piece of Oregon history with a frontier Wo—Romeo and Juliet story thrown in for good measure."

Riley clicked the next slide and a picture of the roofless building filled the screen, graffiti warring with moss on its rough stone walls. "Danford Balch was the first man legally hanged in Oregon after it became a state. This spot in Forest Park was originally the Balch family homestead, where Danford lived with his wife and nine children."

"Nine kids?" Grace, the camera PA, sounded horrified. "I'm surprised his wife didn't save the hangman the trouble and murder him first."

"When was this?" Zack asked.

"Late 1850s." With evidence that a few of the crew had at least a passing interest in the story, Riley's nerves subsided and he settled into his lecture groove. "He was well-off enough to employ a hired hand, a teenager named Mortimer Stump. Stump's family lived on the other side of the river, and likely were not as high up socially or financially, since their eldest son was working for someone else rather than his own family."

Max propped his feet on the coffee table with a thump. "Who cares? Halloween is coming up. Can't we do a story on Houdini?"

Riley reeled in a sigh. *Okay. Fascination not universal. Got it.* "Everybody does stories on Houdini at Halloween."

"Exactly. Proves he's popular. A guaranteed audience. I can totally do his look too." Max sat up and fixed Scott with a goggle-eyed stare.

Jeez. If Max intended that expression to be intense, he'd missed it by a mile, landing somewhere in the middle of constipated.

"Max," Julie said in her humor-the-star voice, "we can discuss a Houdini show at another time. Besides, this show won't air until January, so the Halloween connection is irrelevant. Let's hear what Riley has to say." Max thrust his lower lip out, and Julie played her trump card. "Afterwards, we'll discuss the promotional appearances I've got booked for you."

Max's eyes took on the manic glow of a kid anticipating trick or treat, and Julie nodded for Riley to continue.

"Balch's eldest child, Anna, was fifteen in November of 1858. She and Mortimer fell in love, and Mortimer asked Balch for permission to marry her. Balch refused."

"Oooh. Bad move," Grace said.

"Exactly. For everyone. Anna defied her father, and she and Mortimer eloped. A week later, when they'd come to town for supplies along with the rest of the Stump family, Danford ran into them at the tin shop on Front Street. He demanded his daughter back. The Stump patriarch, Cuthbert, insulted his new daughter-in-law, and Danford stormed off. He returned with his shotgun and caught up with the group at the Stark Street ferry."

"If anyone *cares* about my input, I think the Houdini story would be better," Max grumbled. "We could restage one of his escape routines."

"Oh give Houdini a fucking rest, Max," Scott said, and Max's mouth dropped open. "Go on."

Riley shared a quick stunned glance with Julie. Was Scott taking his part against Max, or simply moving the agenda along? *Okay, then. Stakes raised. Maybe. Better make it good.* "Danford Balch shot Mortimer Stump in full view of his daughter, the entire Stump family, and a crowd of onlookers."

"So who's the ghost?" Grace asked. "And what does the Witch's Castle have to do with it?"

"Well, that's the thing. The second legend about the Witch's Castle haunting involves not just a single apparition, but a full-on ghost war. A family feud between Stumps and Balches, a sort of replay of the events leading up to the hanging of Danford Balch on October 17, 1859."

Julie looked up from her clipboard, where she'd been furiously scribbling notes during his presentation. "Riley? Can those dates be correct? According to this, he wasn't hanged until nearly a year after the murder."

"He might not have been hanged at all if he hadn't been an idiot. They jailed him immediately after the shooting, but the jail was no Alcatraz. He escaped. He could have run anywhere. Instead, he hid out near his own home and had regular meals with his family. He was rearrested, and this time he couldn't escape, but he contended all the way to the gallows that the shooting had been an accident. They hanged him, apparently much to his own surprise, in front of a crowd that included his wife and daughter." Riley turned off the projector and closed his laptop. "The daughter, by the way, sat with the Stumps."

Scott stood up. "Right. Everybody's dismissed. Julie, schedule change. I want to complete the principal photography tomorrow night. You stay on with the second unit crew to film all the supporting shit."

Riley inched his hand into the air. "Scott? Sorry, but while we can film the preliminary interviews with witnesses beforehand, we can't film the ghost war until October seventeenth." He gulped under Scott's narrow-eyed glare. "From everything I've been able to uncover, the full war only materializes, complete with an unbreachable perimeter, on the anniversary of the hanging of Danford Balch. The evidence of sightings on other days is sporadic and not especially reliable."

Scott scowled and poked at the screen of his smartphone as the crew straggled out of the suite. "Fuck. I was counting on getting back to LA by Thursday night. Why'd we get here so early?"

"We've all got plenty to do, if that's what you're worried about. Aside from the background shots, we've got PR appearances, red tape to cut through with the city, meetings with Parks and Rec. I gave you a rundown of the timeline in the pitch, Scott. It's been in the production schedule for over a month." Julie rose from her chair, clipboard at attention. "But if you really need to get back to LA, I can handle the main shoot, no problem."

Scott shot her a look from under his lowered brows. "Don't dance on my grave yet, Ainsworth. This is still my show, God help me." He stalked to his desk and cracked open his laptop. "Now get out. I need to call my agent."

Riley scrabbled his computer and water bottle together and escaped into the corridor with Julie on his heels. She followed him down the two flights of stairs to his floor and into his room.

"That went well." She collapsed onto the lumpy desk chair.

Riley set his laptop on the desk, flipped up the screen, and plugged in the power supply. "Yeah. The crowd went wild. Huzzah."

"Shut up. You did great. At least we're not doing that stupid Houdini story. Max's usual camera-ready poses are bad enough. Can you imagine him trying to channel Houdini?"

"You gotta admit. The fans love him."

"Yeah, but do they love him for the right reason? Is he just camp now? Something they use as background for a drinking game? How many times will Max Stone say, 'Chilling... if true'?"

Riley chuckled. "We know that answer. Once per commercial break."

Julie slid down until her butt was at the edge of the seat. "He's starting to ignore the script and ad lib them now. The last episode had eight instances. We had to edit them out in post." She pushed her bangs off her forehead and laced her hands on top of her head. "Scott's the only one Max listens to, but he refuses to engage. I was stunned he actually told Max to shut up in the meeting today."

"I think he just wanted everyone to leave, and letting Max go on about his Houdini crush would have kept us there forever."

She nudged his knee with her foot. "You were right, Rile. This is a good story. Not the usual paranormal crap. A pretty heartbreaking tale, really." With her chin resting practically on her chest, she grinned at him. "See how smart I was to get Scott to hire a real folklorist and not just a generic researcher?"

Riley sat on the edge of his bed and fell backward. "Brilliant."

"Oh, come on." Julie could wheedle with the finesse of a roomful of kindergartners. "You wouldn't have taken the job if you hadn't been interested in it a little bit. I know it's not folklore fieldwork, but…"

Riley glanced at her. Her eyes were focused on his laptop, her expression grim, and he raised himself to his elbows to see what had caused the sudden change.

He stifled a groan. His wallpaper slideshow had frozen again. On *that* picture. The single piece of evidence that his relationship with Logan hadn't been a product of his fevered imagination. Documentation of the only time Logan had touched him in public.

So embarrassing. Someone had taken the picture at a barbecue during his last spring break. He and Logan, his arm draped around Logan's shoulders, one of Logan's hands resting on Riley's leg, the other wiping something off Riley's bottom lip with his thumb. Logan was smiling—laughing, probably, at Riley's awkwardness—looking hot, as usual, his dark hair rumpled, his chin darkened by the perpetual scruff that Riley couldn't resist. Riley just looked… besotted.

Guys like Logan hated that shit, hated evidence of big stupid feelings, especially those they didn't return. No wonder he'd walked out.

Riley launched himself off the bed and closed the laptop lid. God, he'd been stupid to believe Logan had cared that much about *him*, but nothing else had made sense. Why stick with Riley for a year and a half, especially when dozens of more attractive guys had made it perfectly obvious they'd be willing to take Riley's place? *Shows how spectacularly love can blind you.*

He rested his hand on his laptop, tracing the Apple logo on the lid with a finger. "I saw him last night. Logan."

"Shit, Riley. I don't *believe* you." She shifted sideways on the chair, the better to glare at him. "I didn't tell you about him being in Portland so you could *stalk* him. I told you so you could *avoid* him."

He dropped back onto the edge of the bed and hunched forward, hands between his knees. "Is it so wrong to want the truth from him? This isn't the first time I've been ditched, but usually the guy can't resist listing every single reason why he'd leave a loser like me. I figured Logan would jump at the chance."

"You're not a loser. You're the world's sweetest, most caring guy."

Riley squinched up his face. "Kiss of death, Jules."

"It beats the hell out of being a user douche bag. But you—" She smacked his arm. "You can't give up, can you, not until he tells you to fuck off to your poor little face."

Riley frowned. "I don't have a poor little face."

"Yes, you do. Everything you feel is right there for everyone to read. If I could convince you to get in front of the camera, you'd be an instant hit."

"If I can't hide anything, how could that make me an actor?"

"Not an actor, doofus. You're not self-absorbed enough for that. I mean a host. An interviewer. No one could doubt your sincerity."

"Yeah, that'd go over great." As soon as stage fright kicked in, years of speech therapy would vanish like smoke, and he wouldn't be able to pronounce his own freaking name. He pulled in a deep breath and blew it out. "By the way, he did tell me to fuck off. Not in so many words, but the subtext was pretty damned clear."

"You gonna listen to him?"

Was he? Riley hadn't missed the bulge in Logan's jeans last night. For an instant, he'd let hope for something more than a closure discussion creep into his heart. That was the only reason he'd tried to invite Logan back here to talk. *Yeah, to talk. That's so not what you wanted.* Then Logan had tossed that insulting twenty on the ground, and the hope had died, although the need for closure remained. The question was how to arrange the discussion if Logan wouldn't stand still long enough to exchange more than twelve words and a sneer.

"Guess I don't have much choice." The nail-gun-to-motorcycle-boots option looked better all the time.

Julie slanted a look at him that clearly said, *I'll see your nail gun and raise you a chainsaw.* "We'll see."

Uh-oh. When Julie hatched a plan, virtual death and untold destruction were sure to follow. Trouble was, he didn't know who was in the most danger: Logan or him.

CHAPTER FIVE

Logan dumped an armful of clean clothes onto his bed. Last load of laundry he'd ever do, so what was the point of folding it? He pulled a T-shirt out of the pile and yanked it over his head.

He didn't have a shift tonight, but he needed to drop by the bar to pick up his final check. Enough to settle his remaining expenses. Anything left over, he could shove into the Audubon Society mail slot on his way down the trail on Saturday.

The apartment building's dryer sucked, so his clean jeans were unpleasantly damp. He didn't want to wait for them to dry, so he put them on anyway, the waistband clammy against his skin. As he transferred the contents of his pockets from yesterday's pair, his hand closed around the hard links of a chain.

The rings. He'd taken them off last night and hadn't put them back on.

Why the fucking hell did Riley have to show up and remind Logan not only of what he missed, but of the only time he'd considered setting aside his obligation?

Riley's proximity had tormented him all day. Logan had tried to fill his time with stupid shit—laundry being a case in point—to keep his mind off the knowledge that the man was a mere ten-minute bike ride away. Facing his fucking destiny had been a hell of a lot easier when Riley was out of reach.

What would Riley think of him if he found out the truth? Logan's father, politically invested in keeping his son's public nose clean, had lied to the police investigating Trent's disappearance with a concerned frown on his face—he'd made sure Logan hadn't been implicated.

With anyone other than Riley, Logan wouldn't have been worried—he'd learned plausible denial at his father's knee, after all. But Riley was a smart guy, and it was his job to track down connections in stories. Shit, that's how Logan had found him in the first place, why he'd first been attracted to him. If Riley ever found out Logan had lied to him during their entire relationship? It wouldn't matter that his lies were ones of omission—he couldn't depend on Riley forgiving him for them, no matter what his reasons.

The first year after Trent disappeared, Logan had gone back to the park every night, violating the park's posted hours through the cold, wet winter and the colder, wetter spring. All summer and into fall, he'd continued, dodging the authorities, risking discovery and pissing his father the hell off. All for nothing, because not once in three hundred and sixty-four days, had anything shown up other than bats, raccoons, and the occasional deer.

Then exactly a year later, at midnight on October seventeenth, when he'd been huddled against the dank mossy stones of the Witch's Castle, drinking himself into a stupor in Trent's honor, it had happened again. Or mostly. The barrier rose, but the floating blobs of greenish light that populated the battlefield hadn't resolved into transparent pioneers as they had that night with Trent.

Why had everything been so clear then? His grandfather's story spoke of recognizable figures too. What was the difference? Was it the weather? The brand of beer? Did it need two trapped men to engage the whatever-the-hell-it-was? He'd decided he either needed to seriously consider a lobotomy, or try to find a solution. After all, Trent had somehow made the leap in, so there must be a way to pull him out again. Logan just needed to find it. The key. The trick. The fucking magic word.

That had launched him on his quest. He'd visited every medium he could find—every spiritualist or shaman or new-age practitioner from Oregon to Florida, from Maine to Baja. Some of them were obvious charlatans. Some weren't interested. Some seemed legit, and were more than happy to sell him powders and potions and incantations, but none of that shit did anything except make him sneeze, retch, and feel like a fucking fool.

Although he hated to risk interference from some grandstanding paranormal investigator, on the fifth anniversary of Trent's disappearance, he'd paid a medium from Sarasota—a woman with the unlikely name of Marguerite Windflower who looked like a new-age flake, but swore like a sailor—to go to the park with him. She'd paced around the clearing, studying the perimeter barrier, peering at the greenish blobs, at the last place he'd seen Trent alive, and at one or two other spots that Logan would prefer to forget.

Every once in a while, she had studied a spot immediately to her left and nodded as if she were consulting with an invisible colleague, which lifted the hair on Logan's neck worse than the Witch's Castle ghosts.

When the barrier finally dissipated, she'd lit a clove cigarette and said. "Can't help you."

"Why not? Are you a fake too?"

"You tell me. I don't mind people calling me a fake as long as they pay me. But the last thing you want is for me to lay these spirits." She speared him with a narrow-eyed glare. "'Lay' means exorcise. You got that, or are you going to make the usual stupid-ass remark about *fucking mediums*?"

He raised his hands, palms out. "Hey. No disrespect. I just want the truth."

"Fine." She blew out a stream of smoke. "I might be able to kill the manifestation. But if it dissipates, everything'll vanish. The end. Poof. That what you want?"

"What? No! I want to find out how to release a real person from wherever the hell he is."

She snorted, smoke curling out her nostrils. "These were all real people once. But you know something, Slick? I'm not sure they're ghosts."

"How do you know?"

Her gaze flicked to the left again. "I've got some experience with those. These don't feel the same. I could try the banishment ritual if you want—"

"No! Not if it means they could... He could..." Logan ran shaking hands through his hair. "Just no. I'll find another way."

Pity flickered across her face, softened the hard look in her shrewd eyes. "Good luck with that."

"If I wanted to do that—find another way, I mean—what should I do?"

"How the fuck should I know? I told you about ghosts. You don't like the answer? Ask a different question."

"How—"

"Don't ask *me*, genius. Find someone who knows about other woo-woo shit and ask them." She cast an irritated glance at the rain beading her flowered poncho. "Christ on a pogo stick, how can you people live like this? I'm surprised your balls don't mildew in the wet. Get me the fuck out of here."

He'd delivered her to the airport—and although she'd kept up a sporadic conversation with her imaginary friend, he'd let himself hope for the first time since Trent vanished. While Marguerite hadn't had the answer he wanted, she'd made him believe an answer existed. Just his goddamned luck that he'd found the answer from the one man who made him wish the quest was hopeless.

"Seriously, Jules, why here? This is inviting disaster." Riley resisted as Julie practically frog-marched him through the door of Stumptown Spirits. "Why don't we do this meeting at

Starbucks, or Burger King, or someplace else where I haven't been kicked out?"

The heavy door closed behind them with a final-sounding *thump*. Ominous.

"That waitress told you the mean boss wouldn't be here tonight, right? What are you afraid of?"

"You. We could just as easily have interviewed those witnesses at the hotel and... Wait a minute." He eyed her giant shoulder bag. "You don't have your taser in there, do you?"

"I don't know what you're talking about." She blinked her big brown eyes as if she were as honest and innocent as Bambi instead of as wily and merciless as Shere Khan. "I'm just in a good mood. Max's local promo spots today were very well attended. His ego is sufficiently inflated to reconcile him to being in Portland, and he's actually stopped whining."

"Whatever." Riley chose a booth that gave him a clear view of the hallway, early warning in case the waitress had been wrong and the barkeep from hell descended on him again like a cross between the Furies and the cast of *The Walking Dead*. As a bonus, he'd see Logan before Logan saw him, and have a chance to arrange his expression into something less than love-stricken.

Julie flounced down onto the wooden settle across from him, humming under her breath. God, she really was in a good mood, and it freaked him out a little.

"Seriously, Jules. This is a beer-and-burger dive. Not exactly your usual venue for interviewing potential witnesses."

"Both these guys live nearby, so it's a convenient location for them." She retrieved the file with *HttM*'s release forms from her bag and plopped it on the table. "The show has to pick up the tab for the meetings, and the prices here are in line with the budget. I checked. Besides..."

Here it comes. "Do I want to hear this?"

The Bambi-eye disguise vanished, and Shere Khan pounced with a roar. "Maybe I want to see what that asshat fucktard Logan Conner thought was worth breaking your heart for."

"Jules—" A movement in the hallway caught Riley's attention. The gleam of the overhead light on dark, wavy hair. Broad shoulders outlined by a snug white T-shirt. A brush of black fire from the dome of the motorcycle helmet in one arm.

Logan.

Logan saw him. Riley was certain, because their gazes clashed long enough for his heartbeat to stutter, stop, and reboot.

But instead of taking his place behind the bar, Logan turned on his heel and vanished down the hall, his retreat punctuated by the clang of a metal panic bar followed by the slam of a heavy door.

No way was Riley letting the big jerk run a second time. He jumped up. "I'll be back."

Julie pursed her lips. "Nothing good *ever* follows that particular line."

"Please. Cut me a little slack for once in your life."

"Fine." She picked up the menu. "I'll order french fries for you. And eat them all myself."

He squeezed her shoulder, craning his neck to see down the hall, but a couple of servers were blocking his view. "Perfect."

As he bolted for the front door, he heard her mutter, "*Men.*"

Riley circled the building at a run until he found the entrance to the alley that cut behind the bar. *There.* The caged light over the rear door shone on Logan, who stood next to a motorcycle, his back to the mouth of the alley.

"Logan."

Logan jerked and dropped his helmet. "Shit." When he bent to retrieve it, Riley got a good look at the bike, and his mouth fell open.

"A Harley? You're kidding. You hate Harleys."

"You were expecting a Vincent '52?"

The air left Riley's lungs in a whoosh as if he'd just cornered out of a steep downhill swoop of a monster roller coaster.

Eugene. The first time. He remembers.

When Logan had approached Riley about the Witch's Castle ghosts, he'd dropped the name of the bar where he worked. Riley had started hanging out there on dollar-beer night in the hope of sharing a word or two with the gorgeous bartender, even if it was only to order another IPA.

One night, a couple of weeks after he'd started haunting the bar, he'd been making the usual fool of himself, attempting to prove to a table full of business and computer science majors that his folklore degree wasn't obsolete. He'd been going on and on about how Richard Thompson's song "1952 Vincent Black Lightning" was evidence that the traditional narrative ballad structure was alive and well in modern popular music. That the forms, the patterns, the mythic cycles, were as viable in the twenty-first century as they'd been in the fourteenth.

Logan must have heard Riley's whole pathetic diatribe from behind the bar, but hadn't laughed along with the rest of the audience, which, by the time Riley had finished, seemed to include half the UO student body, all of them three-quarters sloshed.

Instead, as Riley had trudged home in the chill of the late November night, Logan had rolled up alongside him on his Ducati.

He pulled off his helmet and jerked his thumb at the seat behind him. "It's not a Vincent '52, but at least it's not a Harley. Want a ride?"

The lopsided grin accompanying the amusement in Logan's bedroom baritone sent its own streak of lightning down Riley's spine. He took the offered helmet, climbed on, and wrapped his arms around that lean waist, using the excuse of seat's slope to snug his crotch to Logan's ass.

Logan chuckled, and Riley felt the vibration in his balls, with the inevitable result that his cock hardened behind the fly of his jeans. Logan pressed his legs against Riley's inner thighs. "Hold that thought, folklore boy. I'll get you there."

And he had. Over and over, for the next year and a half.

And then, he'd disappeared.

But still, if he remembered that first ride as clearly as Riley did after all this time, it must mean something to him. Now, another bike. Another chance.

But not if I don't get some freaking answers.

Although the prospect for that wasn't good, not when Logan was refusing to look at him. Instead, he dug a towel out of the Harley's saddlebag and scrubbed at his helmet, a scowl on his face.

"Logan, we need to—"

"Why are you here, Riley?"

At least he acknowledged me. Riley counted it as a win. "That's the reason."

"What?"

"Not what. Why." Riley gulped and took another step into the alley. "I want to know why."

Fuck, Logan was losing it. He'd barely managed to hold it together last night, and repeated Riley-sightings were guaranteed to test his willpower to its limits. *Get on the bike and blow. You did it before.*

He scowled at his helmet as he wiped the crap off it. "Why the hell aren't you in Europe?"

"Because I didn't get the grant."

"Why? Nothing to tie you here. Unless..." Logan pasted a sneer across his face. "Did you think I'd come back?"

"Not everything's about you, Logan." Riley shrugged. "I didn't qualify. The grant recipient has to hold a master's degree. I don't."

Logan was stunned out of his sneer. "What the fuck? You were a week from graduation. One final and your thesis, that was it."

"Didn't take the final. Didn't turn in the thesis. Hence, no master's."

"Jesus, Riley. You worked your ass off for that. Why bail at the last minute?"

"Gee, I don't know." His voice was laced with scorn. "What could possibly cause someone to take off with no warning, leaving a shit-ton of unfinished business behind?"

"That was different."

"Weally? How exactly?"

That little slip, the *W* for *R* that Riley didn't correct, kicked Logan right in the heart. *He used to lose it like that when we made love.* "I didn't..." Logan balled up the soiled towel and shoved it in the Harley's saddlebag. "I didn't want you anymore."

"Maybe I didn't want the degree anymore." Riley moved out of the shadows, the wan moonlight turning the lenses of his glasses silver. "Is that truly the reason why?"

Fuck no. But if I'd stayed one more day, I wouldn't have been strong enough to go. He'd have told himself one more night, one more fuck, one more kiss, until he'd have stayed forever.

"I'm a fucking mess, Riley. You deserve better than that."

"So you left me for my own good? You know, the whole self-sacrifice motif never ends well. Fate has a way of making sure it comes back to bite you on the butt."

Like right now. Logan fumbled his helmet and dropped it again, this time on his foot.

Riley coughed, but Logan swore it was to cover a laugh. "You know, when I think of it..." His face lit up, and Logan groaned.

God, that look. I'm fucking toast.

Whenever a shiny new notion captured Riley's imagination, he followed it all the way down the rabbit hole, ignoring everything else. Logan had always been able to distract him, though, with a kiss on his neck—or in extreme cases, a hand down the front of his pants.

All too tempted to try the same tactics now, Logan took a step back, but Riley was in the zone now, and he followed, shoving at his glasses with one knuckle.

"Mythic concepts are universal, but their expression changes with the culture, with time. These days, your destiny is just as likely to be slapstick as a sword point. The Fates are less likely to drink your blood on the battlefield nowadays than to squirt cosmic seltzer down your pants. Three Fates." He held up three fingers on each hand. "Three Stooges. So forget Clotho, Lachesis, Atropos. Larry, Moe, and Curly have got you in their sights."

Retreat. Retreat. "Look, kid. Sure, we had some good times." He kept his own tone harsh, verging on contemptuous, killing that seductive glow on Riley's face. "That's all. You should know that a guy like me could never—"

"Right. Sorry. I didn't mean to get all..." Riley took an unsteady breath and studied the ground at his feet. "I get that I'm not worth your time."

Logan clenched his eyes shut and regretted it immediately. He could smell Riley's crazy herbal soap better this way. Mint. Rosemary. But no lavender. Riley hated lavender. "No. That's not it. You're totally worth the right guy's time. Me? I'm not that guy."

"Is there— Is there someone else?"

He opened his eyes. Shit. Riley was way too close, and Logan decided he'd been mistaken: Riley wasn't devastated. He was pissed as hell. "Yeah. Guy I met on the road. Crazy good sex. No strings. Just the way I like it." Logan took another step back, his fingers twitching with the urge to run them through Riley's hair. Stroke the column of his throat. Cup his ass. Christ. *I've got to get out of here.*

"You're lying, Logan. I can always tell."

"I'm not. It's true."

"Nope. The muscles in your cheek bunch right there." Riley's finger paused an inch from his cheek, and Logan held his breath. *Don't. I can't stay strong if you touch me.* Riley closed that last inch. A feather touch. Logan's breath shuddered as he exhaled.

"And you start to talk like a telegram, as if you're being charged by the word."

"I—"

"You were lying then, and you're lying now. What can it matter? If it's over for you, it's over. Fine. I'll deal, but I need to know why. What I did. So I can do better with the next guy."

The idea of Riley in someone else's arms sent a spike of possessive fury from the base of Logan's skull to his balls. He grabbed Riley around the waist with one arm and caught the back of his head with the other hand. Crushed their lips together in a clash of teeth, a tangle of tongues. Swallowing Riley's moans and giving back some of his own.

Would it be so bad to take this little time? To have these last few precious days with the man he loved, before he paid his final debt and left warmth and joy and life behind for good?

Keep him safe, damn it.

Logan pushed Riley away and took a huge breath. A mistake, because the air was full of the scent of their combined arousal. Prelude to Sex, the designer fragrance of lust. "I'm not doing this, Riley."

Riley wiped his mouth with the back of his hand. "Why? You seemed on board a minute ago."

"We're in an alley. It's public. It's also fricking cold."

"Same old Logan." He shook his head and gave a tired chuckle. "So hands-on in private. So hands-off in public. You're worse than a closeted quarterback."

"Go home. Find another guy who'll treat you the way you deserve. Just get the hell out of Portland."

"Not until you tell me why. What I did wrong."

Damn it. Logan had pulled out all the stops in douchebaggery when he left Eugene—precisely to keep Riley away from here, away from danger, away from him and his fucking *fate*. He grabbed Riley's arms and got into his face, almost nose to nose. "Listen, you can't—"

A whistle echoed off the bricks of the alley. Alarm sizzled at the base of Logan's skull, and his head snapped up. *Exposure. Not an option.* A knot of young guys stood on the sidewalk a dozen feet away. He couldn't tell whether their grins signified encouragement, a desire to join the party, or to break it up with violence, but he wasn't waiting around to find out.

"Come on." He towed Riley through the rear door of Stumptown Spirits.

"Logan, wait. I—"

He propelled them into the stockroom and kicked the door closed, facing Riley amid the stacked cases of beer, and backing him against the wall between the Widmer and the Weinhard.

"Goddamn it, Riley." Logan's voice, muffled by the crowded storeroom, was nevertheless overloud in his own ears. "What do I have to do to keep you—"

Heavy footsteps sounded in the hallway, followed by a jingle of dropped keys and Bert's muffled curse. Logan clamped a hand over Riley's mouth.

"My boss," he murmured in the vicinity of Riley's ear. God. *Right there.* That tender skin below Riley's earlobe at the feathered edge of his hairline. Logan didn't think. He couldn't think with Riley this close, chest pressed to chest, thigh pressed to thigh, and everything in between getting into the act.

Hell and damnation but he'd missed this man, and he wasn't made of stone, although part of his anatomy was rapidly doing a first-class impression.

Lowering his head, Logan brushed his lips over the secret spot behind that ridiculously perfect ear. Riley inhaled, sharp and sweet, and Logan traced the path with his tongue. "Why did you have to find me?" he breathed. "How am I supposed to resist you?"

Riley laced his hands in the hair at Logan's nape. "Well..." His voice was low. Husky. Bedroom-infused, the way he'd always sounded right before he begged Logan to fuck him. He was about to say it. About to beg, and with his dick hard to the point of pain, Logan didn't have the strength to say no.

Then Riley shoved him away and whacked him on the chest. "Guess you'll have to figure that out, won't you?" He sauntered to the door and paused to flip Logan off. "So long, Logan. Have a nice life."

CHAPTER SIX

Riley speed-walked down the sidewalk, texting Julie that he was heading back to the hotel. Between the encounter with Logan and dodging his scary boss, Riley's nerves were vibrating like the strings of a lute. He'd freaking done it. He'd walked away, but he'd been *this freaking close* to caving. His traitorous brain had whispered, *Go on. Do it once more. What could it hurt? Use it to flush him out of your system.*

This might be the first time ever that he hadn't listened to that insidious voice, at least where Logan was concerned.

God, when Logan had boxed him in between those cases of liquor? Riley hadn't been able to breathe, and his cock had tried to sproing out of his briefs.

No gay man on earth would have blamed him, not if they'd ever had Logan pressed between their legs. Logan, with his slate-colored eyes, cheekbones any sculptor would kill to reproduce, dark hair that would be shaggy if it didn't sport enough curl to keep it under control. No wonder Riley's heart had thudded louder than a giant's footsteps.

Yet even though his voice had wobbled, Riley had finally done the smart thing.

He'd turned his back on temptation.

But by the time he boarded the light rail train—called MAX, in a truly cosmic joke, thanks no doubt to the Three Fateful Stooges—he'd come down off that *screw you*-moment high.

He didn't get it. He'd left. Finally gotten the last word. Why didn't he feel vindicated or satisfied, instead of like Prometheus chained to his rock, with vultures pecking at his heart? Okay, so with Prometheus, it was an eagle after his liver, but whatever.

Closure. Wasn't it supposed to feel better than this?

Then, as he waited for the connection to the streetcar, he figured it out.

He hadn't gotten closure. He still had no idea why Logan had dumped him. Still no answer to that riddle, no moral at the end of their story to teach him what to do the next time.

Strike that. The moral was that Riley was an idiot to still love someone who couldn't even commit to not committing.

Logan held out for three minutes tops after Riley's big exit before taking off after him. Now that he'd had a tease, a taste of Riley, he was done pretending he could resist.

With his life already on the chopping block, he'd have nothing, be nothing, possibly less than nothing, by this time next week. Wasn't every condemned man due a last meal?

He wanted his last meal to be Riley.

All arrogance aside, he knew Riley could be convinced to go along with the program, despite his rebellious exit line. Riley wasn't a guy who could hide his feelings, and he'd given Logan the full spectrum tonight. The man was still hurt, still pissed—and still in love, or he wouldn't *be* so hurt and pissed.

If Logan played things right tonight, he could fix that too. Because he had a Plan.

Logan didn't rush the ride to the Vaughn Street Hotel, both to give Riley time to get there, and to convince himself that he wasn't acting like a total selfish son of a bitch.

As his tires sang on the wet pavement, he told himself he wouldn't let this momentary lapse in his willpower deflect him from his goal. One night, and then he'd return alone to the final countdown. *But after five months of doing nothing but shit I hate, don't I rate this one perfect reward?*

Logan parked his bike in the far corner of the hotel's parking lot and stood behind a spindly fir where he could monitor the entrance. Half an hour ago, he'd have sworn what he wanted most in the world was for Riley to stay as far away as possible. He hadn't counted on the overwhelming desire—as sharp and bright and deadly as a knife in his gut—to touch Riley again, to hold him, to kiss him, one more time before the end.

If he was careful, he could meet both needs—have a last night with Riley, yet convince him that Logan was not worth mourning. If he pulled out all the assholery stops afterward, maybe Riley would be so disgusted he'd break it off himself. Yeah. That was the Plan.

A fucking stupid plan, but it was the best his case of blue balls would let him come up with.

He caught the gleam of Riley's hair under a streetlight at the corner a couple of minutes later as the man trudged up the street, head down as if his shoes held a fricking GPS.

A growl rumbled in Logan's throat. What was Riley thinking, walking alone in this part of town, paying zero attention to his surroundings? Did he have no sense of self-preservation?

Not if he's willing to fuck you. Although that remained to be seen.

Logan waited until Riley walked into the lobby, then followed him in. A bunch of people clustered around the elevators. Riley veered away from them and took the stairs, and Logan followed undetected because Riley never looked back, up, or sideways.

On the second floor, Riley exited the stairwell, so Logan took the last steps two at a time, slipping out the door before it clicked shut. He caught up with Riley outside his room as he wrestled his key card out of the pocket of those painted-on jeans.

He reached past Riley's shoulder and slapped his palm on the door.

Riley jerked, breath catching, and dropped the key card on his shoes. He didn't turn around. "What do you want, Logan?"

Showtime, Conner. Break out the dickhead behavior, no matter what you truly want. Logan lowered his head to murmur against the nape of Riley's neck. "You think you can walk out on me like that?"

Riley shivered, but didn't turn. "Why not? You did."

"That was different."

"Weally."

Christ. That adorable wayward *R*, this time with a snarky attitude chaser. Logan's dick awoke at the clear evidence that Riley wasn't indifferent. He backed off a step, giving Riley some space. "Pick up the key and let me in."

Riley's shoulders rose and fell in a giant breath. "Fine. But I still want some answers." He opened the door and walked inside, turning to face Logan at the end of a short vestibule as he shucked off his jacket.

Logan's breath stalled in his chest. The man was so fricking beautiful, his eyes shining behind his glasses, his hair like chocolate silk. Quirky. Smart. Extraordinary. Like no one Logan had ever met, before or since.

Don't start mooning like a teenager, dumbass. Remember your part.

Logan stalked into the room, his gaze never leaving Riley's face. He kicked the door shut.

"I can't tell you why, but I can tell you what. Straight-up, no-strings, no-frills fucking. Rough and ready." He crowded closer to Riley. "As in you're ready. I'm rough."

In the dim light from the desk lamp, Riley's pupils were indistinguishable from the irises. "You're not like that." Beneath the doubt in his tone ran the same undercurrent of excitement Riley had always displayed whenever they'd tried anything new in the bedroom. *Thank God.* If Logan hadn't heard it, he could never have gone through with this.

"I am now." He advanced on Riley and spun him to face the wall, trapping him with his body. "No beds. Fucking. Dirty, plain and simple. You onboard with that?"

"Y-y-yes. I'm good." Riley trembled against him, and Logan's cock strained behind his fly. Shit, he wouldn't last two minutes at this rate.

"As long as we're clear." Logan flipped Riley around to face him again. "Take off your clothes."

When Riley hesitated, eyes wide and startled, Logan forced menace into his voice that he didn't feel. "Rough and ready, remember? So get ready. Now."

Riley hooked his thumbs under the hem of his Henley, his gaze locked on Logan's. He raised his shirt, slowly. Too slowly, damn it, giving Logan way too long to trace the smooth muscles on hip and belly and chest. Riley's skin was as honey-smooth as he remembered, although maybe a shade paler, all the better to show off his spreading flush.

Logan stifled a groan. "Now the pants."

Riley paused with his hands at his waist. "What about you?"

Logan unbuckled his belt and unzipped his fly, freeing his cock from his boxer briefs to bob against his belly. "I'm ready. Pants, Riley."

Riley fumbled with his belt, his fingers trembling. He slanted a look at Logan from under his lashes and caught half his plump bottom lip between his teeth, sending a spike of heat from Logan's throat to his balls. His heart beat like a monster bass, sending the blood roaring in his ears. Could Riley hear it? See it? He forced a sneer onto his face, the better to hide the truth.

When Riley pushed his jeans and briefs down, baring his rigid cock in its nest of dark curls, his balls already tight against his body, Logan had to cross his arms over his chest, sinking his fingers into his biceps, distracting himself with the sharp pain. He wanted to drop to his knees and worship Riley as he deserved. Nuzzle that glorious cock. Take it into his mouth and throat until Riley writhed against him.

Christ, it had been so fucking long.

He inhaled, harsh and deep. *Don't give in. Do your job. Be a douche bag.*

Right.

So when Riley tried to toe off one of his sneakers, Logan thrust his knee between Riley's thighs.

"Leave 'em."

"But my jeans. I can't get them off over my shoes."

"I said leave 'em. This'll do. For now."

He wanted full-body skin contact. Wanted to feel every inch of Riley with every inch of himself, but he couldn't give in. Couldn't weaken. He had to keep up this pitiful charade of Logan-as-uncaring-asshole, so Riley wouldn't mourn him too deeply.

This night would be enough. It had to be. It was a damn sight more than he'd ever expected and a shitload more than he deserved.

He repositioned his legs, trapping Riley's between his, and held up his right palm. "Lick it."

Riley's tongue darted out, licking his lips, and Logan had to fight the urge to follow it back into Riley's mouth with his own.

"I—"

"No talking. Do it."

Riley nodded, Adam's apple bobbing as he swallowed. Gaze never leaving Logan's, he dragged the flat of his tongue from the base of Logan's palm to the tips of his fingers, then sucked the middle finger into his mouth, cheeks hollowing with perfect suction that was simultaneously heaven and hell.

Logan ground his teeth and snatched his hand away before he shot from nothing but the heat of Riley's mouth on his finger.

"Don't pad your part. I'm running this show. Get it?"

Riley nodded, his tongue darting out to moisten his lips. "Got it," he whispered.

Logan leaned in and fastened his teeth on Riley's earlobe, wrapping his hand around their cocks. "Good."

Yes. So fucking good. Thank God for his oversized hands. He pumped them both, skin against hot silken skin, pre-come adding extra slick to his Riley-damp palm.

He captured Riley's mouth in an almost feral kiss, tongue-fucking him in time with the increasing speed of his fist. A nip of that swollen lower lip as he swiped his thumb over the heads of their cocks.

Riley gasped. "Logan. God. I—" He threw his head back, and Logan caught it with his free hand before it could hit the wall.

Riley shuddered, spilling hot and wet over Logan's hand and onto the smooth skin of his own belly. The intoxicating musky scent pushed Logan right to the edge.

But it was the sight of Riley, gorgeous in the throes of his orgasm, that sent Logan soaring out into space. His jaw tightened as shudders rippled up his spine, his spunk painting Riley's skin from nipples to navel.

With a sound that was part sigh, part chuckle, part snort, Riley nestled his cheek against Logan's shoulder. That sound, totally ridiculous and incredibly dear, torpedoed the last of Logan's resolve. Instead of pulling away, zipping up, and walking out as he ought to do, he wrapped his arms around Riley, holding him close, heedless of the cooling mess that transferred from Riley's chest and belly to his own T-shirt.

Fuck it. I'm taking this. Just for a little while. Just until the end. He buried his nose in the soft hair tickling his jaw, and gave up on the Plan.

Damn thing was fucking stupid anyway.

CHAPTER SEVEN

With all Logan's talk of no-strings fucking, Riley hadn't expected him to stay the night. But after their second round, when they'd made it from the wall to the floor—with the inevitable rug burn on Riley's knees, but he didn't care—Logan had dragged him onto the bed and fallen asleep with his hand cupping Riley's balls.

Not about to remind him that cuddling didn't exactly line up with the no-strings agenda, Riley had snugged his ass against Logan's groin and slept better than he had for months.

Although Logan might talk tough and act like he didn't care, Riley hadn't missed the almost reverent way he'd stroked Riley's skin, or his kisses more tender than raw.

It let him hope.

As daylight crept in through a gap in the curtains, he rolled onto his side, and tucked his hand under his cheek, studying Logan as he slept. God, he always looked so hot in the morning: hair rumpled, scruff another day scruffier, a satisfied smirk on his face even in sleep. Riley had taken a picture of that look with his camera phone once and shown it to Logan, who'd called it "the sleep of the well-fucked."

He lifted the sheet and peeked at Logan's body; it was still the toned work of art it had always been, although he might be a little leaner. Just what the man needed. More muscle definition.

Riley's gaze strayed to Logan's cock, already half-hard. Well. Nobody had ever accused Riley of leaving a job undone, and he wasn't about to let this be the first time. He grinned and crawled under the covers, the sheets enveloping him in a smooth white tent. Just him and Logan's gorgeous cock. Yeah. The perfect way to start the day.

Riley licked his lips, but before he could lick anything more to the point, a determined rap sounded on the door.

"Who's tap-dancing on the walls?" Logan muttered and buried his head beneath the pillow.

Riley struggled out from under the sheets, and scrambled out of bed to the accompaniment of another round of knocking. He yanked open the drawer of the junior-sized dresser. Pants, pants, somewhere he had pants.

He pulled a pair of sweats out of a tangle of T-shirts and underwear, shoved one leg in, caught his toes on the elastic, and nearly took a header onto the rug. Hopping across the room on one foot, he finally got the other leg in and the drawstring cinched around his waist.

More pounding. "Hold on. I'm coming."

Logan's evil chuckle was barely muffled by the pillow. "Not yet. Soon though."

Heat infused Riley's bare chest, and a grin ambushed his face. "Shut up." *Shut up? Seriously?* God, could he sound any more like a seventh grader? He probably looked like one too, the kid who'd just found out that his secret crush wanted to meet him under the bleachers after school. He leaned one bare shoulder against the wall, unhooked the privacy chain, and cracked the door open.

Julie stood in the corridor, tapping her foot in time with the drum of her pencil against her clipboard. "Where did you go last night? I needed to go over..." Julie stared at him. "Oh my God. You had sex with Logan."

Her voice echoed in the hallway and a middle-aged man passing by with three pink Voodoo Doughnuts boxes in his arms turned a startled gaze their way.

"God, Jules." Riley glared at her. "Keep it down, will you? How can you possibly know that?"

"How? For one thing, you have sex hair. For another." Julie drew on her yellow pad and held up a picture of an alleged face —a circle with two dots for eyes and a zigzag for a mouth. "You've looked like this since rat-bastard sucktard Logan walked out last May."

Riley scowled. "My head is not that round."

She bent over her pad, pencil flying. "This is what you look like today." She held up the pad with a new drawing, the zigzag replaced by a half-circle that extended all the way past the eye dots.

"Shut up."

Her eyes widened. "Holy shit. He's here now, isn't he?"

Riley clenched his teeth and nodded.

"You want me to go away, don't you?"

He nodded again, more emphatically.

"And I'll bet you don't want me to remind you..." She poked the knob of his shoulder, the only spot she could reach through the door. "...that the asshole scum-bucket walked out on you without a freaking word five months ago."

"No. Now go away."

"Fine, but we've got a production meeting at ten, and if you're not there, I'm sending Max down here."

"You wouldn't."

"Try me. Ten. Don't be late." She disappeared down the hallway.

He hung the *Do Not Disturb* sign on the doorknob and shut the door. Not that it would deter Julie, but what the hell. He could say he tried.

He crawled onto the bed and lay on Logan's back on top of the blankets, digging his chin into Logan's shoulder.

"I ever tell you your chin should be registered as a lethal weapon?" Logan rumbled from under the pillows.

"No one can accuse me of carrying concealed. Pretty hard to miss it."

"Who was that?"

"Julie."

Logan emerged from under the pillows and propped himself up on his elbows, toppling Riley off his back. "Julie Ainsworth?"

Riley rolled to his knees. "The same."

"That chick has always hated my guts."

"Not really." *Not always, anyway.* "But she thinks I'm too good for you."

Logan snorted. "No shit. Last time I saw her, I thought she'd serve my nuts as a side dish in a salad bar."

"She's the one who got me this job."

"Job?"

"That's why I'm in town."

At the dumbfounded look on Logan's face, laughter bubbled up from Riley's belly, and he fell sideways onto the bed. "Oh my God. You thought I only showed up in Portland because of you."

Logan rolled onto his back and tucked his hands behind his head, staring at the ceiling with a muscle jumping high in his cheek. *Okay. Lie on the way.* "No. Of course not."

Riley shucked off his sweats and burrowed under the blanket, straddling Logan's hips and poking him in the ribs. "You did. You totally did. Are you hurt because I didn't seek you out like my personal Holy Grail?"

"No." He batted Riley's hands away. "What job? I thought you were doing research. On that study grant."

Riley wiggled his hips from side to side to line up their cocks more efficiently. Neither of them were fully hard yet. He'd work on that—with pleasure. "Not eligible, remember? Took a job with Julie's TV show instead. We're based in LA."

"She landed a gig in Hollywood and decided to share the love, eh?" Logan ran his callused palm along Riley's side and rested it on his bare hip. A shiver chased it all the way down.

"Yup. My old thesis advisor may never forgive her. Or you." Riley pressed a kiss to Logan's collarbone. "She had visions of me, I don't know, trekking through the Balkans with nothing but a rucksack and a tape recorder, discovering original folktales under every village idiot."

"Dude. Who carries a rucksack anymore? Hell, who even *makes* rucksacks, let alone tape recorders?"

"Well, she's old-school."

"So what's the show? Documentaries? A reboot of *Faerie Tale Theatre*? X-rated folklore exposés?"

"Ever hear of *Haunted to the Max*?"

"You're shitting me." Logan's eyebrows rose halfway to his hairline. "That piece of crap?"

"Now you're being judgmental."

"Damn straight," he growled. "You're better than that."

"Don't be an ass." Riley pushed Logan flat against the pillows and propped his hands on the broad shoulders. "Think about it. Ghost stories, urban legends—they're living folklore, as relevant today as the traditional tales like 'Alison Gross' or 'Tam Lin' or 'Thomas Rymer' were to the audiences who first heard them. They touch people, or their friends, or friends of friends." He grinned at Logan's skeptical scowl. "They're like the social networking of the supernatural."

"Try the social networking of the stupid and gullible."

Riley smoothed the knot between Logan's brows with his thumb. "There you go with the judgment again. You're looking at it the wrong way. The appeal of this show, of any kind of supernatural investigation, isn't what actually happens. It's the anticipation, the thrill, of what *might* happen. Like Christmas morning, only with no presents." He dropped a kiss on the corner of Logan's frown. "And more screaming."

"Screaming, huh?" He pulled Riley down and rolled on top of him. "I can think of better reasons to scream."

"I suppose…" Riley trailed his hands across Logan's biceps "… in a way, you *are* the reason I'm here."

Logan's grin was positively wolfish. "I knew it."

"Don't get a swelled head."

Logan shifted his hips, and his dick, hot and hard, slid against Riley's leg.

"Well, okay, that head can swell all it likes. But think about it."

"I'll think about it later. Right now, I'm going to fuck you." He licked a path from Riley's shoulder to his ear, and Riley shivered, parting his legs so that Logan rested between them, both of them fully hard. *Yes! Ready for round three.* "You got time?"

Riley undulated his hips, loving the feel of Logan's weight on him, of the slide of secret skin. "An hour." Logan sucked on the spot behind his ear, and he gasped. "We're touring the Witch's Castle site this morning but—"

"What?" Logan pushed himself up on his hands, staring down at Riley with eyes suddenly gone flat. "Why?"

"That's the story we're doing. The hanging of Danford Balch and the alleged supernatural family feud in Forest Park."

Logan tossed back the blankets, and rolled off Riley to sit on the edge of the bed. Gooseflesh rose on Riley's skin that had less to do with the chill air and more with the rigid line of Logan's bare spine.

"Logan?" Crap, why did his voice have to sound so tentative? "What's wrong? You're the one who told me the story in the first place. Your grandfather—"

"I didn't tell you so you could broadcast it to the world."

Riley scrambled to his knees. "I'm pretty sure the show's total audience is closer to the population of Winnemucca, Nevada. We don't have a world kind of reach." He rested his palm on

Logan's back, but Logan flinched away and stood, spine rigid, and moved to the window.

Damn it, Logan, don't shut me out. Not again.

Logan hunched forward, his fists propped on the window ledge. "You won't be able to get permission to film in the park at night."

"Already done. Everything's in place. Even Max is reconciled to being here." Riley wrapped the blanket around his shoulders. "It's a real chance for us to rescue this show from its descent into camp. Even if the ghosts don't manifest, the history itself is still compelling."

Logan swore under his breath. "Do you know what that fucking ghost story did to my family?" He stared out the window, his scowl superimposed on the freeway vista beyond the rain-speckled glass. "My grandfather was a war hero. They gave him a fucking parade when he came back from France. But after that night in the park? After the ghost war? Nobody would talk to him. He lost his job. They accused him of murder, for Chrissake."

"Why did they accuse him of murder? The ghosts had been dead for nearly a century by then."

"Because… because he wasn't alone when he saw the ghosts. The other man, the man who was with him… he disappeared that night. Never found. Granddad swore the ghosts took him." Logan's laugh was closer to a sob. "They decided Granddad was too crazy to go to trial so they institutionalized him. Hell, they wanted to fucking lobotomize him, but my grandmother wouldn't stand for it."

"I'm sorry, Logan," Riley whispered around the lump in his throat.

"Sometimes I think it would have been kinder. At least he wouldn't have known how contemptuous everyone was of him. All he had to do was say it wasn't true, and they'd have let him out. But he believed in honesty, and he wouldn't."

"There have been other witnesses, other anecdotes. The ghost war shows up on a half-dozen different paranormal tracking websites. We can leave him out of it. We won't mention his name."

Logan snorted. "His name. That's a laugh." Logan unfurled his left fist and stared at the thick scar that ran diagonally across his palm. "My dad was so freaked about the scandal of having a crazy father that he changed our fucking name."

"Your name's not Conner?"

"O'Connor." He held up his tattooed forearms. "I got the Celtic knot work just to piss Dad off. I think my father would have preferred a murderer to a lunatic in the family. Once he hit adulthood, he never visited Granddad again."

"Why didn't you tell me? If I'd known—"

"So kill it." Logan leaned his forehead against the window, and his shoulders lifted in a deep, shuddering breath. "Please. Kill the story."

"I can't. Not now. I don't have the kind of clout to pull an episode that's already in production." Riley drew the blankets tighter, wishing they were Logan's arms, an option that seemed to be slipping further away by the second.

"Then wait a week." He shoved away from the window and paced to the end of the bed. "What can it matter?"

Riley raised his eyebrows. "Seriously? Do you have any idea how much of a budget drill sergeant Julie is? If I suggest even a day's delay, her head's likely to explode. Besides, from everything I've been able to dig up, the full ghost war only manifests on the anniversary of Balch's hanging, the seventeenth. If we delay, we won't have a story. I'll seem like the incompetent idiot half the crew already thinks I am."

"So get another job."

"Maybe I like this one."

"Why?" Logan's face had lost all trace of the lazy lust of the morning. He wore the locked-jawed, hard-eyed expression from their first encounter outside Stumptown Spirits. God, Riley hated that look. "It's not like this is your real career."

"Jesus, Logan. You're as bad as my old advisor. Why do you assume this show has no value? That it's less valid to try and make something real out of it than it would be to sit in a library somewhere, cross-referencing articles about Vlad the Impaler?" Riley snagged a pillow and pulled it inside his blanket cocoon to give himself something to hug. "Why did you tell me this story the night we met anyway, if you didn't want help clearing your grandfather's name?"

"Maybe it was just a pickup line, folklore boy. The quickest way into your ass. Worked, didn't it?"

As Riley struggled out from under the blankets, Logan squatted to sort through the tangle of clothing on the floor so he wouldn't be tempted again by that smooth skin, or distracted by the hurt tugging the corners of Riley's mouth and wrinkling his forehead.

His temples throbbed like the engine of a badly tuned motorcycle. Consequences. Christ, they sucked. The night Trent disappeared, Logan, in teenaged-male hysterics, had run to his father for advice. He'd wanted to go to the police, tell them the whole story, but his dad had told him to shut the fuck up.

"Do you know," his dad had shouted, "how long I've worked to make people forget we're related to a psycho murderer?"

"But, Dad, don't you get it? Granddad wasn't either of those things. He was telling the truth."

"Yeah? How do you plan to prove that?"

Logan pulled out his phone. "I took a picture of one of the ghosts. See?"

His dad squinted at the screen. "That? Looks like a guy on his way to a Halloween party."

"He wasn't a ghost then. He was real. As solid as me. But he's a witness, right? If we find him—"

"Do you hear yourself? Your grandfather claimed he had a witness too, and it got him accused of murder."

Logan fought the sob clawing its way up his throat. God, he was stupid. Why hadn't he thought to take pictures of the other ghosts when he'd had the chance? "We could go back tomorrow. Take the video camera."

"Try that, and you'll look like a chip off the old loony block. Your grandfather pulled a dozen different people into that park before they locked him up. Nobody ever saw a damned thing."

"But—"

"Care to explain your shirt? It's covered in blood. You telling me ghosts bleed?"

Logan glanced at the red Rorschach on the tail of the T-shirt below the waistband of his hoodie. "It's not Trent's. It's mine. I cut my hand on a bottle." He'd forgotten. He held out his palm, the gash still oozing. "Do I need stitches?"

"Forget that. The hospital would ask for details. They might connect the injury to Trent. I've got butterfly bandages that'll work fine."

He trailed after his father into the bathroom, the pain in his hand awakening now that he was back in familiar surroundings. "But Dad, I need to tell them. The police, school. God, Trent's family. They need to know."

His father slapped the first aid kit onto the counter. "They only need to know three things. One, you were here with me all night. Two, you cut your hand on a bottle. Three, you haven't seen Trent since yesterday. End of story."

"Dad—"

"I mean it, Logan. You don't want this following you the rest of your life." He dug a wad of bandages out of the kit. "And my candidacy will never survive another scandal."

But even though Logan had caved at first, following the party line and covering up Trent's fate, the incident had caused a breach with his father that had never healed. A gay son his dad could stomach because it had made him approachable and earned him some liberal constituency cred. But a crazy son had no place on his conservative party platform.

As far as Logan was concerned, a father who sacrificed an innocent kid to political expediency didn't deserve his loyalty. In spite of his dad, Logan had searched for a way to make things right. To atone. Then, like a goddamn idiot, he'd let his libido take the wheel a year and a half ago.

He should have moved on once he'd realized Riley was more than a quick fuck. *If you'd done that, dumbass, you'd never have learned the answer.* Yeah, without Riley, he'd never have learned that this year was his best chance to rescue Trent unless he waited another seven fricking years. But *with* Riley? *Admit it, asshole—you'd just as soon wait forever.*

He'd let his desire overrule his conscience again, as soon as Riley was within reach. *You should have done a better job keeping him out of reach.* If he'd been crueler. Said something unforgivable rather than just disappearing. Screwed some random guy and arranged for Riley to catch them in the act.

But unable to bear laying the tracks of another man's hands over his body where Riley's had been, he'd hedged. He'd tried to give the appearance of cheating without the actual deed.

He should have known it would turn around and bite him on the ass.

Goddamn fucking *consequences.*

"Logan?" Riley's tentative tone shoved another spike of guilt into Logan's gut.

"Yeah?" He located his jeans, his boxer briefs still inside them, and pulled both on at once. "What?"

"You don't mean that. Do you? It wasn't just a pickup line, I know it."

"You don't know shit about it, and that's the way we're keeping it." His T-shirt was rank with half-dried semen. Rather than put it on, he shoved his arms into his jacket and zipped it up over his bare chest. "I'm out of here." He pocketed his keys and wallet and tucked his helmet under his arm.

"But this is your chance, don't you get it? We can prove the ghosts exist. Clear your grandfather's name and—"

"No." Logan bunched his T-shirt in his fist and pointed at Riley. "*You* don't get it. I want this story buried along with my grandfather. I don't want you or Julie or even that idiot Max Stone anywhere near it. Stay the fuck away from Forest Park, Riley." Logan shoved his T-shirt in the pocket of his jacket on his way to the door. "And stay the fuck away from me."

CHAPTER EIGHT

What the hell just happened?

Riley wrapped his arms across his bare stomach. Logan was lying. Again. That muscle in his check had twitched in time to the frantic flutter of Riley's heart as soon as Riley had pushed him about his grandfather. *Just. Freaking. Swell.* He'd found another of Logan's buttons, but had no idea why pushing it had launched Logan back into flying douche bag mode.

But even though Logan had bolted—again—Riley didn't have the slightest urge to curl up and whimper in a corner this time. For one thing, he had a job to do and a production-crazed best friend who wouldn't stand for it.

But for another, Logan wasn't as good at hiding his emotions as he thought. He still cared, dang it. Every stroke of his fingers on Riley's skin last night, every kiss, every long slow thrust into Riley's ass while he murmured endearments had said so, as clearly as if he'd shouted it in the middle of Pioneer Courthouse Square.

Besides, Logan may not have said the words, but his actions just now screamed, "It's not you, it's me."

This might be the first time in the history of forever when that excuse made anyone feel triumphant rather than eviscerated. *Oh yeah.* His stubborn Galahad was back on his white horse, and in order to boot him out of the saddle and save him from his own stupid honor, Riley needed to figure out why.

He scrambled out of bed and into the shower, his brain abuzz with the thrill of intellectual pursuit. While he washed his hair and scrubbed the scent of sex off his body, he cataloged possible sources in his mind, each new idea spawning others like the hydra sprouted heads.

When Logan had originally told him the story of his grandfather's experience, he'd kept it so generic that Riley had focused only on the ghost war legend in his research. Clearly that had been wrong, wrong, wrong.

There was more to this story than frontier tragedy, and Riley would find it. Because degree or no degree, he could be totally relentless tracking down the connections, the answers, the reasons why.

This time, he had something to go on. This time, he had a name. This time, he knew there was something to find.

And this time, he had one hell of an incentive to get it right.

All the way home, Logan mentally kicked his own ass for being such a clueless loser. He'd dedicated himself to his purpose, and he should be strong enough to stick to it. He had no business indulging himself, especially at Riley's expense.

As he climbed off his bike behind his apartment building, his cell phone buzzed in his jacket pocket. He pulled it out and glanced at the screen. Deke, one of his old trucker buddies.

"Yo."

"Logan. I been trying to reach you all night."

"Sorry. I was—"

"I saw that guy."

Logan's stomach plummeted. *That guy.* The ex-ghost in the picture. The one he'd been searching for for almost seven years. Fuck it to hell and back. What unbelievably shitty timing.

"Where?"

"Truck stop in Chehalis."

"You pick him up?"

"Nah. He was scavenging food in back of the Burger King, but he bolted when I got close, maybe heading for the train station. Might be riding the rails. No way any trucker I know would let that guy in his rig. Stinks like month-old fish dipped in piss."

"Nice image, Deke."

Deke's deep chuckle rolled over the line. "Call 'em like I see 'em. Anyway, I spread the word. Everyone'll be on the lookout for him. Hell, you'd be able to smell him coming from across the state line."

"Thanks, man. I owe you." Not that Logan would be around to make good on that debt. Maybe he'd leave Deke the Harley. The guy had always had lousy taste in bikes. "Later."

He climbed the stairs, entered his craptastic furnished apartment, and tossed his helmet onto the threadbare recliner on his way to the bathroom. After splashing cold water on his face, he stared at his hollow-eyed reflection in the spotty mirror. What the hell had he been thinking last night? He was old enough now to tell the difference between a good idea and total fricking disaster.

Not like back then. In his first year of college, he'd been the typical stupid teenager masquerading as an adult, adjusting to the heady freedom of college after growing up with his father's image-conscious rules. He'd scored a jackpot with his roommate —a seriously gorgeous gay guy who had his own family drama. He and Trent had bonded over contraband beer and controlling-asshole-dad stories, and transitioned to fuck buddy status within the first week.

That night, the night that had changed the course of his life, he'd been studying in a half-assed way, waiting for Trent to return from the final auditions for the winter production of *Blithe Spirit*. Trent had been confident he'd land the lead, and Logan had plans for a suitable celebration. Who knew? Maybe they'd take their relationship up a notch. *Boyfriends?* He wasn't sure he was ready to go that far, but hey, anything was possible.

A key rattled in the lock, but instead of bursting through the door and posing in his own virtual spotlight as usual, Trent stalked into the room with a script rolled in his fist and face-planted on his bed.

"Trent?" Logan set his book aside and got up to close the door. "You okay, man?"

"Understudy." Trent's voice, muffled by pillows, lacked its customary confidence. He tossed the script on the floor with a flick of his fingers.

"What?"

"I didn't get the part." He rolled over and flung one arm out and the other over his eyes. "Un-fucking-believable. Three callbacks. My chemistry with the rest of the cast was off the charts. The director told me it was the best audition he'd seen in years."

"So why didn't you—"

"Because I'm a freshman. I have to pay my *duuuuues*." He smacked the side of the bed. "He made me the understudy, like it's some kind of reward."

Logan sat sideways in Trent's desk chair, his knees against the bed. "Well, what is it you theater geeks say on opening night? Break a leg? You could always hope the lead guy actually does."

Trent peered out from under his arm. "Dude. Do *not* mock the sacred traditions of theater."

"Sorry. So who got the part?"

"Wayne fucking Peterson. Just because he's a senior. Asshole."

Logan frowned. "But isn't he a friend of yours? Part of that club that spends all its time hanging out in cemeteries?"

"We don't hang out in cemeteries."

"You so do. Three times in September and once already this month."

"We *reenact*. We don't 'hang out.'"

Logan chuckled and poked Trent in the ribs. "Right. You're... what? Spirit stalkers? Ghost groupies?"

"Legend trippers, dickhead. As if you didn't know."

Yeah, some people liked bungee jumping or skydiving or extreme sports. The thing that turned Trent's crank was hanging out in cemeteries, hoping to get goosed by a ghost. Go figure.

"Can't say I see the appeal, but whatever."

Trent toed off his trainers and turned on his side to face Logan. "It's the adventure, dude, a total rush, like real-life theater. If we do it right, we could raise the legend."

"Raise it?"

"Make it happen again."

"Have you ever succeeded?"

"Not here. Not yet. But people legend trip all over the world. A group in France actually saw a werewolf."

"You mean they saw someone shift from man to wolf?" Trent shook his head, but didn't offer an explanation. *Fine. Guess we're pulling teeth then.* "Vice versa, wolf to man?"

"No, but they saw the wolf."

Logan raised his eyebrows. "And that means it's a werewolf... how?"

"Dude. The last wolf in France was shot in 1947. It had to be a shifter."

"Or else it was somebody's German shepherd."

Trent sat up and propped his back against the wall. "Fine. Be an asshole. But I've witnessed something myself. Back home, this one college had a ouija board door."

"You mean a door with a ouija board on it?"

"No. You'd ask it questions, and it'd slam once for yes and twice for no."

Logan snorted. "Seriously?"

"Hey, it was right for me, both times."

"Yeah? Did you ask it if legend tripping was a bogus waste of time?"

Trent threw a pillow at him. "No, asshole." He ducked his head, tracing a pattern on his blanket with a finger. "I asked it if my parents would be cool with me coming out."

"That didn't take a haunted door to figure out. From what you've told me about your folks—"

Trent's face closed up shop, his usual sparkle completely snuffed. *Just fucking great.* As if Trent wasn't already bummed enough about the play, Logan had made him feel worse. "Shit, man. Sorry."

Trent shrugged. "You know the worst thing about losing the part to Peterson? Other than, you know, not having the part? That asshole will get major tripping points."

"Points? Your club has points?"

"It's not a *club,* dude. We're serious about this."

"And points are serious? How can he get points for a Noël Coward play? It's not like the thing is based on an actual ghost story."

"It still counts. He'll be reenacting the story, re-creating it every night. He gets points."

"Who made that stupid rule?"

"Peterson did."

"Figures."

Trent's mouth drooped. "I know, right?"

Logan's chest tightened with the need to do something, anything, to reignite Trent's spark, but it wasn't as if he could magically give him the part in the play. But maybe there was another way to cheer him up, even if it made the hair stand up on Logan's own arms.

Yeah, he and Trent had shared some family history, but Logan had never told anyone about his grandfather, not after the lessons his father had pounded into him about the fragility of public opinion.

So don't tell him the whole story. He'll only care about the ghosts anyway. Leave Granddad out of it. He could give Trent a harmless thrill, let him score off Peterson, and then they'd come back here and banish the rest of his depression with some leisurely sex.

"Know what, man? Fuck your parents and fuck the director and fuck Noël Coward."

A smile wavered on Trent's mouth. "Might have gone for it with Coward, if he, you know, wasn't *dead*, but I'll pass on the others, thanks."

"Noël Coward ghosts aren't real ghosts, dude. Too mannered and polite. Real ghost stories are raw. Messy." He dropped his voice into Cryptkeeper range. "Daaaangerous."

"Oh, and you're an expert, I suppose?"

"Hey. I'm a Portland native."

Trent hugged his knees. "Non sequitur much?"

"So sadly ignorant." Logan shook his head, pasting a pitying look on his face. "I'll cut you some slack, since you come from one of those little bitty New England states—some island or other, wasn't it?"

Trent shoved Logan's knee with his foot. "Fuck you."

"You can't be expected to know the really big stories from really big places like Oregon." Logan grinned. "Ever hear the story of Danford Balch?"

"What do you think?" Trent scowled at him, crossing his arms over his chest. "Get on with it."

"Well then. Just warning you, I plan to be an architect, not a singer." Logan cleared his throat. "'Coooooome and listen to a story 'bout a man named Dan. A poor pioneer and a tortured fam'ly man.'"

Trent barked out a laugh. "Dude. Is that the theme from *The Beverly Hillbillies*?"

"If you don't recognize it, my singing's worse than I thought. God knows the stupid tune's been stuck in *my* head after you made me watch that marathon with you last week."

"It was for your own good. You young people today have no appreciation for the classics."

"I'm only two months younger than you. And excuse me—classics? *The Beverly Hillbillies*?"

Trent flipped off his script. "Beats Noël Coward."

"Then get a load of this." Logan grabbed a pen off the desk and held it like a microphone. "On this very day in 1859,

Danford Balch was hanged for murdering his son-in-law. But did he stay dead? *You* be the judge."

He told the whole story—leaving out references to his family, of course. "And they say the two families still battle it out on the banks of the creek that bears Balch's name—ghosts locked in a bloody feud—forever." He bowed his head. "The end."

Trent nudged his knee again. "Anybody you know actually witness this?"

"Let's say…" Logan swallowed, his stomach clenching. *Don't mention Granddad.* "… a friend of a friend."

"Dude, that's a *quintessential* hallmark of a true urban legend." Trent's blue eyes sparkled. "Come on. Tonight. Let's do it."

Logan peered out the window. It was raining, the businesslike showers of October in Portland. Had he really thought this would be a good idea? "Maybe we could wait until it's not raining?"

Trent scrunched up his face and tossed his discarded shoe at Logan. "A native Oregonian, afraid of a little sprinkle? You said it yourself: He died this very day. What better time to catch sight of his ghost?"

"Daylight, blue skies, and about twenty additional degrees in temperature," Logan grumbled, unease creeping up his spine like a palm-sized spider. His grandfather's debacle had occurred on this date too. Not that he was superstitious—much —but maybe it wasn't the best night to mention this story.

"You're missing the point of a good legend trip. It's not supposed to be cushy. It's supposed to be *authentic*."

"Then why does your group end up at the Heathman Hotel or Old Town Pizza half the time?"

"Hey, those places are haunted. It's documented."

Logan snorted. "You read it on Wikipedia, so it's gotta be true."

"Don't mock—"

"The sacred traditions of legend tripping. Got it."

Trent stood and pulled Logan to his feet with a come-hither smile, hooking his fingers in Logan's belt loops and snugging their groins together. "Wouldn't it be hot to blow each other out there?"

"Is that what you do in your cemeteries? Blow each other?"

Trent grinned, grinding against him. "Jealous?"

"No." *Yes. Maybe?*

"Come on. Nobody will see us but the ghosts." Trent leaned forward and licked Logan's earlobe. "If we're lucky."

"The park's not open this late."

"So we'll sneak in. Even better." He slanted a look from under his lashes. "Please?"

Logan ignored the dread creeping up on him. His grandfather's ghosts were probably as real as that ridiculous fortune-telling door. For Trent, surely he could man up for a couple of uncomfortable hours in a dark soggy park. That is, as long as nobody caught them—his dad would freak if his son got caught violating a city ordinance.

"Okay. But we'll have to be careful."

They left Trent's car on Upshur, down the street from the Lower Macleay trailhead. The parking lot was deserted, thank God, but there was enough light from cars passing on the Thurman Street overpass that they didn't have to risk turning on their flashlights until they got into the trees. Logan's belly fluttered like a captive bird. Nerves? Excitement? Fear? He wasn't sure, but he began to see the attraction legend tripping had for a thrill-seeker like Trent.

They reached the Witch's Castle sooner than Logan expected. It sat back from the bank of Balch Creek, at the Y intersection with the Wildwood trail.

"Hunh." Trent played the beam of his flashlight over the building. "I thought it would be bigger."

It wasn't a particularly impressive sight, for sure. Roofless, with empty windows staring out at the woods, its rough stone walls defaced with graffiti. A flight of shallow stone steps on either end led to the upper story. On the ground floor, a couple of empty doorways gaped at the creek.

Trent poked his flashlight through the smaller door, illuminating a small windowless room, its walls tagged with a pentagram and one or two *Fuck You*s. "This must be where the ghosts come to take a piss." Next to the narrow room was a wider alcove with a concrete slab floor. "And this must be where they park their bikes."

Logan ducked under the overhang and beckoned for Trent to join him. "It's got a roof and a floor. It works for me."

After they sat with their backs to the wall, Trent opened his backpack and pulled out two artisan microbrews. Although Logan's nerves still skittered at every noise in the woods—afraid more of discovery by very real cops than of ghostly pioneers—he chuckled.

Trent paused while opening his beer. "What?"

"You. Trust-fund Trent and your old-money silver-spoon sensibilities. Even when you want to get wasted, it's an *upscale* wasted."

"Fuck off, politico spawn. We all have our issues." He clinked the necks of their bottles together. "Cheers."

The edge of excitement that had fueled their arrival dissipated from the cold and damp, despite the slight alcohol buzz from the beer. No wonder Trent's legend trippers stuck to hotels and bars when they could tear themselves away from cemeteries. Had to be more interesting—not to mention warmer —than this.

Logan slung an arm across Trent's shoulders and pulled him close—to stave off hypothermia rather than as a prelude to anything else, but Trent immediately snuggled close and nuzzled his neck. Logan's dick made a valiant effort to respond, but the concrete slab under his ass was fucking cold. Not exactly a mood-enhancer.

"So." Logan shifted on his tailbone, trying to get comfortable. "Your haunted ouija door warned you about you parents' reaction to you being gay. What else was it right about?"

Trent took a swig of his beer and rested the bottle on his knee. "I asked if I'd meet the love of my life if I stayed in Rhode Island." He cuddled closer, placing a hand on Logan's thigh. "It said no."

Logan's heart lurched. Did Trent just say—? Did he mean he thought Logan was—? Sweat broke out on his forehead. *Not ready to go that far. Not yet.* He slid his arm from around Trent's neck. "Look, man. I—"

Trent scooted away, hurt clearly visible even in the funky shadows cast by the flashlight. "Yeah, sorry. Guess it was too much to hope you'd feel—"

"It's not that." Hadn't Logan been toying with the idea of *more* himself? "But we've known each other a month and a half. You're my best friend. Maybe if we give it some time—"

"Fuck time. Time sucks. You never know what'll happen in the next year, the next month—hell, the next *minute*. Everything could change, and shit you counted on, shit you believed in—" He pressed the heels of his hands against his eyes. "One fucking conversation, one wrong word, and *poof*. Gone."

"If you mean your parents—"

"Fuck my parents." He dropped his hands and stood, looming over Logan. "I thought I could count on *you*."

"You can." Logan scrambled up. Tonight, in the uncertain light, Trent's eyes shone almost green, with the manic gleam that always heralded the worst of his reckless behavior. "I'm here for you, I swear. But this isn't the best place to have this convo. Maybe—"

Trent's empty beer bottle slipped from his fingers and shattered against the alcove's concrete floor. "Oh my fucking God. Logan. Look at that!"

Logan whirled, and all the hair lifted on his arms and the back of his neck under his damp hoodie. A line of mist snaked across the clearing. Not the usual Portland gray fog—this mist was tinged a bilious green and it sparked like a downed power line.

"I've got a b-b-bad feeling about this. Let's get out of here." He shoved his empty in the backpack and searched for the pieces of Trent's broken bottle in the shimmer of arcane light.

"Are you kidding? This is bigger than anything I've ever heard of. Bigger than that French werewolf sighting. Bigger than the ouija board door. And it trumps *Blithe Spirit* all to fucking *hell*. Peterson will shit his pants when he hears about this." Trent smacked Logan's biceps. "Dude, you are the *king* of legend trippers."

From the paths that converged at Witch's Castle, amorphous balls of light pushed out of the mist, and Logan's heart tried to bound out of his chest. "Seriously. We need to leave. Now." He reached for the last piece of glass near Trent's foot.

"I don't fucking believe it," Trent whispered. "Orbs. Actual *orbs*. Dozens of them." He punched Logan's shoulder, and Logan stumbled, slicing his left palm on the jagged shard.

Pain shot up Logan's arm as blood dripped onto the muddy ground. "Shit." He pulled the hem of his T-shirt from under his hoodie and bunched it in his fist to stem the flow.

Trent gasped and let it out on a slow, "*Ooooooohhhh.*"

"It's not that bad." Logan peeked under the shirt, wincing at the length of the gash. "I can—"

"Look, man. Just *look* at that."

Logan looked, and his breath stalled in his chest. The formerly featureless blobs had resolved into distinct figures, and more were joining them by the second, stepping out of the mist as if it was a curtain over a doorway to hell. Men and women in old-fashioned clothes. Wagons. Horses. Mules. All the trappings of the legend, exactly as his grandfather had described.

Trent clutched Logan's arm, his eyes as wide as a kid's on Christmas morning who'd just opened the gift he'd been begging for his whole life. "We did it. We raised a legend."

The ghosts advanced; some were brighter than others, like the stars of the show. Logan had no idea what the Balches or Stumps looked like, but the young couple spotlighted by the wagon had to be Anna Balch and Mortimer Stump. Danford appeared on cue to confront them and the story unfolded, playing out in the muddy clearing next to the rushing creek like a time-lapse tragedy.

Trent watched it with an incredulous smile, edging forward despite Logan's attempts to pull him back into the dubious shelter of the alcove. When the ghost of Danford stormed off and vanished, Trent turned to Logan, disappointment clouding his face.

"Is that it? There's no more?"

Christ wasn't that enough? Logan shook with more than the damp and chill of the air. "N-n-no. He'll be back. With his gun. Let's go, Trent. Please." He knew what happened next. His grandfather had repeated it to anyone who would listen whenever he had the chance. "You've seen enough to score off Peterson."

"No fucking way. Nobody I know has *ever* gotten this close. Come on." Trent let go of Logan's arm and dashed out of the alcove. When he reached the outermost figures, he posed next to one of them with a cheeky grin. "Check it out. Trent Pielmeyer, ghost pioneer."

Logan groaned. "Christ, Trent, don't push it."

Trent flipped him off and turned to watch the tableau again.

At the far side of the clearing near Anna and Mortimer, Logan spotted a man in a flat-brimmed hat and jawline beard loading a bag of flour into the back of a phantom wagon. The terror on his face as he gaped at the other ghosts probably matched Logan's own.

Logan's stomach jolted in shock. *That must be the guy. Joseph Geddes, the man who disappeared into the war.* His grandfather hadn't been crazy. He'd been telling the truth. About all of it.

He needed to warn Trent, but when he tried to force himself to get closer to the ghosts, panic cramped his belly.

"Hssst. Logan." Trent pointed to the left, where the phantom Danford Balch had returned with his shotgun.

"Trent, wait. There's some stuff I didn't tell you. Stuff you should know."

"Later."

Logan expected Balch to storm down to the spot where his daughter stood with her bridegroom, but instead he slowed, head turning to focus on Trent. Surprise registered on his semitransparent face, and he glanced down at the gun.

Trent stared at Logan, goggle-eyed, and mouthed, *What the fuck?*

This isn't what happened, and the last time something deviated from the story —

Balch beckoned to Trent, offering him the gun.

And Trent reached for it.

"No! Trent, you idiot. Don't." Logan lurched forward and grabbed the sleeve of Trent's jacket.

Trent frowned and jerked his arm away. "Are you crazy? It's the role of a lifetime, and I'll be the star, not the fucking understudy." He bowed with a flourish of one hand. "You may applaud my many curtain calls."

"You don't understand. This isn't a fucking play. You—"

Trent seized the gun.

As soon as it was in his grasp, Balch fell to the ground next to Logan, as solid as he was himself, as if Trent had pushed him aside. And Trent—Trent was suddenly as transparent as the rest of the spirits, the jagged stump at the edge of the creek clearly visible through his chest.

Then... God. Mortimer stepped out from behind the wagon, and he looked... so scared. How many times had he played this scene? He had to know what was coming next.

But Trent, who always buried himself in every part, either didn't notice or didn't care. He raised the gun to his shoulder, a crazy grin visible in his ghostly face, and pulled the trigger.

The shotgun blast echoed in the clearing, bouncing impossibly among the trees, the sound all the more shocking because the rest of the action had been silent.

Mortimer toppled onto his back, his face and neck an open wound. His blood, obscenely red, steamed in the cold.

Horror banished Trent's grin. He thrust out his arms, the cords on his neck distended as if he were fighting to throw the gun down. "I want it to stop now. Why can't I—" He tried to back away, but the crowd swallowed him up.

Clutching his bleeding hand to his chest, Logan staggered toward Trent, but someone grabbed his shoulder and pushed him to his knees. He stared up into the haunted eyes of Danford Balch.

"Let me go, you bastard." Logan struggled, but Balch's hand tightened with bruising strength.

"You can do nothing now."

"I didn't mean— God, I'm sorry, I'm sorry." Trent's voice was faint, echoing as if he were at the bottom of a well. "Help me, Logan, please." Beyond the shifting backs of the townspeople, Logan glimpsed a sliver of Trent's face, his eyes wide and terrified. "I—I want to go home."

"Too late," Balch said.

Logan writhed in Balch's steely grip. "It's not. It can't be."

The hangman stepped up with the noose, flinging it into the air where it dangled as if from an invisible tree, and the crowd raised Trent on their shoulders in lieu of gallows steps.

Trent strained against invisible bonds, shaking his head wildly, in a futile attempt to evade the rope. "I'm not the guy. I swear. I'm just the—the understudy."

"Trent!" Logan wrenched himself out of Balch's clutches and stumbled forward. "Hold on, man. I'll get you out. I'll save you, I promise."

Trent shared one last agonized glance with Logan before the crowd dropped him and the rope took his weight, breaking his neck with a sickening crunch.

"No!" Logan fell to his knees, the pain in his hand nothing compared to the agony in his chest. He doubled over, arms wrapped across his belly. *My fault, my fault, all my fucking fault.*

"It worked." Balch's voice was rough, disbelieving. "Before, I thought it chance only."

Logan caught his breath, fighting off sobs that threatened to choke him. "What did you do?"

"I did nothing. He.... he did it of his own free will. Now my fate is his, and I..." He ran trembling hands over his clothing, his face, his neck. "I am granted another chance."

"You can't. It's his life, not yours."

"It *was* his. But he gave it to me."

Logan glared at him. "You won't get away with this. The police—"

Balch laughed, a hollow sound. "You think your lawmen will pursue a man so long dead?"

"They will if I prove you're alive." With his uninjured hand, Logan wrestled his cell phone out of his hoodie pocket and snapped a picture of Balch, who flinched from it, flinging up his hands to shield his eyes.

The light partially blinded Logan too, and by the time his vision cleared, Balch was gone. Along with the ghosts. Along with Trent.

All these years, he'd tried to find Balch. Get some answers. Why had he been able to do what he did? How had he trapped Trent? How had he himself escaped? But Balch had vanished. In the years Logan had spent on the road, wandering aimlessly between Octobers, he'd circulated that grainy cell phone picture in the trucker network, and to every biker he knew.

He'd heard a few rumors. Someone who might have been Balch in Montana once. South Dakota. Passing through Anchorage. But no confirmed sighting until now. *Damn it.* This was as close as Logan had ever been to the bastard since that night, and he had no time left to track him down. No chance to confront him before the end. No chance to try to force him to undo what he'd done.

Logan sat on the edge of the sagging bed, his head in his hands. It was his turn. Time to finally keep his promise to Trent, and nothing—not Riley's job, not Riley's feelings for him, not even his love for Riley—could stand in his way.

CHAPTER NINE

Riley fidgeted his way through the production meeting, barely listening to anything anyone said, depending on Julie to bring him up to speed later.

His fingers twitched with the need to get back to his laptop, to start finding the truth about Logan's grandfather.

The instant Scott stopped nattering on about the budget, Riley launched himself out of his chair. As the crew filed out, he caught Julie's arm.

"Jules. Something's come up."

"To do with the show?"

"Yeeess." It wasn't exactly a lie. Not really. Logan's reaction told Riley he'd missed something in his preparation for this episode. Something big. Sure, it might end up having more to do with Riley's battered heart than Danford Balch, but his scholar's instincts pinged like crazy, telling him to dig deeper, find the clue, make the connection. *The answer's out there, and you can find it.*

After all, *wesearch* was his middle name.

Julie pulled her top lip between her teeth, like a hellhound with an underbite. "I don't like it. You need to remind Scott of your value. If you're not in his face at least once every three hours or so, he'll forget who you are and why he should listen to you."

"I know. But this is critical. Anyway…" He leaned forward and lowered his voice to a stage whisper. "Are you telling me you can't handle Scott?"

As he'd hoped, she rose to the bait. Nose to nose with him, she growled, "In my sleep, with no hands and a hangover."

"Excellent." He fumbled in his messenger bag and pulled out the map of the site with the boundaries of the ghost war clearly marked in signature *HttM* neon-green marker. He hesitated for an instant, smoothing a crease in the paper. The expression on Logan's face had been so bleak earlier. What would it hurt if Riley fudged a little, redrew the lines so the crew set up in the wrong spot, or let Scott film a day or two early? He would give Logan what he'd asked, yet give the show's audience exactly what they expected: Max Stone strutting around some creepy scenery in his fedora and bomber jacket while precisely nothing supernatural occurred.

When he thought of it that way, the fans might be outraged if a real ghost *did* show up.

No. Absolutely not. Riley never freaking *ever* falsified his findings. He hadn't abandoned his professional ethics when he dropped out of school, and he wasn't about to start now, with so much more at stake.

A few days ago, this story had been nothing but a way to prove himself in a job he wasn't sure he wanted. Now? It was personal. He needed to get it right for Logan's sake, whether Logan admitted it or not.

He thrust the map at Julie. "Here. Make sure they don't get distracted by pretty camera angles or spooky atmospheric shots. This is where we need to film."

She peered at it, tracing the green line with one finger. "The Witch's Castle is barely in the picture. Just that one little corner. Scott won't like it."

"If Scott wants ghosts, he'll pay attention to the map."

She shook her head. "I don't know."

"Jules. You trust me?"

"Of course."

"Then engage those UPM superpowers. Do your job and let me do mine."

She rolled her eyes and heaved an exaggerated sigh. "Fine."

As soon as she left, he raced back to his room and booted up his laptop. Saturday. God, so little time to figure this out, especially since his schedule was already packed with Production Bitch errand-running and preparation for his first time at the shoot location.

So he'd better channel Hercules and get on with the labors.

It was almost too easy. With the right name, Riley found what he was looking for immediately.

Sean O'Connor and Joseph Geddes had been trapping rabbits —illegally—in Forest Park on the night of October 17, 1952. O'Connor had been seen running from the park near midnight, but Geddes was never seen again.

In the sensationalist journalism style of the time, reporters had trumpeted foul play, but xenophobic, not supernatural. With the country in the early throes of the Cold War, they'd been quick to blame the disappearance on conspiracies by agents unknown.

Then Logan's grandfather had been arrested, and the shit had well and truly hit the fan. The newspapers had been merciless, launching a positive feeding frenzy with Logan's grandfather as hapless chum. They'd torn him apart.

Logan's grandmother had been a schoolteacher before her husband's arrest. She'd lost her home and her job, and from what Riley could discover, had lived the rest of her life with her sister, as a house cleaner, sometime seamstress, and eventual unpaid caregiver for her brother-in-law.

But as rabid as the reporters had been about Sean O'Connor, his arrest, and subsequent institutionalization, none of them had spared an inch of ink on the family of his alleged victim. Joseph Geddes's wife and two children had been mentioned in the reports of O'Connor's arrest, but Riley couldn't find a single story that mentioned them afterward.

The death rolls told their own tale.

The youngest child died not six months after her father's disappearance. Their mother later the same year. Of the eldest child, he could find no trace at all, as if with no adult to care for him and protect him, he'd ceased to exist.

God, Logan's grandfather hadn't been the ghost war's only victim.

But if Sean O'Connor hadn't been a delusional homicidal maniac, if his claims were correct and the ghost war had somehow captured a living man...

Holy shit.

Riley leaned back and clutched his hair with both fists. What if the Witch's Castle legend was more than a ghost story? What if its mythic roots went even deeper?

Folklore annals had tons of instances of humans lured or forcibly abducted to places outside the normal plane of existence. Hades, Faerie, Annwn—the lists went on. The flow of time in the alternate world frequently tracked differently than the human world, and when the victim returned, years, decades, even centuries had passed.

The odds were that Geddes was dead, and had been since the night he disappeared, but what if he wasn't? What if he was trapped in the ghost war in a kind of supernatural stasis? What if he could be released? No matter what Logan had said about burying the story, it would have to mean something to him to clear his grandfather's name. Joseph Geddes, freed from ghostly captivity and able to bear witness, could do it.

Riley plunged back onto the net, searching for every ballad, myth, legend, or folktale with a "rescue from the other world" scenario. As he cataloged each of them—and a depressing number ended in spectacular failure—he discovered a disturbing motif: The odds were heavily weighted against the rescuee, either because the rules governing their imprisonment were fricking *secret*, or because the boneheaded rescuer knew the rules but screwed them up anyway.

For Persephone, it had been eating six lousy pomegranate seeds when nobody had told her it meant she'd be stuck in Hades for one month per seed. How was that fair? For poor Eurydice, it had been a husband who couldn't wait another five lousy minutes before he turned around to look at her. Sure, all the odes were for poor bereaved Orpheus, but he was the one who had screwed up and Eurydice had paid the price by dying —again. Orpheus just mooned around demoralizing everyone with his dirges until the Maenads finally got fed up and had him for lunch.

If the ghost war followed the classic pattern, it could have a number of its own booby traps, and tripping any of them could cause the rescue to fail, sending Geddes down the path of Persephone, Eurydice, or even Orpheus, if the ghosts decided to take exception to outside meddling.

Crap, crap, crap. If there was an answer to the Witch's Castle riddle, he'd never figure it out with so little data. He needed more, damn it. A single verified incident wouldn't cut it statistically.

He got up and paced the narrow alley between the foot of his bed and the dresser. Was he limiting his options because of invalid assumptions? He'd tracked every recorded witness account when he'd prepped the pitch for Scott. But what if he'd been looking in the wrong place? He'd been treating the ghost war as the effect of the Balch–Stump feud—but what if he turned it around and viewed it as the cause of real-world problems, like the fate of Geddes's family?

If he wanted to find other incidents, maybe he needed to look at the response, not the stimulus—not only on October seventeenth in that year or any other, but in the days and weeks and months afterward, when the fallout began to affect the people left behind. That's when atypical behavior would surface, when the pattern would begin to emerge. Once he had more data to analyze, he'd stand a better chance of discovering why a man could be caught in a supernatural snare, and clues about how to release him.

He plopped back onto his chair and pulled up a new browser window, modifying his Witch's Castle search criteria to include any crimes, disappearances, or anomalies that mentioned Forest Park since the date of Geddes's disappearance. Scrolling down the list of stories, he discarded all the standard DUI, domestic disturbances, and misdemeanors.

Ha! *There.*

Seven years ago this month, Trent Pielmeyer, a nineteen-year-old PSU student, vanished without a trace. The official story was frustratingly bare of detail. Trent's car had been abandoned near the Lower Macleay trailhead. The police had discovered blood at the intersection of the Wildwood and Lower Macleay trails—the location of the Witch's Castle—but it hadn't matched Trent's type. With no body or motive, the story ended with nothing but a request for any information leading to the whereabouts of the missing man.

But then, buried at the end of an article published two weeks after Trent's disappearance, Riley discovered an account of police questioning Trent's PSU roommate, an architecture student.

Logan Conner.

Fingers numb, Riley slumped in his chair and stared sightlessly at the door. How likely was it that Logan knew nothing about his own freaking roommate's disappearance at the same place his grandfather had witnessed a ghostly kidnapping?

Exactly zilch.

Was this why Logan had rabbited this morning? Not because of his grandfather, but because he was afraid the show might link him to the later scandal? Riley had always assumed Logan never touched him in public because he was ashamed—either of being gay or being seen with someone as dorky as Riley. Could it have had nothing to do with Riley at all?

After public testimony, public outcry, and public reaction had destroyed his grandparents' lives, maybe Logan had overcompensated, adopting an obsessively low profile to avoid similar danger.

Or maybe...

Riley's fingers stilled on the keyboard, his stomach suddenly hollow. Could Logan be complicit in Trent's disappearance?

No. Not my Galahad. But odds were even that Logan knew more than he'd let on about the ghost war, and Riley intended to ferret the rest out, one way or another.

Before he faced Logan, though, he needed to do his homework.

As he started to type, to cross-reference source material and plan his attack, his nerves settled, his breathing deepened, panic sloughing off and leaving confidence and certainty in its place.

No matter how awkward he was with people, how often he screwed up his social life, *this* he could do. This was his life, his blood, his purpose.

He pushed up his sleeves and settled his glasses on his nose. "Move over, Production Bitch. Folklore Boy is in the house and ready to throw down."

CHAPTER TEN

When Logan arrived for his shift that night, still raw from the scene with Riley, he found his boss holed up in his office in a more-than-usual foul mood.

"Infernal *toorists*. Asking for something called a tropical piranha."

Logan tucked in his smile. "Maybe a tropical caipirinha? Cachaça, coconut rum liqueur, and pineapple and lime puree."

"If they wanted golblamed fruit, why'd they come to a saloon?" Bert slammed the top file drawer closed with a *clang*. "Why can't they order whiskey like any normal man?"

Logan chuckled as he stowed his helmet on top of the bookshelf and hung his leather jacket on the peg behind the door. "Why'd you ever decide to run a bar, Bert? People come with the job."

"That's why I hire fellas like you. To put up with all that bull-pucky."

"Yeah. About that." Logan rubbed the back of his neck and stared at the six-year-old calendar above Bert's ancient rolltop desk. "You do remember Wednesday's my last bartending shift, right?"

Bert's shaggy white eyebrows shot up, making his face look even longer and narrower than normal. "Thursday'd be better for me."

Trust Bert to cut to the chase. "Sorry. Like I told you, I'll do the stockroom Thursday morning, but that's it. I've got stuff to take care of before I... head out."

"Bah. Get out there, then. The place is full of folks with more money than sense."

"Better take care of 'em, then."

He stopped in the stockroom. Yesterday, he'd nearly run out of drink umbrellas, and if the bar patrons were in the mood for tropical drinks, he'd need a fresh supply. He grabbed the first box within reach and headed down the hall. Heather met him outside the kitchen.

"Hey, Logan. Full house tonight." She brandished her order pad. "I think they're about to eat us out of burgers."

"Rowdy ravenous frat boys?"

Heather giggled. "No. Way more fun. It's the entire crew of a television show that's filming in Portland."

Logan's heart lurched sideways. How many shows could be on location here at one time? "Do you know what—"

"Heather!" one of the cooks called. "Order up."

"Oops. Gotta run. Later." She ducked into the kitchen.

Logan crept the rest of the way down the hall and peered around the corner into the main part of the bar. Yep. A bunch of guys in black and neon-green *HttM* show T-shirts, with *techie* written all over their scruffy faces, clustered around an island of tables in the middle of the room. Their no-talent asshole of a star sat at one end, and judging by the empty chairs on either side of him, the crew's opinion of Max Stone wasn't much higher than Logan's.

Logan ignored Max and held his breath, searching the room for that thatch of board-straight dark hair, the glint of narrow rectangular glasses, but Riley wasn't there. Logan didn't know whether to be relieved or disappointed. *One more glimpse. What could it hurt?*

It could hurt one hell of a lot, that's what. Looking, but unable to touch, forced to pretend disinterest if he expected to pay his debt to Trent and keep Riley safe as well.

He scowled at the box of drink umbrellas in his hand. *Shit.* They were the special ones Heather had conned Bert into ordering for Halloween: black, with red-eyed grinning skulls. She'd shoot him if he used them up before the holiday— although he'd be out of her reach by then.

Wait a second. He opened the box and took out one of the kitschy things. Maybe this was his golden opportunity. How many times had this crew faced actual paranormal phenomena? Exactly never. If that idiot Max Stone ever encountered anything more threatening than a five-martini hangover, Logan bet the guy's vanishing act would put Penn and Teller to shame.

So if Riley wouldn't step up the plate, Logan could try his own hand at killing the story.

Heather approached him, balancing three plates, the aroma of burgers and fries reminding him he'd skipped both breakfast and lunch. No matter. He'd eat later. As for now… A smile tugged at his lips. *I've got other priorities.*

"Whoa." She wrinkled her nose as she brushed past. "Whoever you've got in your sights had better watch out. That is one evil look, my friend."

"No clue what you're talking about," Logan said, and sauntered into the bar, ready to scare the shit out of the *toorists.*

He counted heads while the burly guy at the end of the table tried his level best to impress Heather.

"It's not just anyone who can film this stuff, right? We work in the dark so standard tools don't cut it. We've got special…" Mr. Bear tucked his chin in and waggled his bushy eyebrows at Heather. "… equipment."

"You don't say." She slapped his plate on the table in front of him. "Takes a brave man to face ghosts, I guess."

He puffed out his barrel chest, probably under the mistaken notion he was about to get lucky. "You know it."

"Takes a braver one to announce the shortcomings of his...
equipment... to the whole bar."

He reddened while the rest of the men hooted with laughter.
Heather turned away, caught Logan's gaze, and rolled her eyes.
He beckoned her over.

"Guys giving you trouble?"

She snorted. "No. But if they expect to get anywhere, they
need to try it with someone who doesn't spend forty-plus hours
a week with guys drunk enough to think that's a good line."

"I've got a couple of ideas about how to handle them."

"There's that evil smile again." She leaned over the bar.
"Whatever you've got planned, I want in."

"You're on."

Logan lined up a shot glass for each guy and poured doubles
of the mid-shelf whiskey. He plunked a black umbrella in each
one. "Hand these out to their table? I'm buying."

Heather loaded the drinks onto a tray. "Only if you promise
there's more to this plan."

"Count on it."

He followed her to the table. She served the shots, saving the
last one for Mr. Bear. "You're in luck, boys. These drinks are on
the house, courtesy of our bartender."

The men set up a ragged cheer except for Mr. Bear, who
poked at the umbrella. "What's this?"

"I heard about your plan to shoot at Witch's Castle. Figured
condemned men could use a last drink."

A square-jawed guy, the only clean-shaven one at the table,
gave Logan an appreciative once-over. "You know something
we don't?"

"Couldn't say. You've heard about Sasquatch."

Max blew a raspberry. *Attractive.* "That's for the tabloids,
man. We're serious paranormal investigators."

"Could be. But this is the Pacific Northwest. You shouldn't
turn down tips from the natives."

Mr. Square Jaw aimed a flirty grin at him. "If you're the native in question, sign me up." He pulled an empty chair from a nearby table, parked it next to his, and patted the seat.

Logan sat down and leaned back, giving Mr. Square Jaw a good view of his package. He had no intention of following up on the invitation, but anything that made the group more likely to pay attention to his bullshit was a good thing. "Sasquatch doesn't hang out in Forest Park, so you're safe from him. But ghosts... yeah."

Max scoffed and downed his shot. "I've heard big talk about these ghosts, but they sound pretty tame compared to some of the things we've faced."

"Really?" Logan drawled. "Where are you staying?"

"Up in the industrial district," Square Jaw said. "Vaughn Street Hotel. Need directions?"

"Thanks, but no."

"It's practically a dump," Max grumbled. "Our unit production manager is too cheap to swing a hotel for us downtown. You'd think she could at least manage a suite for me at a more upscale place."

"She may have done you a favor. You don't want to be too close to Nina."

"Nina? Wiley didn't mention any Nina in that briefing."

"How would you know, Max?" Mr. Bear asked. "You were too busy lobbing paper wads at the poor guy to listen to anything he said."

Max didn't acknowledge him, but his knuckles whitened around his glass. "So. Nina?"

Logan shook his head. "Very sad case. A working girl who got tangled up with some mobsters, about a hundred years ago. She was about to turn them in, but then..." Logan put his palms together and mimed a dive. "Took an unscheduled trip down an elevator shaft, sans elevator."

"Where does she... uh... walk?"

"Building that used to be the Merchant Hotel, not far from here."

"So we're safe up on Vaughn, right?"

"Well..." Logan screwed up his face and squinted at the ceiling. "Probably. But they say she's got a real grudge against elevators. I can't tell you what to do, of course, but..." He leaned across the table and tapped Max's empty glass. "I always take the stairs."

Max's mouth had gaped during Logan's spiel, but he shut it with a snap and cut a glance at the other guys at the table. All of them appeared very interested in their drinks, empty or otherwise. Square Jaw winked at Logan. Obviously Max's crew wouldn't lift a finger to keep him from hanging himself.

Excellent.

"So." Max cleared his throat. "Elevators. Check."

"Then there are the tunnels."

"Tunnels?" Max's gape was back, his eyes nearly as wide.

"The shanghai tunnels. Lots of port cities on the West Coast have 'em, they say. San Francisco, Seattle, Port Townsend... Portland's are notorious. You mean you never heard of 'em?"

"I have," Mr. Bear volunteered.

Logan shot him a thumbs-up. "Crimps used 'em to kidnap men and sell them to ships that were short of crew. Fifty bucks a head for an able-bodied man, no questions asked. A cowboy or farmer or lumberjack would drop into a bar, and get an on-the-house special from a friendly stranger or bartender." Logan nodded at Max's empty shot glass, its umbrella tilted at a tipsy angle. "Next thing they know, they're unpaid labor on a ship bound for who knows where. And let's say they didn't have a very attractive retirement plan."

Max gulped and pushed his glass aside. "So the ghosts of the kidnapped men—"

"Oh, not them. Most of them died at sea, some of 'em chained below decks. It's the crimps you've got to worry about."

"I'll bite," Square Jaw said. "Why?"

"Fifty bucks a head isn't money they'd walk away from, even after death. I've heard of men disappearing off the sidewalk between one block and the next if they stray over the tunnels after dark."

Max scoffed. "Right. Where'd they take the guys? Ghost ships?"

"Could be." Logan shrugged. "The tunnels used to lead to the docks and this bar is supposed to sit over one of the spurs. But why worry? You're the professional. You've got the respect of the entities on the other side of the veil, am I right?"

"Uh… right." Max's gaze cut to the other guys at the table, who offered him nothing but bland expressions. "Other side of the veil. We've got it covered."

"Then you're golden. Unless, you know, you run into a ghost who likes a challenge." Logan stood up and clapped Max on the shoulder. "Then things could get ugly."

Riley typed feverishly, cross-referencing his private research files with the data he'd located online and at the local historical society. Julie had tried to convince him to have dinner with the guys in the crew tonight, but he'd passed. If he expected to find the truth without any help from Logan, he had no time to waste.

What had he missed, what critical piece had escaped him because he hadn't known the real story of Logan's grandfather? What if it made the difference between catching the war on camera to prove it was real, and having it devolve into another anticlimactic *HttM* hoax?

Worse, what if some scrap of lore he'd overlooked put the crew in real danger? That was what had Riley shaking in his sneakers.

A knock on his door interrupted his search through the barely legible scans of old police reports. "Just a minute." He saved his work and scrambled out of the chair to open the door.

He'd expected Julie, but instead, Max stood there, visibly shaken and also quite obviously drunk off his ass.

"Wiley. Buddy. This town is seriously freaky." He stumbled past Riley in a bob and weave that would have been impressive if it had been intentional, and stood swaying at the foot of the bed, blinking at the room. "What is this? A fucking broom closet? You need a serious upgrade in accommodations, man."

Riley checked the hallway, but nobody else from the show materialized to take custody of its inebriated star. He sighed and shut the door. "I'm just the newbie PA, Max. I don't rate a suite."

Max squinted at the single chair, then at the one-step-up-from-plastic flowered bedspread on the bed. "Where am I supposed to sit?"

Riley's eyebrows shot up, and he shoved at his glasses with a knuckle. "You want to sit?"

Max never spent time in his presence voluntarily, unless it was to order him to fetch a latte or a bottle of tequila.

"Yeah." Max turned and nearly fell over. "We've got shit to discuss."

"We do?" A seed of warmth sprouted in Riley's chest. Maybe he'd finally made a place for himself in the crew as someone who knew more than everyone's preferred sandwich orders. "About what?"

"This freaky-ass story, *mowon*. What do you think?"

The seedling shriveled and died. Okay, so Max wanting to talk didn't mean he wanted to be buddies, or even cordial. "How about we take this upstairs to your suite?"

Max belched behind pressed lips. "Nah. I don't roll that way."

Jesus. "That's not what I meant." Riley pulled Max toward the door. "Come on, big guy. When you pass out, I'd prefer it if you weren't occupying all the available real estate in my room."

He shouldered Max out the door and steered him toward the elevator banks, their path not as direct as it could have been given Max's increasingly unsteady gait and his tendency to lean. Why did drunk guys always revert to mouth-breathing?

The alcohol fumes in Max's breath were enough to make Riley woozy from the backwash.

"Evelators? No way, man." Max veered toward the door to the stairwell. "Shtairs."

"Yeah, I don't think so." In his state, Max would probably fall all the way down and break his neck. Luckily, Max's alcohol level impaired his willpower, and Riley was able to haul him back on track. If the star took a fatal header while in Riley's custody, he'd be so fired.

"You take me seriously, wight, Wiley?"

"Uh…" *Can I plead the Fifth?*

"'S what I thought. Knew I could count on you."

"Sure, Max. You bet."

He propped Max next to the elevator, but before he could hit the Up button, the doors slid open, and Julie charged out. She halted when she saw Max sliding down the wall, relief replacing the concern that knotted her forehead.

"Thank God. You found him." She helped Riley heave Max upright, supporting him from the other side.

"He found me. Unfortunately. Let's get him upstairs before the inevitable occurs." It took both of them to pull Max into the elevator, since the guy was listing as if the floor were the deck of the sinking *Titanic*. "Do you know what his problem is? He seemed kind of freaked."

"Now he seems kind of semiconscious." On cue, Max sagged against Julie, drooling on the shoulder of her fleece vest. "Ewww. He's gonna pay for my dry cleaning. Or better yet, a new vest."

The elevator pinged, and they staggered out, towing Max along like a sack of potatoes with really good hair.

"Where's his room?" Riley panted.

"Four thirteen. End of the hall."

"Where's his key?"

"Probably in his pocket." Julie met his gaze over Max's lolling head. "You do it. You're used to feeling up guys' junk, right?"

"Excuse me? You've got as much experience as I do, bi girl."

"But I'm, like, management. If he comes to while I'm playing pocket pool he's liable to file a sexual harassment claim."

"Max? Are you kidding? He'd probably invite you in for drinks."

Julie heaved a giant sigh. "Just do it, Riley, okay?"

"Fine. But you have to hold him up."

"Yeah, that'll happen," she grumbled. "The guy weighs a ton. Help me lean him on the door so he doesn't squash me flat."

They shuffled around in the corridor, Max's awkward weight draped over Riley like a lead overcoat, until they offloaded him. But instead of sliding down onto his butt or lurching back onto Riley, Max fell backward as the door creaked slowly open.

Riley caught Max's arm and the front of his jacket, and managed to break his fall, although Julie's swift intake of breath made him glance up.

Jesus. Max's suite looked like the aftermath of a wrap party for a zombie movie. The furniture in the main room had been upended, chair and sofa cushions scattered from wall to wall, although they all seemed intact. The bottles on the wet bar were overturned but not shattered. However, shredded paper covered the carpet like glossy black and white ash.

Riley nudged a clump of the scraps with his toe. "Guess Max'll need to replenish his supply of autographed photos."

Julie didn't answer. She was staring at the chaos, her hand over her mouth, her brown eyes wide.

Riley put his arm around her shoulders. "Could he have done this himself? Does he usually trash his room?"

She shook her head. "No." Her voice was a broken croak. "He's actually pretty meticulous. Besides, he'd never trash his own photos."

Riley eyed Max, now sprawled on the floor, adding a guttural snore to his continued drool action. Lovely. "What are we going to do? We should probably notify someone. The police? Hotel management?"

"No!" She whirled, arms out as if to block him from digging the phone out of the litter on the desk. "Are you nuts? If Scott hears about this, he might start paying attention to the show again, and I'll be back to a glorified gofer."

Riley gave her the *thanks-a-lot-pal* look. "You told me the glorified gofer job was a chance in a million when you convinced me to take it."

"And it was, right? Any day now, Scott'll promote you to content developer."

"What do you bet I'll still fetch the coffee, regardless of the title?" Riley craned his neck in an attempt to see beyond Julie. "We should probably check the bedroom too."

"Later. We need to stash him somewhere since we can hardly leave him here." Max twitched on the floor between them, snorting like a feral pig. Julie shot a disgusted glance at him. "Help me get him to my room. It's in reasonable shape."

"Where are you going to sleep?" Riley knew the answer before she blinked her doe-eyes at him.

"I'll crash with you. Won't be the first time."

"I know. That's not the point. If we—"

"Please, Rile? This story is important to both of us. I need it to prove I've got the chops to run the show on my own. You need it to prove you're more than the guy who knows how to google."

Riley glanced at the shambles of Max's room. "Jules, this looks pretty major. What if something important is missing? What's Max going to do when he sobers up tomorrow and finds out he has no pictures to hand out to his adoring fans?"

"We'll spin it. Say it was, I don't know, poltergeist activity."

Riley primmed his lips and folded his hands at his waist. "But that would be a lie."

"We work in television, Riley. What makes you think *truth* is a priority?" Julie lifted one of Max's limp arms and nodded for Riley to do the same. They pulled him to a sitting position only to have him fall over sideways, his head hitting Julie's belly instead of the wall. "Ooof. Jesus. When I produce my own show, I'm signing a smaller star."

Riley stepped over Max's legs and into the corridor. "Wait here. I've got an idea."

He raced to the end of the hall and took the elevator to the lobby, where he snagged one of the luggage carts and returned to Max's suite.

Julie grinned at him. "You're brilliant."

"Yeah, well, guess you learn a thing or two as Production Bitch."

They wrestled Max onto the cart and wheeled him onto the elevator. When the doors slid open on Julie's floor, Wes and Charmaine were standing in the hallway.

Riley tensed, waiting for the inevitable questions, but the two staffers only stood aside for Riley to push the cart out of the elevator before they stepped inside.

"Evening, Julie. Riley." Wes ignored Max completely. "Missed you at dinner."

The elevator doors closed. Riley exchanged a sidelong glance with Julie.

"Right," she said. "Let's offload the baggage, shall we?"

By the time they wrestled Max onto the bed and got him face-planted on the pillows, they were both panting.

Riley wiped his forehead with the back of his hand. "What do you suppose he'll do when he sobers up and discovers his headshots are nothing more than a carpet of confetti?"

"Don't worry about it. I can handle Max."

"But should you? Jules, the place was trashed. I still think we need to notify the police."

Her eyes lit up with the manic glee he'd learned to recognize —and fear—from their college days. "I've got a better idea. Let's get one of the handhelds and film the scene. We can get Max to record a voice-over later." She strode out of the room and power walked down the hall.

"Julie." Riley scuttled after her, catching her arm as they passed the elevator bank. "Come on. The hotel must have some kind of policy for loss. They won't want it known that their guests aren't safe here."

She rounded on him and poked him in the chest with her forefinger. "Can you guarantee that Max didn't leave the door open himself? He's always flipping the stupid security bolt to the outside so he doesn't need to take his key with him when he goes to the ice machine or cruises someone else's room."

Riley's eyebrows popped up. "Max gets his own ice?"

"My point is that the fault might be judged to be ours. And in the dance of blame, I can guarantee you nobody's gonna want to step up and be our partner."

"You mean—"

"Yup. We found it, so it's our fricking problem. Now come on. The equipment suite's on this floor. Let's go get that camera." She sped on her way.

"The equipment has a suite? I think I'm insulted it rates a better room than I do," Riley grumbled as he tried to keep up with her determined stride. That was the problem with being on the low side of average height for a man with a best friend on the high side of tall for a woman. He was always in a half run whenever Julie was in a hurry.

"Sorry to break it to you, hon, but the equipment is worth more than..." Julie's steps slowed, and she stopped in the middle of the hallway. "Oh, no."

The door to the equipment's deluxe suite gaped wide. Riley put a hand on her shoulder. "Wait here."

"Why? So you can get brained by the maniac with a grudge against *HttM*?"

"No. But, like you said, finger-pointing is bound to ensue. When it's time to spread the blame around, I've got less to lose than you do."

"No, you don't. We're in this together." She linked arms with him. "Come on."

They slipped inside the suite. When he switched on the light, Julie whimpered and clutched his arm in a death grip.

Most of the molded plastic equipment crates were out of kilter, but intact. However, several lay upended in the middle of the room, their two night-vision cameras little more than a pile of very expensive electronic pasta next to them.

Riley eyed the carnage. "I'm guessing this is not good."

"You think?" Julie let go of him and shuffled forward, picking up a short boom with a microphone dangling off it like a dead fish on a line. "Whoever it was, they knew what to hit. Everything else is generic. But these? You almost certainly can't find replacements in the local surplus or camera shop."

Riley picked his way around the mess and eased open the door to the other room in the suite. The crates in there were undisturbed, but the light caught the glitter of broken glass on the carpet next to the bed. He crept forward.

The shards of a crystal vase lay there, along with the sad broken stems and scattered petals of what had been one of the small welcome bouquets hotel management had placed in each of the higher-end rooms. Needless to say, Riley hadn't rated flowers. He'd barely rated enough floor space to turn around.

Riley heaved a sigh, snagged the wastebasket from beside the dresser, and squatted down to collect the clutter of flowers and glass. When he picked up the first battered plants, however, something silver glinted underneath the litter of leaves.

Careful not to nick himself on the slivers of glass, he pushed the detritus aside with one headless rose.

On the sodden carpet lay an adjustable wrench the length of his forearm.

"The murder weapon," Riley muttered, flicking a thorn with his thumbnail. He squinted at the handle and the breath stalled in his throat, his vision blurring at the edges like an out-of-focus camera shot.

There, just above the hole at the end of the handle, were two letters in a navy-blue enamel paint he knew all too well.

LC
Logan Conner.

The broken flower dropped from his nerveless fingers. God, how far would Logan go to kill this story?

"Okay, Riley. You win," Julie called from the next room. "We need to bring in the cops. And Scott, damn it all to hell in a little tin cup."

Alarm jolted down Riley's spine, and he rocked back on his heels. "No." This was his fault. Regardless of how self-absorbed Logan had grown, *HttM* would never have raised a blip on his radar if Riley hadn't shown up and demanded his stupid freaking closure.

Besides, he wanted the chance to kick Logan's ass himself first.

He wedged the wrench up the tight leg of his jeans and down his sock, lodging the lumpy handle next to his ankle under his high-top.

As he stood, the head of the wrench gouged his calf. *Ow, damn it, ow.* He shook his foot experimentally and only succeeded in catching what felt like half the hair on his leg in the adjustment-gear-thingie. When he turned around, he nearly collided with Julie. For a tall woman with a drill-sergeant stride, she could move silently when she wanted to. Sweat broke out along his hairline. Had she seen him hide the wrench?

"You were right before." He wiped his damp palms on his jeans. "We keep this internal."

"Riley. Get real." She brandished her dead-fish mic. "We have no cameras. Someone might notice when the director yells, 'Action,' and there's nothing for the camera operators to hold."

Hold it together. Don't let on you know who did it. Not yet. "We can figure it out. There's a couple of places in town that do TV production support. I researched them when I was, well..."

She raised one eyebrow. "Cyber-stalking Logan?"

"When I was developing the story." He walked back into the other room, mustering as much dignity as he could manage with a foot of chrome-plated steel doing its best to merge with his flesh. "I told you I didn't know he was here."

Julie followed him. "Whatever. We..." She poked him in the shoulder until he faced her. "Why are you limping?"

"It's nothing. My leg's a little stiff. Now don't worry. I'll take care of this." *All of it. One way or another.*

"I told you. We're in this together."

"Not this time." He spun her around, propelling her out of the room with both hands planted on her shoulder blades. "Don't you have a shoot schedule to revise? PAs to terrorize? A slacker showrunner to coddle?"

"Yes, but—"

"Jules. Go do your job. This is *my* job, remember?"

She scowled at him from the middle of the hallway, her arms wrapped across her stomach. "You're the researcher, Riley. Not the janitor."

He shrugged and managed a half smile. "So you say. But we know the television truth. Go on. I'll be fine."

He closed the door before she could charge back in.

"That's right," he told the pile of ex-cameras. "Production Bitch to the rescue."

CHAPTER ELEVEN

Logan finished mopping up the spill from the damned leaky keg and was turning off the lights behind the bar when a fusillade of knocking erupted from the back.

"I've got it, Bert," he called. His boss had been barricaded in the office nearly all day, and the only thing that made him grumpier than paperwork was after-hours visitors. Nobody needed that shit—not the clueless time-challenged person and certainly not Logan. He balled the soiled bar towel in his fist and strode down the hallway. When he hit the panic bar, the door flew open.

Riley.

Damn it. He thought he'd soaked that bridge with enough gasoline to burn it to ash. Logan stepped back, bunching his fists against the urge to grab Riley's arms and kiss the holy fucking shit out of him.

But Riley muscled in, shoving Logan's shoulder, throwing him off-balance.

"How far, Logan? How far will you go to get your own way?"

Ah. Perfect. His spooky stories must have hit folklore pay dirt. "Don't know what you're talking about."

"You want to get me fired, fine. But what about Julie? The rest of the crew? We've got obligations. But you wouldn't know about that, would you? When the stakes get too high, you just leave."

"Shut up." Logan glanced over his shoulder at the office door. Although Bert had been holed up in there most of the evening to avoid the *toorists*, he could emerge anytime. If he'd booted Riley out on his ass once, he probably wouldn't hesitate to do it again, and Logan wasn't sure whose side he'd take in that particular altercation. He grabbed Riley by one arm and hustled him toward the door.

Riley wrenched his arm out of Logan's grasp, yanking his jacket off his shoulder. "Don't touch me."

The edge in his voice, the disgust twisting his mouth, caught Logan like a sucker punch to the gut. But this was what he wanted, wasn't it? Riley so pissed at him that he'd stay safely free of Logan's personal blast zone. So why did he want to wipe the hatred off Riley's face, tease a smile from him instead? "You can yell at me all you want, but not here." Logan pointed at the back door. "Outside."

Riley shrugged his jacket back on and nodded curtly. Logan followed him into the alley and wedged the door open with the bar towel.

"Right." Logan leaned on the brick wall next to the door, his arms folded. "What's the problem?"

"The pwoblem?" Riley pulled a long metal object from under his jacket. "The *problem* is this." He slapped the thing—hard—on Logan's chest.

"Ow. Jesus, Riley. That's gonna leave a bruise." Logan looked down at Riley's hand splayed against his shirt. *He's touching me.* Damn it. *Focus, Conner.* "Hey. How'd you get my wrench?"

Riley's lips thinned into an unforgiving line. "The scene of the crime."

"What crime? Substandard equipment? A boss who won't spring for his own tools? Bert's skinflintedness is revolting, but not illegal, unfortunately."

"No. You—"

The door creaked open, and Bert loomed in the shadows of the hallway. "Logan. What's the—" He stepped into the wan light of the alley. "You. I thought I told you to stay out of my place."

Great. Logan pushed himself off the wall, ready to intervene.

Riley shoved his hands in the pockets of his jeans and hunched his shoulders. "Not in your place, am I?" He refocused his death glare on Logan. "Why did you do it, Logan? Did you think we'd give up on the story because of your terrorist tactics?"

"Oh come on. Terrorist?" Logan couldn't fight his grin. Christ, that had been fun. "The guy hunts ghosts for a living. You telling me he can't handle a few spooky stories?"

"Stories? What stories? Your vandalism is going to cost—"

"Hold it." Bert took another step outside. *Shit.* Logan shifted his stance to shield Riley from his boss's uncertain temper. "You part of that bunch that's aiming to film at Balch Creek?"

Riley lifted his chin and squared his shoulders. "At Witch's Castle. Yeah." He glared at Logan. "And we're still filming, no matter what happens."

"You don't say. Well. That changes things, don't it?" Bert cackled like a demented hen. "Where's your hospitality gone, Logan?" He jerked his thumb at the door. "Offer the man a drink."

Riley's gaze bounced between Logan and his boss. Yesterday, he'd had no doubt which man belonged in the hero's camp and which one sided with the villains. Now, in the face of a friendly Bert, and with damning evidence of Logan's dark side, his judgment was seriously in question.

Was this why Logan had chosen to work at Stumptown Spirits—because he was colluding with Bert? Why? And how could sabotaging *HttM* possibly benefit them? For once, Riley wasn't sure he wanted to know.

"No. Really." He backed away. Slowly. *Don't startle them. You clearly have no idea what they'll do.* "I've got to go."

"Come back tomorrow. Bring your friends. Burgers on the house."

Logan's head whipped around, and his dumbfounded expression told Riley the free-food offer wasn't SOP.

"Bert," Logan said, "I'll be back in a minute to lock up."

"Take your time." Bert shot one more speculative look at Riley, and returned inside, trailing a rusty chuckle.

Yeah, that wasn't ominous in the least. Riley edged farther toward the street, wiping his damp palms on his jeans. Although the light above the door still shined, the alley seemed darker than it had before, the sidewalk behind him too empty.

Logan scowled at the door, tossing the wrench end-over-end. The slap of the metal hitting his palm was the only sound in the night. *Just two more steps and I'll be on the sidewalk.* As Logan flipped the wrench once more and snatched it out of the air, Riley's heel collided with an empty beer can, sending it spinning across the pavement with a hollow clatter.

Logan's head snapped around. "Not so fast. I'm not done with you." He strode toward Riley, the wrench clenched in his fist, and Riley flinched, stomach plummeting, and raised his hands to ward off the blow.

The shock on Logan's face was almost comical. He glanced from Riley to the wrench. "Seriously? Christ, Riley. You really think I'd hit you? You know me better than that."

"It's pretty evident that I don't know you at all."

Logan swore under his breath and carded the fingers of his free hand through his hair. "Listen, last time I saw this, it was hanging on a nail under the bar. I keep it there to fix our leaky keg, but anyone could've taken it."

"That's not where I found it. I know you don't want us to film this story, but did you have to destroy the equipment?"

"Whoa, whoa, whoa. I haven't destroyed anything."

"Yeah? Where were you earlier tonight then, when the crew was at the bar?"

"I was serving them more beer than was good for them, if they have an early call tomorrow." Logan grinned, a goddamned shit-eating grin so familiar, so *Logan*, that the last of Riley's earlier fear and uncertainty vanished, replaced by the urge to grab the stupid wrench and smack him with it. "That guy, Max. He can't hold his beer as well as he thinks he can."

"Sometime today, between about four o'clock and eleven, someone vandalized Max's suite."

Logan's grin faded. "You think I had something to do with that? I told you. I was here."

"What time?"

"My shift started at six."

It would have been close, but he could have pulled it off. "Someone broke into the equipment suite too. Destroyed both our night-vision cameras. That," Riley pointed to the wrench in Logan's hand, "was on the scene."

"Then I must be guilty. Why even ask?" Something in Logan's tone said *danger*, and fear fizzed in Riley's veins again. God, why couldn't he have fallen in love with some nice geeky gamer? He so wasn't cut out for dealing with this alpha shit.

He gave it his best shot, poking Logan's chest with a stiff forefinger. "Your wrench didn't walk there by itself."

"Maybe it did." Logan advanced another half step, trapping Riley's hand between them. "You should investigate. The Case of the Walking Wrench. Film at eleven."

Riley stared at Logan, at the way his lips tucked in at the corners, at the slight lift of his left eyebrow. "Are you laughing at me?"

"You hear me laughing?"

Riley's eyes narrowed. "It's a virtual laughter. The kind you expect me not to see. The kind at my expense. The kind you share with your friends and aim at me like some kind of cool-guy weapon."

Logan dropped the wrench with a *clank* and grabbed him by the shoulders. "That's not the weapon I want to point at you. And I damn well don't want to share you with my friends." His hand shifted to the back of Riley's neck, and his lips came down in a ruthless kiss with a tongue chaser.

Riley wanted to resist, to salvage some shred of his pride. He tried. God, he tried, clenching his fists and holding them tight against his thighs. But the heat of Logan's mouth, the way his body fit against Riley from chest to knees... *Screw it.* He moaned into the kiss.

But before he could wrap his arms around Logan's waist, Logan disengaged, holding Riley at arm's length. "But I still don't want you to run with that story. Go home, Riley. Stay away from me. Stay safe."

As Riley gaped at him, swaying on his feet, Logan turned and disappeared back into Stumptown Spirits.

Riley raised shaking fingers to his lips. "Well shit."

Logan let the metal door clang shut behind him, the panic bar *snick*ing into place. He leaned his head against the door and closed his eyes, willing his dick to stand down.

Christ, he was a fucking idiot. A weak fucking idiot. How could he convince Riley that the feeling between them was dead when his own body betrayed him, refusing to support the lie? Riley wasn't stupid. If he'd somehow overlooked Logan's glaring mixed signals before, there was no way he'd missed that kiss.

What was it the shrinks said about near-death experiences or about facing a final battle? The urge to mate roared in and took control, a last desperate attempt to pass on DNA before the end. No wonder Logan wanted to fuck Riley every time he saw him. Didn't matter that Riley couldn't do anything with Logan's pathetic DNA. The primal instinct reared its damned head anyway.

He opened his eyes and nearly fell on his ass. Bert stood at the other end of the hall, the light from the kitchen casting shadows on his angular face, turning him into a Cubist's nightmare.

"He a friend of yours?" Bert stepped forward, and his face assumed its usual form, except for one thing.

He was smiling.

"You could say that." Logan picked up his discarded bar towel to avoid Bert's scrutiny. "That TV crew nearly drank us out of the local microbrews. If they're coming back tomorrow, we should reorder."

"You reckon they'll be back?"

"You offered them free food. What do you think?"

This time Bert didn't laugh, thank God, because that was too creepy for words, but he was still smiling, which was almost as bad.

Logan was damn glad he wasn't bartending tomorrow. Between a grinning Bert and a bar crowd that was bound to include Riley, he'd never survive the night, and an unscheduled demise was not part of his plan.

Riley hadn't gotten over his pissed-at-Logan-and-the-world attitude by the time he'd schlepped back to the hotel. Why couldn't the man pick an attitude and stick with it? All this seesawing made it freaking hard to believe anything he said. *Had* he trashed Max's room and the equipment? The evidence pointed that way, despite his denial.

But that same bone-deep disbelief that had made him doubt Logan's motives for disappearing five months ago cautioned him to check his assumptions at the door. He'd told Logan he didn't know him, but he knew enough. Sure, Logan was physically capable of destroying the cameras, although the care he lavished on his motorcycle and every appliance they'd ever owned made it seem unlikely—he respected technical craftsmanship too much. But shredding Max's photographs?

That was just... petty. Logan might have a flash-point temper, but he was never, ever small-minded.

Riley stomped down the dim corridor to his shoebox of a room, jammed his key card in the slot, flung the door open, and hit the light switch.

"Jesus, Riley," Julie's muffled voice emerged from a mound of blankets on his bed. "Throw in a little C-4 and a hand grenade. You'll make less noise."

"Crap. Sorry. I forgot you were here." He killed everything but the bathroom light so he wouldn't maim himself on the furniture, and tiptoed to the dresser.

"Don't bother playing cat burglar now. That ship has sailed."

"I'm pretty sure cat burglars don't sail."

"So I mix metaphors. Sue me." Julie sat up and pushed the blankets down to her waist, her curly blond hair smooshed on one side, and the Marx Brothers T-shirt she slept in twisted around her torso. "Where did you go?"

"I had an errand. To run."

"I guessed that much, doofus. What errand?"

"Just, you know, things."

"Jesus, you cannot dodge for shit. My four-year-old niece is a better liar than you."

"It's my business." He pulled a pair of flannel sleep pants and a T-shirt out of the dresser. "You don't have to worry about it."

"The hell I don't. Come on. Tell me."

Riley sighed. "Julie—"

"If you don't, I'll sing 'Copacabana' all night until you cave."

God, why did he ever think it would be fun to work with his best friend? At least if he worked with strangers, he'd be able to hold on to a vestige of privacy, not to mention dignity. "Fine. I went to see Logan."

"Good lord. Why?"

"Because..." He still wasn't sure whether to believe Logan's denial, but he also wasn't ready to share his suspicions with

Julie. She'd never forgive Logan for sabotaging her show, even if he hadn't actually done it. Julie could carry a grudge further than a Republican congress member, and with as little justification.

She punched her pillow, and he winced. "Cut the bullshit, Rile. I know what's going on."

Crap. How had she found out? Had she seen him stuff the wrench in his sock? Followed him to Stumptown Spirits? He braced himself for the Wrath of Ainsworth.

"You've still got the hots for that ass-bite dick-monkey, haven't you?"

He exhaled a giant breath. Two days ago, this was the worst thing he could have had to admit. Today, he had so much more to hide. "Yeah. Yeah, I do."

Too bad it wasn't a lie.

Under her lopsided hairdo, Julie's face hardened into the expression she reserved for conversations about Logan. "Shit, Riley. Why—"

"Jules." His shoulders slumped, and he scrubbed a hand through his hair. "Can we leave it for tonight? Please?"

"Oh." She blinked at him in the half-light, clearly having trouble rewriting her retribution agenda. "Sure. But..." She plucked at the corner of the pillowcase. "I've got some more bad news for you."

God, worse than trashed equipment? He clutched the ball of clothing to his belly. "Is everyone..." He gulped. "Everyone okay?"

"Mostly. But your prime witness bailed tonight. I got the call about an hour ago."

"But—but he was so adamant about his experience, and pissed that no one believed him."

"Yeah." Julie wrinkled her nose. "Too bad he suddenly discovered an emergency visit to his Great-aunt Tessie in Bozeman."

"You're kidding."

"Unfortunately, no. He really said that."

Riley sank into the squeaky desk chair. "What are we going to do, Jules? That reduces us to a single witness whose experience is restricted to mysterious fog on her shots of the Castle." And it wasn't as if Logan—who'd felt the real impact of the ghost war —would get anywhere near their cameras. "Not exactly compelling television."

"I have another idea."

Over the years, Riley had learned when Julie used that overly reasonable tone of voice, she was about to spring something on him that would make him wish he were in a six-year coma.

"What?"

"Don't sound so suspicious. Don't you trust me?"

"Since you ask? No."

She stuck out her lower lip in a pout so incongruous on her strong-jawed face that Riley nearly laughed. "I'm hurt."

"You're not. Come on. Let me have it."

She grinned, bouncing on her butt in the bed. "Simple. You could do it."

Riley's belly curled in on itself. "I'm not a witness."

"No, but you've got the research, the history. Think about it. Even if the ghosts don't materialize—and given our track record, I think that's a certainty—the backstory is still awesome. Flesh it out. Pull in some local history experts. Then you could narrate it."

"Are you crazy? With my Elmer Fudd speech impediment?"

Julie tossed off the blankets and knee-walked to the edge of the bed. "Riley Morrel, do not let assholes like Max Stone or your stupid family convince you that you're unintelligible. It's very slight. And kind of cute, actually."

Riley stripped off his Henley, wadded it up, and tossed it in the laundry pile. "Cute isn't a selling point when you're trying for credibility."

"Maybe not. But it endears you to viewers, and that can't be bad."

"Seriously, Jules, can you see Max Stone allowing me even a minute of his screen time?"

He met her gaze in the mirror, and she narrowed her eyes. "Unless he wants to ad lib the whole freaking episode, he'd better learn how to share."

CHAPTER TWELVE

Riley would be at Stumptown Spirits tonight.

The thought had plagued Logan all day, through the trip to the bank to close his accounts, the wait at the DMV to prep for the transfer of the Harley title, the visit to the landlord to settle his lease.

Who knew dying required so much fucking paperwork?

Now, halfway through his stint cleaning the bar—another one of those least favorite tasks he'd lined up for himself—that insidious thought remained.

Riley. Stumptown Spirits. Tonight.

Christ, he only had three days left. What would be the harm in seeing Riley again? Spending those last days near him?

The harm, idiot, is that it would be both too much and not enough. It would be too much for Riley, whose grief would be greater if he had to mourn someone he loved, whom he knew loved him. But it would never be enough for Logan, because the one thing, the one person he'd regret leaving would be within his reach. If he gave in, Trent would be doomed, maybe forever. And Riley? What would he have if Logan took the selfish coward's way out again?

A lover who was only half there. Who couldn't leave the past behind because once a year he doomed himself to repeat it.

After he'd discovered that nothing materialized except on the anniversary, he'd tried to get as far away from Portland as he could, searching for an answer. But as the hellish anniversary approached, no matter where he'd run—Nevada, Arizona, Texas, Florida—whenever he'd gotten on his bike, to head to his latest bartending gig, to a club, to the damn grocery store, for Chrissake, he would end up on the nearest highway heading north, unable to pass up one more opportunity to try to rescue his friend. Or if rescue was impossible, to at least honor him with his presence, his vigil.

He'd given up on the mediums and spiritualists after Marguerite Windflower told him the ghosts might not be ghosts. Instead, he'd gone looking for someone who knew about this kind of shit—stories, legends, whatever. As soon as he'd dropped her at the airport, he'd headed south, stopping in Eugene. UO had a couple of faculty members who were big noise in the folklore community—and hadn't it been an eye-opener to find out there actually was a folklore community? He'd sat in (illegally) on one of the lectures.

And seen the teaching assistant, Riley Morrel.

Boom.

Since denial was an old and valued drinking buddy, he'd convinced himself that he'd targeted Riley because he was an easier mark than the professor, and approached with a plan to pump him about information on legends and ghost stories, clues about how to save Trent.

He'd ended up pumping Riley in an entirely different way.

For a year and a half, he'd continued to lie to himself. Pretended he was only staying with Riley until he could find the answer to Trent's rescue. But every day with Riley, every time they made love, the urgency of the search had diminished, his guilt masked under his joy and damn domestic contentment.

After all, he'd tried for almost seven years without turning up a single usable piece of information. It was time to admit he never would, to give up his annual pilgrimage to Forest Park and live his life.

With Riley.

Pretty fucking ironic that the very day he'd been ready to pop the fatal question and put the ghost war in the past for good, Riley had given him the answer.

They'd been making dinner. Logan was a decent cook when he put his mind to it, and kept Riley away from the knives and open flames. He wanted this one to be special, something they'd remember every year on their anniversary, so he'd pulled out all the stops. Riley's favorite mustard-marinated grilled fish. Wine. Crème brûlée for dessert. Logan's nerves were on overload. What if Riley said no? Sure, he'd hinted about taking Logan with him to Europe on the big-deal study grant he'd just been awarded, but maybe he wasn't as certain as Logan that he'd met the love of his life.

Logan would have to persuade him to say yes, that's all. Because he wasn't sure how he'd live without him.

Tonight, Riley was so jazzed about some story he'd been discussing with the kids in his TA session that the salad he was tossing threatened to escape the bowl.

"I love this part of teaching: The first time the students really get the power of these mythic cycles. What they mean in history. How powerful, how weal they are."

Logan grinned at Riley's speech slip. "Real, huh? How can you prove it if this shit happened umpteen thousand years ago?"

"It's a cycle, Logan. A pattern." Riley popped a carrot coin into his mouth. "They repeat in different cultures, at different times." He stopped terrorizing the salad and levered himself up to sit on the counter, swinging his legs so the heels of his sneakers bumped the cabinet in a syncopated rhythm. "Take frequency, for instance. Any time you've got a repeating cycle, whether it's ritual sacrifice or replacement or birth order, it's always a repeating periodicity. Seven and three are the big winners."

"Replacement? You mean your favorite myths have parts that wear out and need maintenance, like the spark plugs on my bike?"

Riley grinned, and Logan abandoned the sautéing onions. He crossed the kitchen to nudge Riley's knees apart and draw him into a tight embrace, because that mouth demanded a kiss. Or three. Or seven. Periodicity. Yeah, he could get into that.

Riley pulled out of the kissing marathon, breathing hard— although no harder than Logan's dick—and leaned his forehead against Logan's. "If we keep this up, your onions will burn."

"Screw 'em." He dove in for another kiss, his hands tightening around Riley's ass.

"And let your work go to waste? Besides, it smells too glorious to ruin." He laced his hands behind Logan's neck. "Let's talk about something else. Death."

Logan leaned back, his own acquaintance with death wilting his erection. "Yeah, that's a mood killer."

"No, it's an answer to your question. Replacement. In a lot of the old tales, a person of power, usually a king, could escape death or another fate that might be worse, if he could get someone to take his place."

Logan scoffed and turned back to the stove. "Yeah. How tough could it be? The king orders some peasant to take the hit, and he's golden."

Riley chuckled. "Not that easy. The replacement has to be a willing volunteer. But there could be any number of reasons why someone would sign up for the gig. Money, for instance— in *The Golden Bough*, Frazer mentions a Chinese custom that paid the family of the volunteer. But there are other reasons. Hubris. Desperation. Love."

"Love?"

"Sure. If the replacement was trying to save or protect a loved one, sometimes the king himself, the sacrifice would hold incredible power." Riley jumped down from the counter and wrapped his arms around Logan's waist, warm against his back, and dug his lethal chin into Logan's shoulder. "Then the king is free, at least until the end of the next seven-year cycle when he has to get another sucker to step up to the plate."

Logan's hand shook, and he nearly dropped the sauté pan. He turned off the gas, black spots dancing in his vision. *Seven years. Get someone to take your place and you're free.*

This was the answer. It was a fucking window of opportunity. Logan calculated dates in his head. His grandfather had seen the fully manifested war sixty-three years ago—a multiple of seven. Seven years ago this October, he'd seen the ghosts himself, although they hadn't been visible since. Seven years ago, Trent willingly took Balch's place and freed him from his fate.

In order to save Trent from the cycle of murder and execution, Logan had to willingly take his place, and if he didn't do it this October, he'd have to wait seven years for another chance.

He wiped his damp palms on his jeans, then peeled Riley's hands from his waist and turned around.

"Have you booked your flight to Sarajevo yet?" His voice was rough, blocked by a lump in his throat the size of his fist.

Riley's forehead got that little pinch between his brows, the corners of his lips tipping down in a way that telegraphed his disappointment. Shit. Logan hated hurting Riley. But Riley deserved more. He deserved a life. He deserved a better man than Logan could ever be. He deserved a man who kept his promises.

"But I thought—" Riley peered at him from under his bangs. "The grant's enough to cover two if we don't splurge. You could... you could come with me."

"No." Logan forced himself to move away, busying himself with the torch on the burnt-sugar crust for the crème brûlée. "Not my scene."

"Logan?" The uncertainty in Riley's voice hit him like a rabbit punch to the kidneys.

"Gotta put the fish on the grill. Dinner in twenty."

He'd claimed an emergency bartending shift that night and hadn't returned until Riley was asleep. The next day he'd staged that stupid sex scene in their bedroom and bailed. He didn't have the right to put Riley through that again. He'd stay the fuck away from Stumptown Spirits and hope the seeds of doubt he planted would do their work and keep the crew out of Forest Park until it was too late.

His cell phone buzzed in his pocket. "Yeah?"

"It's Deke. We've spotted your guy again."

Logan tried to make himself care. "On the outbound freight from Tacoma?"

"No, man. He's in downtown Portland. One of the guys was making a delivery at a bar down on Southwest Second and saw him outside the shelter off Burnside."

Anger bubbled under Logan's skin like molten lead. *Someone to blame.* "Thanks, Deke. I'm on it."

He stashed the mop and pail in the storeroom and peered into Bert's office. Empty. Bert didn't usually arrive until closer to happy hour at four so he could put a damper on anyone's desire to order cheaper fare. Logan scowled at the black eye of the powered-down monitor. The damn computer took forever to boot up, and the map program on his phone sucked. If he didn't want to miss a chance at Danford Balch, he couldn't afford to wait.

He grabbed the phone book off of Bert's desk, thankful for once that his boss was probably the only man in Portland who still used the Yellow Pages. Several sheets of paper fluttered onto the floor—a page of notes in Bert's crabbed block printing, another with a hand-drawn map of the industrial district, because the guy didn't believe in Google Maps either. Logan tossed them onto the desk and rifled through the dog-eared book until he found the list of shelters, flipped one of the papers, and jotted down the addresses on it.

Finally. Something to take his mind off Riley. Something that would give him a little goddamn satisfaction. He grabbed his jacket off the hook and headed out the back door, adrenaline powering his steps. Despite all the years of looking for the guy, he'd had little hope of locating Balch. Now he had the gift of a chance to confront him, to stare down the man who'd condemned Trent and now Logan. Get some fucking closure before the end.

Julie made good on her threat to pull Riley on camera in place of his vanished witnesses, and although his spots would take up little screen time, they were located at six different sites around town. He'd spent all day schlepping around Portland with the second unit crew, hands sweaty and teeth clenched against stage fright.

God, he'd probably looked as terrified as the hunted *wabbit* Max always taunted him with.

To top off his crappy day, he'd made the mistake of mentioning Bert's sinister personality makeover to Julie, thinking the news would guarantee she'd stay away from Stumptown Spirits despite her still-active desire for a face-to-face confrontation with Logan, weapons TBD. That had worked until he'd illustrated his point with the unexpected dinner invitation. Then, she'd spread the word to the crew and packed them all into the van again and down to the bar.

Guess a chance to stretch her budget with free food trumped her habit of protecting Riley or her Fury-like desire for revenge.

Good to know.

He hung back, letting the rest of the crew pile out of the van first and crowd into the bar. After they'd commandeered a couple of booths and a nest of tables in the center of the room, he slunk over and took a chair in the darkest corner.

Julie found him, of course. She tossed her clipboard on his table with a clatter and dropped onto the stool across from him. "Don't hide, Rile. You're everyone's hero."

"Yeah, right." He scrunched down in his chair. Just because Bert had put on his alarming happy face yesterday, didn't mean it would remain in place today.

"I'm serious." She pulled a laminated menu from between the napkin holder and the salt and pepper shakers. "A whole day without Max, plus free food? They may nominate you for sainthood. In fact..." She stood up and hauled him out of his chair. "Come on. You're not allowed to lurk."

She dragged him over to the crew's tables and shoved him into a seat next to Zack, who slapped him on the back, a grin splitting his scruff.

"Good work today, man." He beckoned to the rest of the crew. "Am I right?"

Everyone hooted, and Grace put two fingers in her mouth and let out a piercing whistle.

Heat spread from Riley's chest to the tips of his ears. "Um... thanks."

"Far as I'm concerned," Zack said around a mouthful of pretzels, "Max can be terminally hungover every day."

"Guys," Julie said in her taking-no-shit UPM voice. "No trash-talking behind Max's back." She leaned close to whisper in Riley's ear. "That's my privilege."

The friendly waitress from Riley's first visit arrived. "Hey, ghost hunters. So you decided to brave Stumptown Spirits again. Welcome back."

Zack started chanting "Hea-ther, Hea-ther," and the other guys picked it up.

She grinned and took out her order pad. "Thanks, but I'm still not interested in your special equipment."

"Awww. Not even a little?"

"Get over it."

While Heather jotted down orders and sidestepped Zack's determined flirting, Riley cast furtive glances at the hallway. Would Logan be here tonight? He couldn't decide whether he wanted to see the man or not, although judging by the way his stomach dipped whenever someone who *wasn't* Logan emerged, his stupid heart still cherished hopes that his brain considered futile.

By the time Heather got to him, his belly was so knotted he didn't think he'd ever eat again. "I, uh, guess I'll have a—"

"You're Riley, right?" She tilted her head like an inquisitive sparrow.

He dropped his menu. "Why? Do I have to leave?"

"What? No." She laughed and tucked her pencil behind her ear. "But the boss says your tab is on him tonight, beer and burgers."

"Oh." He gulped and forced a smile. "Thanks. Then a burger, I guess. And, you know, beer."

Heather grinned at Julie. "Is he cute, or what?"

"Hello?" Riley peered at them over the top of his glasses. "Sitting right here."

"That man is toast," Heather murmured and crossed the bar in a bounce and swing of her ponytail.

"How about that, Rile?" Julie smirked at him. "You're famous."

"I could do without the fame, thanks."

"Why? You're getting free beer out of it. Half the guys at the table would turn gay for free beer."

"Jules, half the guys at the table *are* gay."

"Whatever." She settled back in her chair and frowned at her clipboard, shooting occasional questions at the crew, leaving Riley to obsess in peace until Heather and a couple of other servers returned with their food.

Zack whistled when Heather set a flight of microbrews in front of Riley. "Niiiiice. Where's mine?"

"You're getting free burgers, hotshot, so no complaining," Heather said with a flick of her fingers. "Show me your money, and I'll show you the brew."

"How come he doesn't need money?"

"He's cuter than you." Another server set a plate with a burger and fries in front of Zack. "And so's his boyfriend."

Boyfriend. Riley's cheeks flamed so hot they should have lit up the whole bar. "I don't have a boyfw—" He took a calming breath. "Boyfriend."

"Oh, sugar. You do. I saw that scene with those two bozos on the sidewalk the other day. You totally do." She leaned down and whispered, "Whether he admits it or not."

Riley grabbed her hand. "Where is he?" God, was he actually *whining*? He cleared his throat and made a giant effort not to sound like Elmer Fudd. "Logan. Where is he?"

"He's off tonight, but…" She glanced at the rest of the table, but all except Julie were focused on their plates. She pulled a cocktail napkin out of her apron pocket, jotted something on it, and held it out to him. "Here. I got this off the staff contact list. Do him a favor. Go."

Riley took the napkin. *Logan's address.* Any desire for food fled. "Oh. Thanks." *I think.*

"I mean it." She made a shooing motion with her hands as she left their table.

Damn it. Now he had a choice. He didn't have to stalk Logan at work. He could take it straight to the mattresses. God, that kiss last night. Logan still wanted him. He'd said so. Riley could be proactive, but did he want to?

"Holy shit," Zack muttered. "Dead man walking."

Riley's head jerked around. Bert was approaching their corner like a vulture with his sights on some tasty roadkill.

"Nobody told me this was gonna be the zombie episode," Zack murmured out of the side of his mouth.

"Shut up," Riley said, keeping his voice low. "That's the owner. Thank him for the free food if you know what's good for you."

A ragged cheer erupted from the crew as Bert reached them. "Thanks, man."

Bert's lips drew back, reminding Riley of Jim Carrey's old Fire Marshal Bill routine.

"My pleasure, boys." Bert nodded at Julie, Grace, and Charmaine. "And ladies."

"Would you like to..." Riley's mouth went dry as Bert drew up a chair next to him. "Join us?"

"Right neighborly. Now. I hear you folks are looking for some ghosts. That true?"

"Yes?"

"Let me tell you a thing or two about the Balch Creek homestead."

An evening sitting next to Bert versus a chance for Logan to shoot him down for good?

Surprisingly tough choice.

Still, Riley shouldered his messenger bag and stood. "Excuse me. I have to see a man about a... a thing."

As he stumbled to the door, Heather caught his eye and gave him a thumbs-up.

God, he hoped he wasn't making a mistake.

CHAPTER THIRTEEN

The narrow alley where Logan waited smelled of urine and rotting meat. A mud-brown rat regarded him from atop a pile of burst garbage bags, the rustle and squeak from beneath the tattered plastic suggesting it had brought its friends to the party. Altogether, a totally revolting spot.

Perfect.

He bounced on his toes, his hands fisted in his pockets, and tried not to grin like a maniac. Today he might finally have a chance to confront Danford Balch, the bastard who'd hijacked Trent's life and mortgaged Logan's own. He couldn't fucking wait.

The first shelter had been a bust—teens only. But the second one looked promising. As the evening wore on, chill with autumn, a pitiful double handful of men lined up on the sidewalk outside the peeling green door, shuffling forward in the hope there'd still be room by the time their turn came.

There. That one. Second to last in line, his head covered by the draggled fur-lined hood of his parka. The men on either side of him stood twice the distance away from him than from any of the others.

"Stinks like month-old fish dipped in piss."

Yeah, that'd be a reason to cut a wider berth.

As if he could feel the heat of Logan's glare, the man raised his head and stared straight at the spot where Logan lurked in the shadows.

That's right, you bastard. I'm here for you.

When Logan strode forward into the flickering light of a streetlamp, the man bolted for the corner and across the street, the untied laces of his boots slapping the concrete. Logan sprinted after him, grabbing the guy's arm before he could plunge into traffic, and dragged him into the doorway of a closed secondhand shop.

The man held his hands up, protecting his face and his neck. "Don't. Please." His voice was worn and cracked like old leather. "I don't have any money. I don't have anything."

"You got that right."

The man flinched and drew his hands toward his chest, fingers half-curled. "What do you want with..." His breath caught in a rattling wheeze. "You. You were there."

Logan tightened his grip on Balch's arm. "That's right, and on Saturday night, I'll be there again, damn you, Danford."

"I go by Danny now. Danny Ball."

"I don't give a shit what you call yourself—"

"Hey, man. Need some help?" The voice behind Logan was laced with menace and deep enough to belong to someone who could back it up.

Under the shadow of his hood, Balch's eyes widened, his gaze skittering from Logan's face to a point beyond his shoulder. "No. Only a... a chat. Friendly-like."

"If you say so." Footsteps slapped the concrete, fading under the whoosh of passing cars.

"Smart, *Danford*," Logan growled.

He struggled weakly. "Let go. Please. I—I don't know what you want."

Logan pulled Balch forward, ignoring the fetid puff of his breath. "That second chance didn't work out the way you planned, eh?"

Balch shook his head miserably. "No."

"Serves you fucking right."

A ghost of a smile flitted across the man's pockmarked face. "So easy for you to pass judgment."

"I'm not the one who murdered my son-in-law."

"It was an accident!" His wail cut through the blare of a horn in the street. "I told them. I didn't deserve to hang."

"The judge saw differently, and no matter what your story is, whether you deserved the rope or not, I know damn well that Trent didn't deserve it."

"Was he... the boy? Your friend? Did he..." He gulped, and Logan noticed the ring of scar tissue around his throat, under the collar of his threadbare flannel shirt. "I never thought he'd —"

"Get trapped in your place? Hanged in your place? *Die* in your place? How'd you do it? How did you escape?" Despite the stench, Logan crowded Balch against the door. "Tell me."

"I don't know. I only wanted peace. An end to that everlasting hell. Instead..." His gaze tracked the seedy closed storefronts across the street, the graffiti-marred walls, the knots of people—both adults and teens—hunkering down on the sidewalk and in doorways. "I found another."

Logan backed off and took an unsteady breath of the marginally clearer air in the street. "There've been a lot of changes since 1859."

"Some." Balch's hands plucked at the stained nylon of his pockets. "The frontier may have retreated, but the hearts of men are still black as Satan's pitch."

"You should know." He clenched his fists. "I've never wanted to kill anyone, but I'd make an exception for you."

"Have at it then." Balch pulled the collar of his shirt open, baring his throat. "Finish the hangman's job."

"Don't tempt me."

"Please." Balch held Logan's gaze, chest heaving. "*Please.*"

"I—I— *Fuck*." Logan whirled and smacked the wall with one palm. If he took that last irrevocable step, he'd be no better than Balch. "No."

Balch clutched his shirt closed. "I don't think you could anyway. God knows I've tried. A hundred times and more."

He can't die? Marguerite had said she didn't think the apparitions were ghosts. After years struggling to survive in an inhospitable world, could Balch be convinced to do the right thing? A desperate hope took hold of Logan and closed his throat, reducing his voice to a rough whisper. "Can you undo it? If you go back on Saturday night—"

"No!" Balch's eyes reflected the sullen glow of the streetlamp, as feral as the rats in the alley. "I may not know how to make my way in this pitiless stone wilderness, but I know what the end of the rope feels like."

"Then why come back now, after all this time?"

Balch blinked, his brow furrowing under a fringe of filthy grizzled hair. "I come back every year."

"So do I. I've never seen you."

"I hide. Across the creek. In the trees."

"Why bother?" Logan shoved his hands in his jacket pockets and leaned one shoulder against the wall. "If you won't do anything about it."

"For her. My Anna. If I could see her again... just once." He sucked in a breath, a half sob. "But she's never there. Only a wisp of light at the place I saw her last."

"I figured that out the first year. If you knew nothing would materialize, why make the trip? Kind of pointless, wasn't it?" Although that had never stopped Logan.

"It's my home. Was my home." His gaze skittered back to the line outside the shelter. "I'll never have another. Not anymore. Not anywhere."

He shouldered past Logan, trudged to the end of the dwindling line of men.

A chill wind curled around the double row of buildings, cutting through Logan's jeans as he returned to the alley where he'd parked his bike. He ought to feel gratified that Balch's stolen life had been wretched, that he'd been punished for what he'd done. But instead a hot tide of anger swamped his chest, and he kicked a broken brick into the pile of tattered garbage bags, sending the rats scuttling into the shadows.

"What a goddamned fucking waste."

Seven years of Trent's life gone, at a minimum. His own about to be offered up on a platter. Riley on deck to get caught in the same shit-storm.

All because Logan hadn't kept his goddamn mouth shut about the ghosts of Stumptown past.

CHAPTER FOURTEEN

The shabby apartment building squatting on the corner shared all the architectural charm of the finest state penitentiaries. Riley shifted from foot to foot, nerving himself to open the door and go inside.

Stupid. This was stupid. Why did proximity to Logan frenchfry his logic circuits? Any reasonable man would have given up on Logan the first time he bailed.

Any reasonable man wouldn't still be in love, damn it.

Apparently Riley could no longer claim *reasonable* as an accomplishment on his CV.

"Pathetic, yes. Reasonable, no," he muttered, shoving the fatal bar napkin in his back pocket. This wasn't just about the two of them anymore. Other people were involved—Julie, Scott, the rest of the crew. Even Joseph Geddes and Trent Pielmeyer, if they were still trapped in the ritual. He took a huge breath and blew it out, adjusting the strap of his messenger bag. Somehow, he'd force Logan to see the bigger picture. Not that he'd ever managed before. The guy couldn't multitask if his life depended on it.

One of the double front doors sported a sheet of plywood tagged with unimaginative obscenities, but the other still had its safety glass intact. Riley opened it and slipped inside.

The narrow ill-lit stairs might just as well have been the path to any of a score of different underworlds, the cinder block walls breathing damp and cold like the dank bowels of a cave.

The second-floor hallway smelled of cigarette smoke and mildew. Why would Logan, who loved the outdoors and wide-open vistas and the elegance of art deco style, choose to live in this depressing place?

Logan had never been hard-up for money. He'd bartended in Eugene, and he'd done all right, with no expenses to speak of other than food, rent, and his precious Ducati. Riley had tried to talk him into going to school, into doing something besides bartending, but Logan had refused. His whole problem back then had seemed to be a lack of ambition that stifled his potential.

Now, in light of what Riley had learned about Logan's supernatural experience, he recognized that lack for what it was. Fatalism, with a heaping helping of guilt to top off a classic early-Christian martyr complex.

The big overprotective jerk.

Locating Logan's unit at the end of the hall, he knocked, making the flimsy door rattle in its frame. Riley leaned closer, trying to detect any sound from inside above the blare of the television from the next apartment. He knocked again, and the door flew open under his fist. At first he thought he'd actually broken the thing down, and staggered forward in an attempt to grab the knob.

Logan caught him by the arms, steadied him. "Take it easy, tiger."

"Sorry." Riley stepped back, out of reach. "Guess I don't know my own strength."

"That's for damn sure," Logan muttered. "Come inside before the spores invade." He gestured to a vomit-green sofa, cigarette holes dotting its arms. "Have a seat and tell me what brings you to this lovely four-star shithole."

"Heather." Riley shuffled across the faded orange shag carpet. "She gave me your address."

"Of course she did." Logan didn't sound surprised or angry. Just resigned.

That was a good sign, right? At least he hadn't left Riley standing in the hallway, or tossed him down the rickety stairs. Riley sat gingerly on the edge of a stained sofa cushion. A spring poked him in the butt. "Jesus, Logan. Do you have to disinfect yourself every time you sit on this thing?"

Logan leaned one hip against a narrow counter that separated the living room from the galley kitchen. "It's not that bad."

"It's totally that bad. It's worse." Riley wove his fingers together, heels bouncing in a threadbare spot in the carpet. "We need to talk."

Logan crossed his arms and scowled. "Look, I didn't trash your equipment."

"I know."

"You do?"

Riley shrugged. "You said you didn't. I believe you." Besides, given the way Zack and Heather bantered about "special equipment," anyone in the bar could have overheard them.

"Then what's there to talk about?"

"You may not have done it, but someone did." Riley clamped his hands between his knees. "Someone has a vested interest in killing the story. Someone other than you."

"Not my problem."

"I think it is. I think it's been your problem from the beginning." He took a deep breath. "Logan. I know about Joseph Geddes. I know about the whole thing."

Logan grunted. "I doubt it."

"Then tell me. This is the reason you don't want the crew in the park on Saturday, right?"

"Mmmphm."

"Logan." Riley loaded his voice with as much warning as he could. "Don't be a dick. Not now."

"Jesus, Riley. You can't— Why don't you— Ah, fuck." Logan stalked across the room and threw himself into the sagging recliner. He stared at an empty bookshelf as if he could set it on fire with his eyes, his jaw as hard as marble.

"Come on." Riley used the same tone he used to cajole Julie out of production-induced hysteria. "Please? I want to help."

Logan let his head fall back and closed his eyes. "So you know my grandfather and another guy—"

"Joseph Geddes."

"Yeah. They were out in the park, hunting. Not with guns, but still not strictly legal. Geddes's family was in rough shape. Granddad wasn't as hard up, but he knew how to trap small animals, so he went along to help." He opened his eyes and gazed at the ceiling. "They were ready to leave, but Geddes cut his hand while they were skinning the last rabbit, and Granddad was patching him up when it happened."

"The ghost war rose."

"Yeah. But for them, it was different. The figures were distinct right from the beginning. With Trent—"

Riley straightened. "Hold it. You were there? You saw the ghost war too?"

Logan met Riley's eyes. "You said you knew."

"That you were questioned, not that you were *there*." Riley's eyes widened. "The blood at the scene. It was yours."

"Yeah."

"How did you manage—"

"To evade the law?" Logan's tone was bitter. "My father. He lied himself blue that I'd been with him since my last class the day before. He was a city commissioner. They took his word."

Riley stared out the window at the fading light. "So two men have been drafted into the ghost war."

"Not drafted. More like they volunteered."

"What?"

"Granddad said Geddes wasn't interested in trigger-happy Balch and his pathetic story. He fixated on the supply wagon. He had a wife and kids. They were starving, so he tried to intercept one of the bags. Unfortunately for him, he succeeded —but instead of taking food home to his family, he's heaving phantom flour forever."

Riley threaded his fingers through his bangs. "Whoa." These weren't random kidnappings at all. They were purposeful interactions between two planes of existence, instigated by the victim.

"You know the fucking ironic thing? If Granddad had kept his mouth shut, he'd have been fine. He got away clean. But he insisted on giving those rabbits to Geddes's family. He told them about what had happened. Hell, he told anyone who would listen, insisting what he'd seen was real, that he hadn't killed his friend, that Geddes had turned into a ghost. But he could never find that other guy again to back him up."

"Wait." Riley let go of his hair and scooted down the sofa toward Logan. "'That other guy'? What guy?"

"I told you."

"No. I'm pretty sure I'd have remembered a guy."

"Geddes didn't just get sucked into the war. He displaced someone. When he went in, the other guy fell out."

Riley blinked and tried to recalibrate his brain. "You mean... your grandfather witnessed an actual possession?"

Logan shook his head. "Don't think so. That's when a ghost takes over another person's body, right? My grandfather said they swapped places—one here, one in the ghost war."

God, this was bigger than Riley had imagined. An actual corporeal manifestation? Un-freaking-believable. He edged closer. "Go on. What happened then?"

"My grandmother was away, visiting her sister with my father, so Granddad took the guy home. Gave him a meal. A place to sleep. Claimed he stayed for several days but then took off before the police showed up."

"What was his name?"

Logan snorted. "John. John Doe. Yet another reason why the authorities questioned my grandfather's credibility. Nobody believed he existed, but you'd think if Granddad wanted to lie, he could have come up with a more convincing name."

"Do you think he was lying?"

"No." Logan's gaze shifted away from Riley's face to a point over his shoulder. "I know he was telling the truth."

"Because of Trent."

"Yeah. Because of Trent."

"Don't you think it's time to tell me everything? Not just the pieces that are convenient or unembarrassing or nonincriminating, but the whole freaking story. Because I've got to tell you, after what you just laid on me, anything I imagine is bound to be worse than the truth."

Logan ran both hands through his hair. "I doubt that. The truth is fucking horrible."

As Logan told Riley the story of his last night with Trent, his shoulders hunched until they were practically up to his ears. He stared down at his hands, and from the occasional awkward pause, Riley could tell he was censoring his words, damn it. Was it on purpose, though, or from his long habit of hiding the details? If the first, Riley needed to call him on it; if the second, though, Riley would have to tease it out of him. *Pay attention. There'll be a test later.*

When Logan described the point when the spirits had become visible, Riley frowned, something snagging at the back of his mind, something critical that he'd missed. If he could just...

Logan slammed his fist into his thigh. "But I swear Balch could see Trent. He stopped and focused on him, stared right at him, before he offered him the gun."

The hair on Riley's neck sprang to attention. "Hold it. Trent displaced *Danford Balch*?"

Logan snorted. "Yeah. Leave it to Trent. He'd never settle for being anything less than the star of the show, even if it turned him into a murderer and got him hanged at the end of act three."

Riley pressed his fists to his temples. God, and he thought the *HttM* job threatened to detonate his head. That was nothing compared to this. "*Danford Balch* has been on the loose for the last seven years?"

"Yeah. Don't think he's had an easy time of it though. He looked like hell on a biscuit."

"Holy... shit, Logan. You— What the bleeding *fuck*? You've *seen* Danford Balch? Here? In Portland?"

Logan leaned forward and grasped the back of Riley's neck. "Hey. Take it easy. You'll give yourself an aneurism."

Not an aneurism, damn it, but the connections had definitely started clicking in Riley's brain. "God, Logan. This is... this is huge."

"Tell me about it."

"You're right. This isn't a case of possession. I'm not sure it's truly a ghost story at all. It makes so much more sense if you think of it as—" Riley jumped up and paced across the shabby room. "Look. When you cut away the loaded words—Witch's Castle, ghost war—I mean, the Balches and the Stumps had issues, but they never had an actual war. No violent family feud, a la Montagues and Capulets or Hatfields and McCoys. It's more of a metaphor than a battle reenactment."

Logan nodded. "She said she wasn't sure they were ghosts."

"She who?"

"Marguerite Windflower, psychic counselor."

Riley squinted at Logan over his glasses. "You're joking."

"I wish. But she seemed like the real deal, as far as mediums go. She sensed the spirits. Picked out Balch and Mortimer even though the figures weren't distinct."

"Did she have a solution?"

Logan's cheek twitched. "Nope. Not ghosts. Nothing she could do."

Hello, big fat lie. He'd deal with it later. Now he was in the zone, buzzing with the adrenaline rush of discovery. *This is the right trail. I'm sure of it.*

"Think about it. Anna Balch, Cuthbert Stump, the other townspeople—none of them died at the same time or place. Balch wasn't hanged on the same day he shot Mortimer." Riley dropped to his knees, rummaged through his messenger bag and pulled out *The Golden Bough.* "It's more like a... a ritual battle. What Frazer calls a mimic conflict." He located the page and handed the book to Logan. "Here. See? The battle between winter and summer. The Holly King versus the Oak King. The ducks verses the ptarmigans."

"The what?"

"Never mind. The point is that it's not like on a battlefield, with the spirits of dozens of people who all died at the same time haunting the place of their death. But those events—Anna and Mortimer's star-crossed love affair, Balch's crime and punishment—had huge emotional resonance for everyone involved. Energy like that leaves a... a stain. A residue. Especially if so many of the participants had a soul-deep longing for another outcome, the desire to make things right."

"Or wanted vengeance."

Riley's elation dimmed at Logan's terse comment. "That too, but the power of ritual is undisputed. Ask any superstitious hockey player. People engage in rituals because they believe that the actions, the tokens, the trappings, will cause a specific result. They'll win a game, find a husband, turn back winter. That's what this is. A ritual battle that arose because of the emotions and desires of people who desperately wanted a different outcome."

"Good versus evil?"

"I don't think you can make that kind of judgment. Is winter evil? Summer good? For every hockey team that wins, the opposing team has to lose. But win and lose. Love and hate. Life and death." He nodded at Logan. "Vengeance and redemption. It's powerful stuff."

"Okay. I get it, but so what?"

"So these ceremonies, the ritual battles, are exaggerated representations of how to satisfy some primal need for the community. But one way or another, they're driven by belief. By force of will, either of the society or the sacrifice himself."

Logan handed him the book, and Riley stuffed it back in his bag. "Belief? In ghosts?"

"Not that." Riley knee-walked closer to the recliner and gently placed his hand on Logan's arm. "Joseph's family was starving. He wanted those provisions desperately. Trent wanted the ghosts to be real, to be the star." Riley shrugged. "It must have been enough to trigger the exchange. To let them take their place in the ritual."

Logan's brows drew together, eyes narrowing. "Yeah. I guess that would do it."

Riley didn't trust that calculating look, but he couldn't stop to call Logan on it, not with an idea hovering at the fringe of his consciousness. *Almost got it.* Ah. *There.*

He tightened his grip on Logan's arm. "Every ritual has its own power. A life of its own, sort of like the alternator in a car. It generates its own charge, keeps itself going, as long as the initial need is still there."

"So to interrupt the ritual, take it down for good…"

"We have to figure out the need and fulfill it."

"You think we can do that?"

"If not us, then who? Max?" Riley shook Logan's arm, willing him to see. "It's not just about you or your grandfather or Trent. If it happened before, it could happen again. Think about it, Logan. How long before some poor idiot displaces Mortimer?"

Logan's face paled behind his scruff. "Fuck."

"Exactly. It has to be stopped." Riley released Logan's arm and squeezed his knee. "*We* have to stop it."

Logan stared at his lap, his throat working.

Riley's heart sank. *He's going to refuse. He'll bail again and go all loner knight on me.* He sat back, but Logan grabbed his hands, lacing their fingers together, and Riley's heart rebounded, fluttering against his rib cage.

"You're right." Logan raised his chin and looked Riley in the eyes, his mouth grim. "It's already destroyed enough people. We can't let it go on."

There was that twitch again.

He stood, drawing Riley to his feet along with him. "We'll fix this, but you need to trust me. Trust me to make it right."

Riley's lungs seized. He'd made an extreme tactical error. In that instant, he knew that if they couldn't find a way to end the ghost war, Logan planned to offer himself in Trent's place.

It would be just like him, the stupid noble asshole.

God. It was bad enough that Logan's damned savior complex made him ready to take a bullet for his grandfather or Trent or some unknown future victim. Did Riley have to keep handing him ammo?

He raised his chin, fixing his gaze on Logan's face, waiting for the telltale twitch. "The way you trust me?"

Logan trailed the backs of his fingers down Riley's cheek. "I trust you. You're the world's most stand-up guy."

God. *Stand-up.* One step away from *sweet and caring.* Riley clenched his teeth against the shiver that threatened from Logan's continued caress. "I'm not talking about my stupid personality. I'm talking about what I do. What I know. If you can't trust my intellect—"

Realization hit him like a boulder launched by a catapult. He gulped and pulled back from that insidious stroke, the familiar wash of shame starting in his belly and working its way up.

"What's the matter?" Logan murmured.

"You don't think I know what I'm talking about, do you? You think I'm as worthless as Scott does." And despite her championship, her support, her love, he knew Julie believed he was equally hapless. She humored him, the way Logan was doing now, but her priority was her career. She could afford to encourage his contributions as long as he kept the coffee coming and remembered to order extra mayo on Scott's turkey club.

Logan reeled him back with a finger under the collar of his Henley. "If they think you're worthless, they're idiots."

Riley's heart thumped like a drum in his chest. *Resist. Resist.* "Is that why you don't want me anymore? Because you don't respect me?"

The corners of Logan's eyes crinkled with a suppressed smile, and the dimple quivered in his cheek. "I'm pretty sure we settled the *want* question the other night."

Damn it, where had Logan's anger gone? His assitude? His douchebaggage? How could Riley fight with a freaking dimple? "I don't mean like that. Not just to scratch an inconvenient itch."

Logan grinned, deepening the damn dimple. "Nothing wrong with scratching an itch. Sure, we've got shit to do, but if I know you, you've got it half-done already." He hooked the fingers of one hand under the waistband of Riley's jeans, behind the belt, and tugged him forward. "So we've got time."

"T-t-time?" Riley, mesmerized by the scent of Logan's skin, of soap and leather and a hint of musk, of the way his thumb stroked just to the outside of Riley's fly, could only try to catch his breath.

"Riley." Logan leaned forward, his scruff brushing Riley's cheek, his breath warm against Riley's neck. "Take me to your hotel. I can't stand the idea of making love to you in this mold-pit."

"Make love?" Riley pulled back to scan Logan's face, but couldn't detect any mockery or contempt in his heavy-lidded gaze. "Not itch-scratching? Did you decide to abandon your quest for meaningless sex?"

"Sex, yes. Meaningless, no."

"Don't you have that backwards?"

A slow, sinful smile curled Logan's mouth. "You know what I mean."

"You think I'll have sex with you?"

"I know you will."

Riley sighed. There were definitely worse ways to distract Logan from getting stupid ideas about martyring himself. "You're probably right." He poked Logan in the shoulder. "But you'll still have to work for it. Let's go."

Since Riley had thrown himself headfirst into this crapfest, the best chance Logan had of protecting him was to stay close. Really close.

That was his story, and he was sticking to it, damn it.

Back at the hotel, he crowded against Riley's back as Riley tried to fit the card key in its slot.

"Hurry up and open the door if you don't want me to pants you right here in the hallway."

"I'd have better luck if you weren't humping my ass."

"Want me to stop?"

"Hell no." The green light flashed, and they staggered into the room.

Logan locked the door and advanced on Riley. "Clothes off. Now."

Riley shucked off his jacket and backed away, a smile playing on his delectable lips. "You sure? Don't you want something from the minibar first? Snickers? Some overpriced Evian? Cracker Jacks?" Riley waggled his eyebrows. "Nuts and a prize in every…" he swiveled his hips in a slow bump-and-grind that triggered an involuntary thrust from Logan's hardening dick "… box."

"You know what I want," Logan growled, shoving the desk chair out of his path, "and it's not in the damn minibar."

"Ah. I think I know. You want to watch TV." Riley flourished the remote, swinging his other arm wide and making a show of punching a button.

Logan grabbed the remote, and flung it across the room to clatter against the wall and disappear behind the bed. "I don't want to watch the damn TV. I want to watch you. Coming. I want to hear you scream my name when I'm buried in your ass. I want to—"

A burst of pounding on the door cut Logan off midfantasy.

"Yo, Wiley!"

Riley bunched his fists in Logan's T-shirt and tugged him forward, whispering in his ear. "It's Max. Be quiet. Maybe he'll go away."

"Wiley, you jackass. I know you're in there." The pounding recommenced. "Open the frigging door right now."

"Shit," Riley muttered. "Sorry. I better see what he wants before he wakes the whole floor."

He let go, but Logan grabbed him by the back of the neck and kissed him because damn, he hadn't done that yet tonight. Lips, tongues, a slight clash of teeth because he was in too much of a hurry for finesse. "Don't forget the plan. Sex till you scream. Get rid of him."

"I'll try." Riley returned the kiss, with interest. "But you don't know Max."

More pounding. "Wiley. Open the fucking door."

"Christ." Logan released Riley with one last stroke down his spine and across the curve of his stellar ass. "Let him in before he brings the wrath of management down on us."

Riley walked to the door with an awkward stiff-legged gait. He stopped and adjusted his jeans, pulling on the crotch and, judging from the elbow action, repositioning his dick. Logan snorted, even though he wasn't much better off.

"Laugh it up, pal." Riley paused long enough to skewer Logan with a glare. "Tell me how funny it is an hour from now when Max is still yammering at me and your balls are turning blue."

As soon as he unlatched the door, it flew open.

"About time." Max pushed past Riley, pulling up when he saw Logan standing by the window. "Hey, you're that bartender. The one who told us—"

"Yeah." Logan cleared his throat. He didn't want Riley to find out how far he'd gone to sabotage the show with his ghost stories, especially since it hadn't worked.

"Then you know." Max's voice throbbed like a twelve-inch subwoofer. "You know. What. Did. This."

CHAPTER FIFTEEN

Max held up his leather bomber jacket and shook it in Riley's face. The back was shredded as if someone had taken a meat hook to it. "He told us Portland ghosts were dangerous. Look at this. This can only be a warning from beyond." His voice rang with the conviction of a Fox newscaster.

"Or else Wolverine woke up with a fashion hangover," Logan muttered.

Riley shot him a quelling glance. "When did you find this, Max?" When Riley had straightened Max's suite yesterday, he hadn't made more than a cursory pass through the bedroom because it had appeared undisturbed.

"This evening. When I... Well, never mind. And that's not all." He shoved his hand into the pocket of the tattered jacket and pulled out a handful of fabric scraps. "This is what's left of my hat."

Riley checked Logan for signs of guilt or satisfaction, but he only wore the half-pained/half-pissed expression of a man with a hard-on still tangled in his underwear. He was back to his minimum safe arm's-length distance, though. Oh no, wouldn't do for anyone to see him displaying any inconvenient affection.

"Did you have the hat and jacket this morning? Any time today?" Riley asked.

"I crashed all day." Max's gaze slid sideways. "Kinda didn't wake up in my own room, if you know what I mean. Julie..."

His gaze slid the other direction, and he coughed. "Julie brought me a clean set of clothes. She booked me a session with my personal trainer and then sent me to hang with Scott before dinner." He clutched the felt confetti to his chest. "Do you know how long it took me to find this hat?"

"Didn't Charmaine find it for you?" Riley poked through the remains of the jacket for any telltale clue. If Logan didn't do it, then who the hell did? Could *HttM* have picked up a demented fan? Well, more demented than their usual viewer.

"Yeah, but it took her forever. I've been asking for it since our first episode."

Julie had told him about that—she called it the Great Hatscapade. The producers had stalled in an attempt to prevent Max from indulging in his Indiana Jones fetish. She said they'd finally given up, citing Chinese water torture.

"Check out her whereabouts last night," Logan murmured. "She's the one with the motive."

Riley shot a glance at Max, who was mooning over the remains of his hat. *Thank God for self-centered Hollywood tunnel vision.* "You're not helping, Logan." He lowered his voice to a furious whisper. "And if you're not part of the solution, you're part of the pain in my ass."

"Your ass is on my radar, but pain is not part of the plan." Logan grinned and leaned against the wall, his arms crossed over his chest. "Unless you want it to be."

A thrill shivered down Riley's spine. "Logan. Oversharing much? We're not exactly alone here." Sure, Logan was talking about sex, not love, and this was Max, not the entire population of Portland, but a semipublic declaration was more than he'd ever gotten before.

"Him?" Logan scoffed. "He doesn't count. If it's not about Max Stone, he can't see it."

Riley sighed. He should have known he didn't have all the nuances of the Rules of Engagement According to Logan figured out yet. Luckily, Logan was right about Max, who was still obsessing over his costume misfortunes.

"This is— It's *sacrilege*." Max tossed the ex-hat onto the floor and shook the jacket. "A little judicious promo is one thing, Wiley, but—"

"Why do you call him that?" Logan's grin morphed into a scowl. He pushed himself off the wall and took a menacing step toward Max. "Does he do that all the time?"

"Pretty much," Riley said. "It's not a big deal."

"It wouldn't be a big deal if he was doing it out of affection, but for this guy, it's about power and perspective. He makes you feel small so he'll look bigger."

Riley stepped between the two other men. "Logan, now is not the time to go alpha-hole on me, okay?"

"He should treat you with more respect."

"You could try the same for him. He's standing right there."

"I know," Logan muttered. "Damned cockblocker."

Ooookay. He turned to Max, who was gawking at Logan as if he'd just discovered the Ark of the Covenant. "I'm sorry about the hat and the jacket. I'll talk to—"

"That," Max breathed, "is totally awesome. That attitude. That's what I'm talking about. Hey, have you got a few? We'll grab a couple of brewskis and you can tell me how you pump up your mojo."

Logan's eyebrows rose. "'Brewskis'? Seriously?" He shot a sideways glance at Riley. "Where'd you get this guy? A touring production of *Footloose*?"

Riley shooed Logan into the corner by the desk. "Logan." He kept his voice low, although given how Max was staring worshipfully at Logan's face, he probably wouldn't notice if Riley did a fan dance on the desk with a boa constrictor. "Remember the part about my ass? You're not getting anywhere near it if you screw up my job."

"But he makes it so easy."

"Don't think *easy*. Think *hard*." Riley angled his body away from Max and pressed his hipbone into Logan's groin. "Get it?"

Logan clenched his teeth around a moan. "Got it."

"Good." *That's right. Who's laughing now, big boy?* "Max, I'll—"

The door, still ajar from Max's entrance, burst open, and Scott strode in, Julie and Zack at his heels. "Max. There you are. I've been texting you for the last twenty minutes."

Behind Scott's shoulder, Julie's eyes widened, gaze darting between Riley and Logan, who'd retreated to his spot against the wall, safely out of touching distance.

"If this keeps up," Logan said, "you're gonna need a bigger room."

Max flapped the shredded jacket in Scott's face. "Do you see this?" He pointed at the hat litter scattered across the carpet. "And that? I've been *violated*."

Scott's bearded face split into a beatific grin. He looked like Zach Galifianakis on crack. "Outstanding."

"*Outstanding*?" Max's voice quivered in outrage. "You think this is—"

"I think it's perfect. Where'd you find it? Put it back. Julie, we need footage of this ASAP. Zack, you're on it."

"But..." Without his usual support from Scott, Max deflated. "My jacket. My hat."

"Exactly." Scott tapped a cigarette out of the pack in his shirt pocket. He patted his pants as if searching for matches, but Julie snagged the cigarette and tossed it in the trash.

"You're quitting, remember?"

"Damn." Scott's laser gaze lit on Riley. "You. Get me some Red Vines."

Riley sighed and retrieved his jacket from the floor where he'd flung it when he and Logan had arrived.

Logan grabbed his arm. "Why you?" he whispered. "Aren't you the research guy?"

"This episode is supposed to prove they actually *need* a full-time research guy. Until then, I'm a gofer with one hell of a browser history. Excuse me." He held Logan's gaze. "Don't go anywhere. Okay?"

Logan eyed the group—which now included the best boy, two grips, and the second cameraman—crammed into the vestibule like sardines. "Couldn't break through without a battering ram anyway."

Riley took that as agreement. As he threaded his way through the crowd, Charmaine and Grace squeezed in and edged between Riley's bed and the wall. *Jeez. Hope Logan's not claustrophobic.*

Halfway to the elevators, Julie caught up to him, her eyes sparkling, breath catching.

"Rile, can you believe it?"

He shot her a sour look. "Believe that I'm the drug mule for Scott's nicotine withdrawal aids? Why is that unusual?"

"No, doofus. The coverage."

"What coverage?"

"Scott found out about Max's room."

"I thought you were keeping that on the down-low. Why else did I spend all that time cleaning the shit up?"

"I was, but Scott was there when PDX Production Resources delivered the replacement cameras." She buffeted his shoulder with her fist. "Good work on that, by the way."

Riley's heart made a determined effort to climb up his throat. "He knows about the equipment?" Had any other evidence been planted? Would Logan be implicated?

"Yeah. Then Max found his jacket and..." She flung her hands in the air and hopped in a circle in a crazy victory dance. "The rest will make *HttM* history."

He caught her shoulders before she could continue her impression of a whirling dervish. "Focus, Jules. Do we have to give a statement to the police? Will there be an investigation?"

She laughed and hugged him. "Are you kidding? Scott's not about to let the police interfere with his shooting schedule. He told the hotel staff it was an internal issue and they're so pissed at Max that they'd probably refuse him a fire extinguisher if he burst into flames in the lobby."

Riley's shoulders relaxed a fraction. "Thank God."

"Scott is *totally* pumped about this. Apparently, some bartender filled the crew full of stories about vengeful spirits, and Scott's spinning it as a 'cursed' episode. He's got national coverage lined up."

"You mean—"

"Yeah." She wrinkled her nose. "The show is now important to his career trajectory. Something he wants to hang on to. An asset instead of a liability. He actually put his agent on hold for twenty minutes this afternoon."

"Shit, Jules. I'm sorry." Since Riley had a pretty good idea the bartender in question was Logan, if he'd derailed her career plans, Julie now had another reason to resent him. *Definitely not mentioning that little detail.*

"Can't have everything in this business. I'll find a way to work with it. We can totally come up with a plan to prove we're brilliant and indispensable."

"I'll get right on that." He punched the elevator button with extreme prejudice. "As soon as I fetch the freaking Red Vines."

CHAPTER SIXTEEN

Logan eyed the crowd, calculating his chances on a bolt to the relative freedom of the corridor, but the place was packed tighter than a dorm room full of frat boys on a bong bender. He crossed his arms, leaned against the wall, and settled in to wait. They had to leave eventually, and when they did, he was taking Riley to bed and keeping him there, no matter who knocked on the door next.

"What am I going to do about the jacket, Scott?" Max Stone was still dithering in the middle of the throng. "My hat? I can't appear on a national spot without my trademarks."

"Jesus, Max. It's a leather bomber jacket and a fedora. We'll get you replacements. Charmaine." Scott pointed to a woman in owl-eye glasses and a hairdo out of an eighties music video. "There must be a Banana Republic in this town. Go. Shop."

Charmaine's eyes gleamed behind her glasses. "Do I have a budget?"

"Just make us look good. We're booked on a couple of the local morning shows."

"Who's 'us'?"

"Me. Max." Scott ticked off the list on his fingers. "Julie."

"Got it." Charmaine punched notes into her cell phone.

Max sidled over to Scott. "Do you think the episode might be... you know... cursed?"

E.J. RUSSELL

"Hell no. But it makes for great PR. Our fans live for this shit."

Ah, fuck. Logan would've smacked himself in the forehead if it wouldn't have attracted undue attention to himself. This was a paranormal investigation show, for Chrissake, even if it was a lame one. If he'd wanted to get them to decamp, he should have told them the whole thing was a hoax, not fired them up with stories of untold horrors.

"But this time, it actually happened. Isn't it..." Max glanced over his shoulder as if he expected Freddy Krueger to leap out from under the bed, the only square footage of the room currently unoccupied. "Dangerous?"

Scott draped an arm across Max's shoulders. "Maxie. Be serious. Would I put you in danger? You're the star." He turned to Julie. "The locals have promised us a closed set, right?"

She nodded. "Yes, but no police support at the Witch's Castle site itself."

"Good. They'd just get in the way." He disengaged his arm and thumped Max on the back. "We'll contact a private security firm. Get a couple of big beefy guards. Put 'em in mirror shades." He pointed at Charmaine. "Pick up mirror shades. And those temporary tattoos."

She nodded, thumbs busy on her cell phone. "On it."

"Aren't you filming at midnight?" Logan asked. "What do the guards need sunglasses for?"

"Good point. Charmaine, scratch the shades and pick up night-vision goggles instead." Scott waggled his palm in the air. "Or something that looks like night-vision goggles. That'll be cheaper."

Logan shook his head. *Unbelievable.* "How effective are guards who can't see?"

Scott, obviously a guy who wasn't used to opposition, narrowed his eyes at him. "They don't need to see. There's never anything there. They just need to read well for the cameras." He scanned the room, his chin dipping as if he was

172

counting heads, then focused on Logan again. "Who the hell are you anyway? This is a closed meeting. Leave."

"I was here first."

"Why?"

Out of the corner of his mouth, Max said, "He's the bartender. The guy who told us about the curse."

Scott rounded on Julie. "Why's a bartender in the meeting?"

"This wasn't supposed to be a meeting," she said. "We're in Riley's room, not the company suite."

Scott peered around. "No wonder I feel like I'm jammed inside a film canister. Everyone up to the suite. Now."

Max hung on to Scott's arm. "Scott—"

"I'm telling you, Maxie, you've got nothing to worry about. Right, Julie?"

"Absolutely. The city's securing the site for us. Guards at all the trailheads that lead to the site. No one can get in unless they're part of the crew."

Fuck me raw. Logan scowled, drumming his fingers against his leg. These jokers clearly had the resources to keep him out of the park. Regardless of what he decided to do about Trent and the ghost war, Logan had to be on deck to keep Riley from doing anything stupid. Riley might think he could take care of himself, but Logan wasn't about to leave his safety to chance.

He knew jack shit about TV production, but he didn't need a fucking manual to figure out that getting in, getting in place, and making his move would be impossible with the police and the show goons patrolling the trails.

The crew filed out, but Max didn't release his hold on Scott's arm. "I'm telling you, I've been targeted. I need special protection. Maybe a gun."

"No way am I letting you anywhere near a gun. Besides, if ghosts and demons really are haunting you, what good is a gun gonna do you?"

"A bodyguard, then. Someone to watch my back."

Logan allowed himself a grin. The perfect answer. Maybe his luck wasn't fucked halfway to hell after all.

"Hey," he called as Scott reached the doorway. "You need a bodyguard?"

Scott turned. "Why? You know one?"

"Sure. Me."

"Hmmmm." Scott looked him up, down, and sideways, no doubt measuring him against Hollywood's generic bodyguard stereotype. Logan stood straighter and took a surreptitious deep breath, expanding his chest. "You have experience?"

"Nope. But I know the area and I'll work cheap." He yanked up his jacket sleeve to display his Celtic knot ink. "I've got my own tattoos."

"You're hired."

Riley appeared at the door, breathless and clutching a plastic tub of Red Vines the size of his head. "Here, Scott. Sorry. I had to get the extra-large size."

"Bring 'em upstairs." Scott charged past Riley into the corridor.

"Upstairs? Why—"

"Production meeting." Scott's voice carried down the hall. "You, too, tattoo bodyguard guy, whatever your name is."

"Tattoo bodyguard guy?" Riley's voice held amused disbelief.

Logan rolled his eyes in disgust. "Yeah. That's me."

"I've been gone fifteen minutes, and now you're on the crew? How'd that happen?"

"Combination of Max Stone's paranoia and my natural charm."

"Wait a minute." Riley squinted at him. "Does this have anything to do with—"

Logan cut off the question with a quick kiss. "How long do these meetings generally last?"

"Forever, or until Scott has a nicotine fit, whichever comes first."

"Jesus." He added a not-so-quick grope of Riley's ass. "Can we be late?"

"Not... God, Logan." Riley writhed against Logan's hand, and his breathing sped up again. "Not an option."

He nuzzled behind Riley's ear. "What do I need to sacrifice to the Marlboro gods for a speedy intervention?"

Riley took a deep, shuddering breath and pushed him away. "You don't want to know." At the door, he turned and stopped Logan with a hand against his chest. "We're not done with this conversation."

"Yeah, well, better get going." Logan urged him out the door with another ass-grab. "Wouldn't want to be late."

The company suite was large enough to accommodate way more bodies than Riley's room, and every single person had to go over some interminable list that as far as Logan could tell, had absolutely no bearing on the show.

But what did he know? He was just tattoo bodyguard guy. Hired muscle. Might as well be wearing a red shirt.

After a minimum hour and a half, Scott slapped his leg. "Good. Everyone's on the same page. Max, you've got three local spots scheduled tomorrow. Two personal appearances and one TV interview."

Max was sitting in the biggest chair, fiddling with a worry bead on a leather thong. "I don't mind the TV spot, but I don't feel good about the others. Anyone could hide out in a crowd like that."

"So take your bodyguard. Charmaine, make sure this guy looks tough."

Charmaine eyed Logan. "I don't think I could improve on the original." She grinned and gave him a thumbs-up.

As the rest of the crew scattered, Julie snagged Riley for some goddamned reason and towed him across the room. Logan dodged through the milling *HttM* staff to follow them, because if he had only two more days to live, he was damn well spending them with Riley, Julie's agenda be damned.

If he had longer than two days, then he intended to begin as he meant to go on.

"Hey." Max cut in front of him with a smirk and a swagger. "Since you're putting yourself on the line to protect me, guess I should know your name."

"Yeah. You should." Logan tried to ease himself around Max, but a knot of crew guys blocked his way. Max reoriented himself so he was front and center again. Christ. The asshole probably couldn't resist upstaging anyone within a city block.

"So. What is it?"

"Conner. Logan Conner."

"So, Logan." Max displayed more teeth than the average beauty contestant. "Willing to take a bullet for me?"

Logan stopped craning his neck in an attempt to keep Riley in his sights. "Look. Max. This isn't the Secret Service and you're not POTUS. So no. I'm just another set of eyes, a guy with knowledge of the terrain and local history."

"What's your background? What'd you do before you became a bartender? Military? Special forces?"

"I was studying to be an architect."

Max goggled at him. "How does that qualify you to protect me?"

"How does posing in a pretentious hat qualify you as an expert on the occult?"

Max puffed out his chest like an inflatable clown. *Yeah. That hit him at his vulnerable point: his ego.* "I'll have you know—"

Logan loomed over him, despite having barely an inch on the guy. But looming was all in the presentation. "You have no idea of the things I can do with a drafting pencil."

Instead of quailing or getting pissed off, awe dawned in Max's faded-blue eyes. "Hey. That's good. That's exactly the kind of attitude the show needs."

"I'm not interested in appearing on the show."

Max guffawed and slapped Logan on the back. "Good one, man. Not you. Me. That's the persona I want. The *I don't give a shit* and *if only you knew*."

The room had cleared out, leaving no one but the giant walking ego in front of him and Riley, standing by the door with the knowing half-smile that never failed to get Logan's motor racing.

"That's pretty much Logan's life's creed, Max. Very insightful. I'm impressed."

Logan met Riley's amused gaze over Max's shoulder. "That's what you think? That I don't give a shit about you?"

Riley didn't back down, but his expression shifted to dead serious with a hint of sadness in his eyes. "The thing that bothers me, Logan, is that you don't give a shit about yourself."

"See?" Max's voice vibrated with excitement. "That's the look I'm talking about. Women go nuts for that bad-but-vulnerable crap."

Logan rolled his eyes. "Max, you moron. I'm gay."

"So? It works on guys too. Wiley over there is practically panting at your feet. Come on." Max grabbed Logan's arm and attempted to tow him across the room, but Logan dug in his heels next to Riley.

"Know what would help that? For you to trust me. Trust me to make things right."

Riley held his gaze, his eyes somber. "Always taking care of everyone else, aren't you, Logan? Who takes care of you?"

"I can handle myself. But you—"

"Save that for later." Max tugged his arm away before he could caress Riley's face. "It's not like Wiley's going anywhere."

Logan rounded on the asshole. "What did I tell you about showing him some respect?"

"I love this!" Max crowed. "Let's go. I'm a strict method actor, and it's time for serious in-the-field observation. We're hitting a club."

"Remember? Gay?"

"So we'll hit a gay club. I need to see you in action."

"I never go to gay clubs."

"There's that attitude again." Max waggled a finger under Logan's nose. "It's all in the subtext, man. What you say is 'I never go,' but what you mean is 'I don't need to.' And that, my friend, is what I'm talking about."

Riley patted Logan's chest. "Give up. He's impervious to anything but a bad review. I'll see you later."

CHAPTER
SEVENTEEN

Before Riley could follow Logan and Max out of the room, Scott strode back in and grabbed the tub of Red Vines. He pulled out two of them.

"You." He pointed at Riley, one string of candy wagging like a lizard's tongue in the corner of his mouth and the other spouting from the middle of his fist. "Get housekeeping to clean up the meeting shit, but watch 'em. Make double damn sure nobody touches the broken cameras in the equipment suite."

"I'll tell the front desk—"

"Wait. Got a better idea." He transferred the second Red Vine from his hand to between his teeth and pulled out his wallet, tossing a couple of bills on the coffee table. "Tip 'em and keep 'em out altogether. You clear up in here."

"Scott, I think we can trust housekeeping to do their job."

He glared at Riley. "I'm from Hollywood. I don't trust anybody until the wrap." He slapped the fresh stack of Max's head shots that Riley had gotten printed at Office Depot. "You cleaned up Max's room, right? When you're done here, go fuck it up again."

He left, the tub of Red Vines tucked under his arm like a football.

Two hours later, still picking scraps of paper off his jeans and sweater, Riley finally made it back to his room. He checked the clock. It was a little late for a call to Florida, but maybe mediums kept evening hours. He could only hope.

He plonked down in the chair, cracked open his laptop, and dialed the number he'd found online for Marguerite Windflower, psychic counselor.

"Greetings, pilgrim." The faint tinkle of wind chimes backed the woman's plummy tones. "And all the blessings of the season of Samhain."

"Uh... hello? Is this... Marguerite?"

"I... What is it, Hootie? Don't mumble. Oh, thank Christ, a sane one." Her voice dropped two octaves and took on a rasp worthy of Tom Waits. "I've had my fill of idiots and phonies for the day."

"How do you know I'm not either of those?"

She snorted a laugh. "Psychic, remember? I know all, see all, all that shit."

"Really?"

"No. But I've got an associate with, shall we say, connections. He claims you don't need the new-age bullshit. So hit me."

"Wight." Riley cleared his throat and shrugged his shoulders to dispel the tingle creeping up his spine. "*Right*. Well, a couple of years ago, you came to Portland with Logan Conner."

"Yeah." She stretched out the word, infusing it with a boatload of suspicion.

"You saw the ghost war in Forest Park."

"And? Shit. Hold on a minute. Those wind chimes need to fucking die." After the clatter of the phone being tossed on a hard surface and a brisk tattoo of footsteps, the wind chimes cut out. The footsteps returned. "That's better. Christ, those things are annoying. So he decide he wants the procedure after all?"

"The procedure?"

"Because, I'm telling you, I'm not going back to that soggy excuse for a city for less than double the fee. Triple. Hootie hated the damn place, and don't get him started on flying coach."

"Hootie?"

"My... associate."

"Well, I don't think you'll need to come out here if— Well, could you tell me what the... uh... procedure consists of?"

"All-purpose cleansing ritual. Cuts the connection between their plane, whatever the hell it is, and ours. Closes the fucking door."

So no more ghosts. No more threat. And no more Trent. No wonder Logan hadn't gone for that. "If I wanted to perform it, what supplies would I need? What preparations?"

"Forget it. I don't deal in home remedies for DIY exorcists. Damn cheap bastards who think they can do a medium's job without paying the medium to do it. Assholes."

Riley made a mental note not to mention who he worked for. He suspected Marguerite would be less than impressed with *Haunted to the Max.* "I understand. But I'm not trying to avoid a fee. It's just that I have a very tight schedule and—"

"What's Logan to you?"

"My—my boyfriend."

"He know you're doing this shit?"

"Well... no. But I promise my intentions are for his own good."

She snorted again. "That's what they all say, pal. You a medium?"

"No. I'm a folklorist."

"Is that so?" He heard a click and then a long exhale as if she'd lit up. "Convince me you know your ass from a dowsing rod and maybe we can do business."

Showtime. Logan had been sure that the seven-year cycle was the key, but Riley wasn't convinced that was the whole answer. In fact, it might not be part of the answer at all. He clicked on the document with the summary of his findings. Even to him, they looked pretty out there. If a self-proclaimed "psychic counselor" thought they were nuts too? *Ooorg.* He took a gulp from his water bottle to moisten his mouth and throat.

"Okay. First, I don't think the apparitions at the Witch's Castle site are true ghosts."

"Logan tell you I said that?"

"Yes."

"At least you're honest. Go on."

"I think it's actually a—a mimic conflict. Like—"

"Winter versus summer. Holly King versus Oak King."

Despite the clock ticking away in his brain, Riley had to smile. "Ducks versus ptarmigans."

"The what?"

"Never mind." He rubbed his damp palms on his jeans. "The only way for a mimic conflict ritual to become unnecessary is if its target need is permanently fulfilled."

Her low chuckle burred over the phone line. "You learn all those fancy words at folklore school?"

"I also learned that mythic cycles are big on representation. Nothing's ever what it seems. Everything stands in for something else, and I don't think this is any different. This one requires something that represents life essence to activate it. In this case..." He remembered the gash on Logan's palm, Joseph Geddes's accident with the skinning knife. "Blood."

"I'm impressed."

"So will you help me?"

She exhaled again. "If we don't know the original need, it'll be tough to design a counter-spell. I'm not sure you *can* undo it, not without the original players in the field so they can work out their issues."

"I realize. But I've got to try."

She sighed. "How'd I know you'd say that?"

"Can you tell me how I could prevent someone from taking part in the ritual? Make it impossible for him to get sucked in?"

"Hmmmm." He heard repetitive clicking, as if she were playing with her lighter. "You know how with sacrifices, there's a purification or preparation ritual? Something that makes the poor fuckers acceptable?"

Riley remembered *Help!* and how Ringo couldn't be sacrificed without wearing the ring and getting doused with red paint. "So what I need is an anti-preparation?"

"Exactly. If you want to keep someone from joining the party, you've got to anchor him. Make him so much a part of this world that he can't slip into the next."

"How do I do that?"

"How the fuck do I know? This is for the boyfriend, right? *You* figure it out. I'll give you a list of protective herbs and artifacts that should help, but they'll only create the potential, know what I'm saying? It won't do shit unless you find the proper hook."

Jeez. "I'll get right on that." He checked his notes again. "If we can't deactivate the ritual, I'd like to have your cleansing procedure on tap, just in case."

"I— Just a minute." Her voice turned muffled. "Calm down, Hootie. Nobody's threatening you." She muttered something Riley couldn't catch. "Sorry. Back now. Anyway, technically, it's not a true dispersion. Just, fuck, I guess you'd call it changing the frequency of the psychic transmission. The thing'll still be there, but not as easily perceived. Invisible."

"But not dissipated."

"That's the price you pay for ignorance. If you know the trigger and the original need, you can pinpoint this shit like microsurgery. But without knowing? More like removing a splinter with a chainsaw."

Riley wrapped his arms across his belly. Those spirits, possibly including Joseph Geddes and Trent Pielmeyer, would be left reenacting their tragedy, unending and unseen, with no chance for rescue. Could he consign them to that fate? But if he didn't, the ghost war could go on consuming unsuspecting victims forever.

"It's a last resort, but I think I need to be prepared for it anyway."

"Hmmphm. Your funeral. Got a pen? You're gonna need an ass-load of supplies, but you should be able to get most of them at the local pagan magical supply house. Or failing that, the nearest natural grocery. Here's a link to a YouTube video of the banishment ritual." She rattled off a URL. "Be sure to get the hand gestures right or you're fucked."

She rattled off a long list of objects, some mundane and some truly alarming, with Riley typing madly to keep up.

"Okay. Got it."

"You've gotta realize we're just guessing. And even if we nail it, your boyfriend struck me as one stubborn SOB. His will might be strong enough to counteract anything you do anyway."

"I know. But—"

"You have to try. I get it. If it makes you feel any better, Hootie thinks we're on the right track."

"Your associate? Does he have experience with this kind of thing?"

"You could say so. He's been a ghost since 1521."

She hung up before he could say thank you or beg for mercy, he wasn't sure which.

He slid down, resting the base of his skull on the cold chrome tubing of the chair back, and stared at the ceiling as if he could find the answer written there in rough plaster and cobwebs.

He ought to be glad that Marguerite had validated his assumptions, although the fact that she claimed to have a five-hundred-year-old ghost as a partner didn't say a lot about her sanity.

What if he was wrong? Logan could end up co-opted by supernatural cosplay, just like his friend.

Trent.

Was he *only* a friend? Or was he more? Logan had definitely been hiding something as he related Trent's story. Was it the truth about their relationship?

Logan had never talked about his previous boyfriends, but a guy who looked like Logan must have had plenty, or at least plenty of opportunities.

He pushed the doubt aside. Logan's past didn't matter. What mattered was preventing the big jerk from throwing his life away, or if that proved impossible, pulling his ass out of hellfire by the power of folklore force.

He swallowed a bubble of panic. *God, you can't screw up, Riley. Not this time.*

Life and death. *Piece of cake.* No pressure whatsoever.

CHAPTER
EIGHTEEN

Of all the shit jobs on Logan's anti-bucket list, spending the day as Max Stone's fake bodyguard shot instantly to number one. Christ, he was irritating. It was almost enough to make Logan long for the relative peace of ghosthood.

He should record Max's endless litany of nagging, threats, boasting, and borderline bullying. No jury on the planet would convict him for taking the guy out.

Didn't help his mood that between Max's demand for his presence 24-7, and the show's administrative shit—seriously, costume fitting?—the only time he'd attempted to sneak off to Riley's room, Julie had intercepted him and sent him back to Max's suite, where he'd gotten zero sleep on the too-short sofa.

On top of that, Max had started to adopt Logan's mannerisms. It was downright creepy to watch a Stone-translated copy of Logan Conner. The way Logan held himself while waiting to cross the street, poised for the first instant he could dive into traffic. The way he sat back in his chair when the server set his meal or drink in front of him. The way he stared at Max as if he were a roach crawling up the wall. That look, reflected back at him? Just. Fucking. Weird.

But as big a pain in the ass as Max was, Logan had to give him his due—he was one hell of a mimic.

This morning after a quick shower, Logan had tried sneaking down to Riley's room. Before he could knock on the door, a narrow-eyed Julie had waylaid him and dragged him to a breakfast meeting with Scott and Max. Afterward, he'd sat in the darkened production suite during the dailies from yesterday's filming, then been forced to endure brunch with reporters, for Chrissake.

After he'd accompanied Max to *his* costume fitting—which took for-fucking-ever considering the guy wore jeans and a T-shirt under his bomber jacket—Logan had had enough. He'd suggested a tour of Portland, if only to get out of the hotel.

Unfortunately, Max misinterpreted his reason for the field trip.

"Stone, I am not taking you to a gay club."

Max kept pace with him on the downtown sidewalk like the world's most annoying sidecar. "Why not? Be reasonable, Logan. You're being paid for your time."

Dude. There was not enough money in the entire Portland metro area to compensate him for the fallout of Max imitating him in a gay bar.

"Ah." Max tapped the side of his nose with one manicured forefinger. "I get it. You think Wiley might find out. What's the deal with you two anyway?"

Logan stopped in the middle of the sidewalk, ignoring the glares of the other pedestrians. "I told you. Stop calling him that."

"Yeah, yeah. Sorry. But what's the deal?"

Logan took off at a fast clip so Max had to hurry to keep up. "Not your business."

"Of course it's my business. I'm the star. My face is on the screen. My name's in the frigging title." Max shoved his hands in the pockets of his replacement jacket, which Charmaine had spent two hours pounding with a hammer to distress it to his satisfaction. "Wiley's trying to—"

Logan spun to face him, rocking him back on his heels. "Riley. Say it with me or I don't go another step."

"Fine. Rye. Lee," Max said, baring his teeth around the words. "Happy?" Logan grunted, which Max apparently took as an affirmative. "Little shit's trying to weasel in on my screen time. Do you know that all the dailies this morning were of him? Not one of me."

"Weren't you too hungover yesterday to shoot?"

"That's beside the point. The show is *Haunted to the Max*. Not *Haunted to the Riley*."

Logan buried his grin behind a fist. The guy was clearly envious of Riley's appeal, as well he should be. Riley was ten times as charismatic as this poser, without resorting to artifice. He doubted Riley was capable of being less than genuine. But Max, self-centered to the exclusion of anything resembling reality, would never understand that. He'd assume it was all an act.

Christ. *Riley*. If things went to hell tomorrow night—and considering Logan's fucktastic luck, they probably would—he didn't think he'd be strong enough to do the right thing if Riley was *there*, reminding him what he was leaving behind.

Max scuffed along the sidewalk, his mouth turned down like a toddler in the throes of a tantrum, not an attractive look on a man over thirty.

An idea bloomed, sneaky and beautiful. *Why not feed the fucking flame?*

"You know," he said, keeping his voice casual, almost lazy, "if it was me, I wouldn't stand for that shit."

Max's head snapped up. "You wouldn't?"

Christ, the guy was so fucking easy. Logan squinted at the fading sunlight glinting off the pink windows of the US Bancorp Tower. "Nah."

"So." Max matched Logan's pace, settling his shoulders at the same angle. "Hypothetically. If it was you. What would you do? Fire him?"

Alarm hollowed Logan's belly. He needed to remember who he was talking to; Max Stone did not do nuance. "See, that's overkill, Max. He's useful to the show. Knows the routine."

Max squinted at the building too. "True. He gets my lattes exactly how I like them."

"Then there's Julie."

Max's gaze slid sideways, and his Adam's apple bobbed above the collar of his tight blue T-shirt. "Julie?"

"Yeah. Riley's her best bud. If you value your balls, don't mess with her."

"I... uh..." Max swallowed again and shot a glance over his shoulder. "Yesterday, I kinda... woke up in her bed."

A laugh got caught in Logan's throat, and he choked. "Holy shit, Max. You really don't value your balls."

"I was alone. I mean, she wasn't there. That I know of. At least not at the time. But she brought me clothes later."

"She have her clipboard with her?"

"Yeah."

"You're safe, then. Nothing happened. She must have scraped you off the pavement somewhere. But you get my drift? Don't screw with her."

"Totally. So...?"

"So keep him away from the camera. Off the set. Busy elsewhere. Christ, there's enough crap on that tome of a schedule to keep an army of Rileys on the run."

Max nodded. "Good point. He could hang out at craft services, make sure they get my dinner order right."

Christ, if Logan didn't die tomorrow, Riley was going to kill him.

He eyed Max, swaggering along next to him. Jesus, did Logan truly look like that? Max as the happy, sloppy—and eventually freaked-out—drunk from his first night at the bar was easier to stomach than Max, the Logan-clone.

That's the answer. Get him drunk and let him pass out somewhere, and Logan would be off the clock. "Come on, Stone."

Max perked up like a puppy at the hint of a treat. "Where are we going? Are you taking me to a gay club?"

"Jesus. No. Get over it."

"A regular club?"

"Absolutely not. We'll go to Stumptown Spirits. I'll drink a large number of beers. You can take notes." And with any luck, Logan could channel all the alcohol down Max's throat and offload him in time to spend the night with Riley. "Light rail stop's this way."

"Public transportation? Why not a taxi?"

Logan was so not getting in a cab with this guy. Walking around with him was claustrophobic enough. "You'll love it. Trust me. Full of potential fans to impress. Plus," he pointed at the signpost at the MAX rail stop, "it's named after you."

That turned the trick. Christmas, birthday, and lottery win, right there on the guy's face.

"Awesome," Max breathed, and let Logan buy his ticket.

Once they arrived at the stop around the corner from Stumptown Spirits, Logan had to pry Max off the train. He herded him inside the bar and into a corner booth, waving at Heather along the way.

"There. Sit. I'll be back in a minute."

Max stood up. "I'll come too."

"You really want to take notes on how I piss?"

Max pursed his lips as if he were actually considering the possibility, but Heather arrived just then, and Max perked up at having someone of the female persuasion to convince of his awesomeness.

On his way down the hall, Logan ran into Bert emerging from his office, the Yellow Pages clutched in his hands, and a more than usually grim expression on his cadaverous face.

"What're you doing here? I thought you were off doing your fancy important errands."

"I did 'em. Now I'm doing the jack-shit errand instead."

"Thought I saw you down by that mission before."

Logan's eyebrows drew together. "It's a shelter, not a mission, but yeah, I was there. What's it to you?"

"That what was so important? The stuff you had to take care of? Preaching to the hobos?"

"First, since it's not a mission, no preaching involved. Second, I wasn't in it, I was on the street where it's located. Third, they're not hobos."

"Bah. Worthless bums. They should get a job, like everybody else. Stop sponging off the rest of us."

"You know, Bert, sometimes a guy just has a little hard luck. You shouldn't judge."

"In my day, men knew how to work. Didn't whine. Didn't shirk." He whacked the phone directory like an evangelist thumping a Bible. "Didn't pretend they were doing something important when they were doing nothing but prancing around like a damn peacock."

"I'm pretty sure no prancing is involved at the shelter, Bert."

Bert's eyes turned flat and cold. "So why were you there? See someone, maybe?"

"I saw a lot of guys there. Not a single one was prancing. Shivering, yes. Starving, sure. Prancing, not so much."

Logan walked on toward the restroom.

"No man can change his destiny." Bert's voice echoed oddly in the hall.

"That so? Then you shouldn't rag on the homeless guys. But right now? My destiny awaits in the john."

"Hmmphm."

Logan pushed open the door. "Yeah. Couldn't have said it better myself," he muttered.

His hands full of earth-friendly bags, and his neck prickled by the needles of the big-ass pine branch under his arm, Riley shoved his door closed with one foot. He dumped everything on the bed and regarded the impressive pile, fists propped on his hips.

What were the chances he could convince Julie to put all this on the *HttM* expense account? His Production Bitch salary didn't ordinarily run to semiprecious stones and rare herbs, but Marguerite's "procedures"—a little bit Celtic, a little bit Wiccan, with a splash of Vodoun thrown in for kicks and giggles—had included a selection of both. The goth clerk at the Pagan Emporium had been fascinated by the fusion of rituals—and more than happy to upsell.

Riley had taken all her suggestions, just to be sure. He might be down the equivalent of a month's pay, but screw money. If it kept Logan safe, he'd shell out his entire savings.

Logan probably wouldn't thank him—might, in fact, hate him for the rest of their lives—but Riley didn't buy into Logan's apparent belief that Trent was more important than everyone else who might ever come in contact with the ghost war, including Logan himself. Riley planned to do everything he could to level the playing field for all the victims. If he skewed things slightly in favor of Logan? Sue him. He was still in love, dang it.

He stuffed the pine branch and silver censer on its three-foot chain into his locker-sized closet. Somehow, he had to justify the need to sweep the whole Witch's Castle site and all the paths leading to it with the branch. That would probably go over as well as explaining why he had to traipse around the clearing, swinging a pierced silver orb smoking with potentially toxic herbs. *Think about that later.*

He plopped onto the bed and pawed through the supplies, laying out the herb packets in a neat row, labels clearly visible. Wouldn't do to confuse the catnip with the Scotch broom, or the ferns with the foxglove. *Foxglove.* Jeez. Considering all the red tape he had to slog through to get it—registry, references, address, fingerprints, for heaven's sake—buying a gun would have been easier. The clerk had apologized, but explained it was a CYA move after one of their customers had gotten creative with the ingredients and tried to kill his mother-in-law.

He located the little charm bag ("Unbleached muslin, dried in the sun on the summer solstice! Stitched with sterling silver needles! Gluten free!") and dropped in a pinch of verbena, mint, and meadowsweet. Then St. John's wort. A couple of rowan twigs. A rough turquoise the size of his pinkie fingernail.

"Flat stone, flat stone, where the heck is that flat stone?" He found the tiny disk under the bag of sea salt, and studied the sketch of the double-headed axe he had to paint on the stone. The clerk told him that paint made with natural dyes would be most effective, but he could draw the thing with a Sharpie if necessary.

God. A Sharpie? Now there was an authentic ingredient. "I'm sure the druids used them every day and twice on Samhain," he muttered. Could any of this possibly make a difference?

Stop it. All his research confirmed that will and belief were the most important ingredients of all, the primary activators. If he expected to succeed, he couldn't afford to allow so much as a scrap of doubt to creep in.

Fine. He'd believe, and he sure as hell willed this to freaking work. But it would be useless without an anchor.

Think. Think. What would tie Logan to this world?

Before Max had towed Logan out of the hotel, he'd forced Logan into a *Haunted to the Max* crew fleece, so Logan's leather jacket hung on the back of Riley's chair. Although Logan had never been overly attached to most of his clothing, he'd had the jacket for as long as Riley had known him. However, he'd probably notice if it went missing. Besides, Riley could hardly stuff it into a fragile bag the size of a child's fist.

Glancing over his shoulder as if his furtive movements might be caught on a hidden camera, Riley eased Logan's jacket off the chair, and draped the soft leather across his lap. For a moment, he simply stroked its supple surface. The scent of leather had been part of his life with Logan, from their first night together.

After Logan had left, the barest whiff of leather had set off that plummet in Riley's stomach, the same one he'd experienced when he'd realized that Logan had taken off, that he'd never smell the intoxicating aroma of leather-and-Logan again.

Now the scent was comforting. Even—he shifted on the bed, tugging at his inseam—arousing.

He didn't know how he'd bear it if Logan left him a second time, but he could bear it even less if Logan no longer existed in the world at all. If putting the ghost war and Trent out of reach for good meant that Logan would hate Riley forever, then he'd find a way to deal.

But if Logan left afterward, this time Riley would know the reason why, and that he'd made a deliberate choice.

He checked the jacket pockets: Harley keys, a folded paper with an address in Logan's familiar scrawl, a knock-off of a Swiss Army knife, a pair of riding gloves. Nothing that felt anchor-ish to Riley. After all, if Logan could chuck his Ducati, he'd have no trouble dumping the Harley, let alone any of the other stuff.

Riley folded back the lapels and searched the lining. Aha. The inside zippered pocket contained a definite lump. He eased it open and reached inside. Cold metal. A little rough. A chain? He drew it out, its serpentine links gleaming in the anemic glow of the desk lamp. Logan had never been a jewelry kind of guy. Had he changed that much in five months? Riley pulled the chain all the way free, and there they were.

The rings.

His heart beat in his ears, and he whimpered as he lowered them onto one shaking palm.

When he'd discovered the rings in Eugene, he hadn't taken the time to look at them closely. He'd felt too much like a kid who'd stumbled across a carefully hidden Christmas present and who didn't want to spoil any more of the surprise.

Now, he picked up each ring, the chain sliding smoothly through their centers. The wide bands, white gold—or maybe platinum, for all he knew—lay heavy in his hand for such small things. Did their meaning make them weightier in his mind?

Etched inside the larger of the two was a Celtic knot, worked around his name as if binding it to the ring. The smaller one—his own—had the same design around Logan's name.

Tears prickled Riley's eyes, but he took a deep breath and blinked them away.

This was the answer. He could feel it. The notion that *he* could be Logan's anchor… Tears threatened again, *damn it*. He yanked off his glasses and pressed the heels of his hands against his eyes, the rings clutched in his fist, the chain softly bumping his cheek.

Which one would be the correct choice for the bag? Logan's ring had Riley's name on it… but it felt off. It represented Logan and his possessive streak. But his own ring. That felt right. Logan wouldn't stay for himself, but he might—just might—stay for Riley.

He muttered an apology as he unstrung the ring, then reclasped the chain, and dropped it back into the pocket with Logan's ring alone.

If his plan succeeded, Riley would be able to hand the missing ring back to Logan personally.

If everything went to hell, Logan wouldn't miss it anyway.

Christ, the only thing more annoying than Max Stone sober was Max Stone drunk off his ass.

It didn't help that for the first half of his bender, Max had turned hyper-entertainer. He'd ingratiated himself to a platoon of similarly soused frat boys and cadged an invitation to a party.

Since Max refused to go without Logan's dubious protection, they'd both ended up jammed into a cramped apartment down by the Amtrak station until the last potential fan had passed out.

By the time Logan, stone-cold sober and totally pissed off, hauled the idiot back to the hotel and up four flights of stairs to his room—because, plastered or not, Max flatly refused to take the elevator, for which Logan had nobody but himself to blame—the sky behind Mount Hood had already pinked with dawn.

He took the elevator down to Riley's floor, palming the key card Riley had slipped him earlier. As he silently opened the door, the idea of Riley waiting for him, rumpled and sleepy, heavy-eyed and willing, sent wake-up messages to his dick despite a solid thirty-something sleepless hours.

He eased the door shut behind him and crept past the bathroom and around the corner of the short entry, blinking in the dim light from the window.

The bed was empty.

He rubbed his gritty eyes and looked again. Nothing. He switched on the desk lamp. Still empty. The bathroom door stood open, and unless Riley had folded himself in half and hidden in the dresser drawers, there was no place in this room where he could be.

Logan checked under the bed, just in case. Then the locker-sized closet for good measure, but all its space was taken up by a fricking pine tree. What the hell?

"Damn it." Riley had always been an early riser, but he'd had a late night last night too. Maybe he had a breakfast meeting this morning? One of those interminable production marathons?

Logan smacked the desk with his fist and the screen of the open laptop quavered to life, displaying a shit-ton of overlapping documents and browser windows. Riley used to post his to-do list on his laptop. Maybe he hadn't lost the habit.

Logan sat in the chair, only intending to look for clues to Riley's whereabouts, but two words on the top document caught his eye.

Marguerite Windflower.

"Christ, Riley, what are you doing?" he murmured, and maximized the document.

As Logan skimmed it—weird lists and URLs and notations in Riley's odd shorthand—he realized Riley had no intention of staying out of harm's way. In fact, he obviously had an entirely different game plan than they'd discussed.

Scrolling through notes from interviews Riley had conducted with potential witnesses and anecdotal information from Portland residents, including Logan himself, Bert, and Heather, he oughtn't to feel the icy wash of betrayal scudding through his veins, yet he did.

Holy fucking hell. His grandfather's entire story, including Joseph Geddes's disappearance and its aftermath, was laid out from stem to stern. So was his own nightmare with Trent. Riley had tracked lives both before and after that night—his grandfather's fall from war hero to suspected murderer and lunatic; the pathetic deaths and disappearance of Geddes's wife and kids; Trent's trajectory from naive New England preppie to daredevil legend tripper; Logan's boring, pathetic existence before that night, and train wreck of a life afterward.

Logan's belly cramped with nausea. How could Riley bear to look at him when he knew the whole truth about Logan's miserable past?

Names, events, timelines—it was all here. He'd overlaid events and times and people in a funky flow chart under headings like *Persephone, Eurydice, Tam Lin,* and a dozen others, complete with connecting arrows and annotations.

Christ. How many hours of work did this represent? When had he had time to do it? Logan clenched his fist around the mouse until the plastic creaked under his fingers. He clicked on the Marguerite document again.

Two different banishment rituals. *That's what the fucking pine branch is for.*

Riley had promised, hadn't he? Promised to let Logan do the right thing. Yeah, Logan had made a couple of promises too, or at least implied them. But Trent's rescue trumped those promises—trumped everything except Riley's safety.

Pain lanced through his chest. Riley was incredibly passionate about his research. If Logan somehow managed to walk away from the war tomorrow night—an extremely unlikely event—would Riley forgive him for what he was about to do?

Didn't matter. If it kept Riley safe, it was the only possible path.

He deleted each document, a roiling pit widening in his belly with each click of the mouse. He wiped the browser history until nothing remained but the screen wallpaper.

The breath left his lungs at the sucker punch of that picture. The two of them on the one day he'd said to hell with his father's rants and strictures about publicly acceptable behavior, and let his feelings for Riley out in the open.

Christ, it had felt so fucking *good*. Not to hide. Not to worry about who might see, who might judge. To be able to touch Riley whenever he wanted—and he'd wanted, a lot. And Riley —he'd had that look, as if Logan were some kind of hero.

He should have known he'd have to pay for that happiness eventually. After what he'd done, Riley would never look at him that way again.

The keycard *snick*ed in the lock. Logan slapped the laptop closed and leaped to his feet.

Riley elbowed the door open, carrying two extra-large to-go cups. His hair was just as rumpled and his eyes as heavy-lidded as Logan had fantasized, but the cause was obviously not sleep but lack of it. They probably both resembled refugees from a forties noir mystery.

"Logan." Riley smiled at him, lines of weariness etched at the corners of his eyes. He held up one of the cups. "I brought you your favorite hazelnut latte, in case Max eventually released you from servitude." He kissed Logan, a quick press of lips, which Logan steeled himself against and didn't return.

Riley pulled back, confusion in his eyes, and set the cups on the desk. "What's the matter?"

"You promised me. You promised you'd put Trent's rescue first."

"I'm pretty sure I said nothing of the kind."

Logan took a deep breath through his nose. "Damn it, Riley. You'll fuck everything up. Ruin the plan—"

"What plan is that? *Our* plan? Or one of your own?"

"Please. Spare me the mock outrage."

Riley blinked, his face crumpling with hurt. *Christ, Conner, the least you could do is scale back on the disgusted tone.*

Logan carded his hands through his hair. "Sorry. It's just— Don't try to make me the only one with an agenda here."

"Tell me something." Riley's eyes glistened with a sheen of tears or fury. Logan couldn't tell, and one was as bad as the other. "Did you ever seriously consider that I might discover another option?"

"I don't doubt you could, probably a dozen different ones, given time. But we don't have time. It has to be now, this year. If we miss the seven-year window—"

"Stop fixating on the cycle. That may not be the only factor; in fact, I'm pretty sure it's not."

"But we know it happened at least twice."

"Two is not a statistically significant result. For all we know, it could be the goddamn margin of error." Riley clenched his fists at his sides. "For God's sake, Logan. Sacrificing yourself in Trent's place is not a *plan*. It's a misguided, guilt-driven death wish and it *sucks*."

CHAPTER NINETEEN

Logan's chest heaved and his jaw tightened, his face assuming the closed-down, no-trespassing mask Riley hated. The one that said Logan was through listening to anything but his own inner demons.

Riley moved forward, reaching out, but Logan stepped back, and Riley dropped his arm to his side. "Logan, please. You don't have to do this alone."

"Yes, I do. You don't understand. It's my obligation. My job to unravel this mess. The whole thing was my fault."

"No, it wasn't."

Logan folded his arms and turned to look out the window. "I suppose you'll say it's Trent's fault, but he'd never have been there if I hadn't told him the fucking story. He'd never heard of Danford Balch or the Stumps or the Witch's Castle. If it weren't for me, he'd have drunk too much, woken up with a hangover, and shown up for rehearsal with a headache and an upset stomach."

"No. It's the fault of whoever's will conjured up this war in the first place, and the engine that powers it. This isn't just about you, Logan. Or Trent, or your grandfather, or Joseph Geddes. It's a bomb primed to explode, and the blast will reach beyond people caught in the ghost war. For that matter, what do you think will happen if you succeed and Trent comes back?"

Logan's back stiffened, and in the reflection in the window, Riley saw his lips thin and his eyes narrow. "Anything's got to be better than getting hanged once a year."

"I agree. But the transition back to this world holds its own issues, and you can't afford to ignore them. You have to be ready to face them."

"What do you mean?"

"It's like the stories of humans kidnapped into Faerie who return to find that more time has passed in the outer world and everyone they know is changed or gone. You said Balch looked terrible. Granted, Trent's been gone less time, but our world moves fast, and seven years can work a hell of a lot of change. What do you think he'll do when he finds he doesn't fit in?"

"He'll be fine," Logan growled.

"How do you know? You don't know what he's endured or how he'll react." Riley held up his hands, palms out. "I'm not saying we shouldn't go through with the rescue. We just need to consider all the ramifications. Not everyone has your strength of character."

Logan's lips twisted in disgust, and he snorted soundlessly. "And not everyone is as stubborn as you. Why can't you see that I have to do this? Make things right?"

Why is he more important than you? More important than us? Riley was beginning to resent Trent Pielmeyer—and he had no confidence whatsoever in Trent's integrity. He'd stepped into the ghost war despite Logan's warnings, and expected Logan to pull him out. *Doesn't say stand-up guy to me.* "What will Trent say when the police start asking questions? Who will he blame for his disappearance? If it comes down to you or him, I suspect he'll throw you under the bus in a hot minute."

"He was my best friend. He wouldn't—"

"Logan, he already did. Don't you see?" Riley gentled his tone. "You're trapped by this ritual as much as if you'd been in his place. Everything you do or don't allow yourself to do is colored by that event."

"Because it's on me. All of it. I knew what would happen—"

"No. You didn't. Your grandfather didn't know why Joseph Geddes disappeared. You had no way of knowing it could happen again. But now you *do* know. If you let this go on, expose anyone else to the same danger, *that's* on you. It ends tonight, Logan. Whether Trent escapes or not. It ends tonight."

Riley sat, swiveling the chair to face the desk. He frowned as he lifted his laptop's lid. Hadn't he left it open? *Huh. Must be more wiped than I realized.*

His screen flared to embarrassing life—the picture of the two of them at that stupid barbecue. Heat painted his cheeks and the tips of his ears. God. Why hadn't he ever changed it?

He glanced over his shoulder, but Logan wasn't looking at him. Just staring out the window, his shoulders even more rigid than before.

Riley turned back to his laptop, to his sappy expression and Logan's single public act of affection.

Wait. What?

He could have sworn he'd left all his documents open, but there was nothing now. Nothing open in the task bar. Nothing minimized. He checked the directory where he'd stored his research, the links to the banishment video, Marguerite's instructions, his own strategies.

Empty. Every last one.

Fire kindled in his chest, heating his neck, burning at the back of his eyes.

"Logan. What did you do?"

"I erased it."

"Do you realize what you've done?"

"Yes." He turned, his face implacable. "I'm keeping you safe and doing what I have to do. I'm sorry if I've—"

"My work. Not just this story, but years of research. *Everything.* Did you stop to think what that would mean to me?"

Logan shut his eyes briefly, mouth pinched. "They were only words, Riley. You're worth so much more."

Riley shut the laptop with a *click*. "If I'm worth so freaking much, Logan, why is what I do worth so little?"

"I'm sorry." Logan's voice held a ragged edge, but no uncertainty. "But this can't end until Trent returns. If that means I have to take his place, then I'm ready."

Riley hung his head, fists clenched on his thighs. "I'm not," he whispered.

Logan eased his jacket off the chair. "Good-bye."

The feathered touch on Riley's hair might have been nothing but his imagination. Logan took the two strides to the door and was gone.

His limbs as heavy as a Gorgon's victim, Riley pressed his fingers against his gritty eyes behind his glasses, not sure if the tears that threatened from his stupid broken heart would outrank his outrage over Logan's thoughtless sabotage. It didn't matter that Riley backed up his laptop regularly—he was no idiot—but Logan didn't know that, and he'd been willing to obliterate the files anyway.

Logan didn't seem to realize that without his work, Riley amounted to nothing but Julie's all-but-unemployed BFF. The guy who got the coffee. Max's pack mule. Scott's virtual nicotine patch.

Production Bitch.

Maybe it was time he buried himself in the part. Stopped pushing for scholarship and authenticity. Let Scott reorient the shots for maximum scenic effect but zero possible manifestation. Allow the whole episode to peter out like any other *HttM* episode, with Max intoning "Chilling, if true," as the final credits rolled.

But this story wasn't just Hollywood special effects. The ghost war presented a real danger, not only to Logan—who'd insist on sacrificing himself even if Max Stone threw him down in the mud and tap danced on his chest—but to any other hapless victim who got caught in the ritual.

Since Riley knew the risks, and had at least a slim hope of making a difference, it was his responsibility to get the job done and end the war.

"I'm doing this," he told the ceiling. The pine broom, the herb smudging, the banishment ritual that looked like St. Vitus's dance. All of it, no matter how insane it made him appear.

If he believed, if he willed it, and if he didn't screw everything from hell to breakfast, Logan would be safe. He might hate Riley forever, but Trent's fate would no longer be his fault. He could blame Riley instead, and get on with his life.

Riley would have to be content with knowing he'd rescued the big jerk from his savior complex.

It would have to be enough.

He settled his glasses on his nose and dove into damage-control mode.

Thank Zeus, Odin, Osiris, and Bran the Blessed for automatic online backups and the free wi-fi that extended even to his poky little third-rate room. Logan's search-and-destroy mission hadn't wiped out anything but the most recent notes on potential strategies.

Luckily, since he'd been obsessing over those all night, they remained front-and-center in his mind, like Max jostling for a better camera angle. He took a gulp of his coffee. *Ewww.* Tepid. He tossed the nearly full cup into the plastic-lined waste bin with a *thump* and *slosh*.

His gaze caught on the second cup. The one he'd bought just in case Logan had returned by the time he got back. He grabbed it, ready to slam-dunk it into the trash, but his hand trembled at the last second.

He took a sip. Just as tepid as his own had been, but the trace of hazelnut tasted like Logan's morning kisses. He took another sip and set the cup next to his laptop.

Pathetic. But whatever.

He recovered the notes on the procedures he'd cobbled together and uploaded them to his phone, with an additional note to ask Charmaine to tuck the charm bag into Logan's bodyguard costume jacket.

He checked the clock icon on his screen. Seven fifty-four. He had to report for duty in six minutes. Slumping in his chair, he removed his glasses and scrubbed his hands over his face. The buzz he always got from completing a project had already faded, leaving nothing but an empty feeling in his middle and the bitter taste of coffee and betrayal on his tongue.

Don't think about what Logan did. Concentrate on saving the dickhead's ass tonight, whether he wants it or not. Whether he believes you're capable of it or not.

His email alert pinged. Great. Another of Julie's last-minute schedule updates.

He blinked blearily at the screen. Why was it out of focus? Oh, glasses. He shoved them on his face, but even with clear vision, his inbox made no sense.

The message was from Scott. How could that be? Scott never emailed him. Riley wasn't certain Scott even knew his name, since he'd only ever called Riley "you," accompanied by a pointed finger.

The subject line read *Revised Shoot Assignments*. Riley frowned as he opened the document. Usually Julie and her Clipboard of Doom handled scheduling and notification—Scott must be more invested in this episode than either of them had realized.

Riley scanned the list and his blood pounded in his ears as earlier outrage returned. "What the freaking hell?"

He'd been taken off the approved crew list for the Witch's Castle site, relegated to traffic control at the trailhead and, God, *craft services*? Seriously?

No, damn it. Not only was this *his story*, but he had to be on site to ensure Logan didn't do something incredibly stupid, offering himself up on the altar of his guilt like a bloody volcano virgin.

He punched Julie's speed dial on his cell. The call went straight to voice mail. Invoking curses to six different deities, Riley shoved himself out of his chair and took the two and a half strides across his room. When he yanked the door open, he nearly got brained by Julie's fist, which was poised to knock with her usual gusto.

"Whoa. Sorry." She backed up a step, a frown pleating the skin between her eyebrows. "Riley? What's wrong?"

He grabbed the pencil from behind her ear and tossed it over his shoulder. "Do not start drawing pictures of my face."

"I wasn't. I promise. I—"

"What the hell is up with the schedule?"

She dropped her gaze and fiddled with the top paper on her clipboard, dog-earing the bottom corner and smoothing it out. "Scott…" She raised her chin an inch above level. "This shoot has a complicated infrastructure. I need someone I can trust to handle all the off-set arrangements."

Riley clenched his fists at his sides. "Julie, you know this is wrong. This is *my* story. You know I have to be there."

"Riley, please." Her eyes were wide, pleading. "It can't matter to you. Not really. You've said so yourself. This is my career trajectory, not yours, and if this keeps Scott happy and Max off my back—"

"You're caving?" He punctuated his words by jabbing his finger into her fleece-clad shoulder. "Sucking up to Scott because you think he'll give you a shot at the showrunner gig."

She bit her lip and glanced at the oh-so-fascinating mass-produced print of Mount Hood on the wall. "Next season. He promised me if this shoot goes smoothly, if I can keep Max happy, the budget under control—"

He let his hand drop, fingers lax. "You don't believe in the ghost war either, do you? That it could be real?"

"Riley." She spoke in an un-Julie-like calm, as if she were trying to talk a mental patient off a ledge. "This show's nothing but an extended fraud. You know it. I know it. Scott knows it. The only one who doesn't know it is Max."

"Then for once…" He carded his fingers through his hair. "I can't believe I'm saying this, but for once, Max is right."

He tugged the clipboard out of her hands and steered her to the chair, then sat on the edge of the bed opposite her. "This story may be a minor rung on your Hollywood ladder, but it's way more than that to me. I wouldn't ask you to go out on a limb with Scott if it weren't absolutely vital." He tossed the clipboard aside and took her hands in a tight grip. "I didn't tell you before because I didn't want to worry you, but there's more at stake here than either of our careers."

She attempted to tug her hands free. "What could be more important—and since when do you hide things from me?"

"I—"

"Wait a minute." Her eyes narrowed. "This is about that scum-sucking asswipe Logan, isn't it?"

Riley reined in his frustration—barely. He didn't have time to talk Julie down from a Logan-hating rampage. "This is about you and me, Jules. You went to the mat for me to pitch this episode, forced me to participate way more than was comfortable, all in the name of promoting me to Scott. Suddenly you've changed your mind, decided I'm not worth it?"

"It's not that. I mean, it's not like we've scrubbed the whole shoot, and with all those background scenes we filmed, you'll have almost as much screen time as Max."

"Except I never wanted screen time. Jules, you realize you're treating me the same way you treat him, don't you? Like a child who has to be kept occupied so he won't interfere with the adults' important work, and won't notice their condescension."

She scowled. "I do no such thing. But I know the industry and I know Scott, and you don't. It makes sense for me to keep you where—"

"Where he won't notice I can't do my job?"

"You can so do your job. The first one who says you can't—"

"Jules. That would be you."

Her scowl faded, and she blinked. "Shit." She pursed her lips and puffed out a breath. "Fine. If I ever imply that you can't do your job, or if I ever treat you like Max again, you have my permission to kick my ass."

"Consider it kicked." He gave her hands a final squeeze, picked up the clipboard, and held it out. "Here. You know where I need to be."

"But Scott wants—"

"The only way Scott knows what he wants is if you tell him. Come on." He poked her shoulder. "Are you the UPM—soon to be showrunner—or just another Production Bitch? Who makes the damn schedules around here anyway? Max freaking Stone?"

She straightened and snatched the clipboard from his hands. Yeah, that was his Jules. Challenge her territory and the Valkyrie donned the horned helmet, the brass-plated bra, and charged.

"Fuck this pencil shit." She pulled a Sharpie out of the pocket of her fleece vest and wrote his name in giant black letters under the list of crew assigned to the Witch's Castle location. "You're on. After all..." Her wicked grin wouldn't be out of place on a Viking berserker. "It's your story."

CHAPTER TWENTY

After he left the hotel, Logan had tried to catch some sleep, but the look on Riley's face had haunted him every time he closed his eyes—the total betrayal, when Riley had realized that Logan had destroyed his work on purpose. It was enough to keep him tossing on his mattress, despite his bone-deep weariness.

Christ, he hadn't thought, had he? Hadn't made any attempt to remove only the Witch's Castle files. Maybe he should have been less ham-fisted about it, but nothing he could do about it now. He'd taken his shot, and now he had to live with it. Or not live. Depending on how the next twenty-four hours played out.

Better this way. He'll hate you, but at least he'll be alive, and when you're gone, he won't miss you as much.

At noon, he still hadn't gotten beyond staring at his ceiling when Max called him on his cell phone, demanding his presence at another of those fucking production meetings.

Could he sit in one of those meetings and watch Riley not meet his eyes? A cold fist closed around Logan's heart. Shit. Riley would take the fall for the stuff Logan had wiped from the laptop. He was likely to get reamed by his boss. Maybe he'd get fired after all.

A double-helix of guilt and relief spiraled up Logan's core. Was he a total shithead for half hoping Riley lost his job?

Probably, but it was the one foolproof way to keep him and his home-grown ghost remedies away from the site.

Riley could go back to school, to the kind of folklore fieldwork his advisor had always intended him to do.

It would be good for him. Logan had to believe that.

"Logan? Did you hear me?" Figured that Max's petulant tone carried perfectly on Logan's crappy phone. "The meeting starts in twenty."

Call him a fucking coward, but he couldn't watch Riley's humiliation play out in front of a room full of jaded Hollywood types.

"Sorry, Max. I can't. You shouldn't need a bodyguard at your own production meeting. I'll pick you up afterwards, and we'll hang for the rest of the day."

"Weeellll, I guess that's okay, although Scott may wonder where you are."

"Scott doesn't even know my name. Just tell him tattoo bodyguard guy will be at your back tonight."

He hung up and wandered around his shitty apartment. Was it worth packing anything up? Other than his clothes, he had nothing except a few dishes. A couple of towels. Some bedding. The landlord was free to add them to his library of crappy furnishings and soak the next tenant for them.

It only took him twenty minutes to stack everything on the counter and leave a note for the landlord. He sat on the revolting sofa, resigned to a couple of hours waiting for Max's call, but it came before the broken spring in the cushion had a chance to bruise his ass.

"Hey, Logan, change in plans. You need to report to makeup at six."

"Makeup. Why?"

"You can't appear on camera without it. You'll look washed-out."

"I'm not going to be on camera. Besides, it'll be dark."

"Yes, you are. Scott likes your style. He says it'll read well for the story."

Logan closed his eyes and pinched the bridge of his nose. *Unfucking-believable.* "Why six? It'll take them that long to smear me with whatever?"

Max's chuckle burred over the scratchy connection. "They'll finish with you in no time, but you have to be there with me. We'll be at the trailhead, so you know, the spirits might sense that we're there and get pissed."

Only if they had to report to makeup too. Christ.

So after another fun-filled afternoon with an amped-up Max, Logan reported to the fucking makeup trailer for ten minutes of prep, and then kicked his heels while Max plunged into his own interminable session.

As they approached hour four of Max agonizing over his hair and the angle of his hat, Charmaine poked her head into the trailer and motioned him outside.

Thank God for small favors, but... He scanned the tents and trailers scattered around the graveled staging area. No sign of Riley. He took a deep breath and conjured up a smile. "Hey. What's up?"

She held out a leather bomber jacket. "Here."

"What's this?"

"Your costume."

Logan held it up in the light from the craft services tent. "It looks exactly like my real jacket."

"But if you wear your own, we have to pay you a costume piece-rate."

"And that's less than buying a whole new jacket?"

She shot a glance over her shoulder at the dozen or so crew schlepping mysterious equipment around and mainlining coffee. "It's one of Max's extras, but don't tell anybody." She held out her hand and wiggled her fingers. "Gimme yours."

He shrugged his jacket off and traded it for its clone. She spun on her heel and took off.

"Hey, hold on." He caught up with her. "I've got stuff in those pockets."

She peered at him over her giant glasses. "I'll keep it secure. You'll get it back after the shoot."

Not likely. For him, there'd be no *after*.

"I still want my stuff."

She sighed, but held out the jacket.

"Charmaine!" Square Jaw shouted from the trailhead. "Scott needs you. Now."

"Coming." She shook Logan's jacket. "Hurry up."

"Yeah, yeah." After he jammed both hands into the outside pockets and transferred each fistful of stuff to the costume jacket, Charmaine tried to escape. "Not yet." He unzipped the inside pocket, gathered the chain into his hand, and pulled it out. He waved her on. "Go for it."

"Take this." She handed him a folded bandana. "For the mud." Then she sped away.

He shoved the bandana in his pocket and ducked behind the makeup trailer. No matter what waited him at the end of the trail, he refused to abandon the rings. When he unzipped the inner pocket of the jacket to stow them—Christ, it really was exactly like his own—the chain slithered out of his fist and dangled from his hand. He frowned. It felt... off.

He held the chain up so it caught the dim light and stared at it stupidly for a full thirty seconds. Only one ring hung suspended from the chain. His own.

Riley, damn it.

Had to be. He was the only one with the opportunity, although what his motive might be, Logan couldn't guess.

"Shit." He dropped the chain into the pocket and zipped it up. Riley must have something in mind beyond Marguerite's banishment ritual. Something Logan had missed in his skim-read of the documents before he'd axed them. Who the fuck knew what the stubborn idiot had planned? Just as well Logan had sabotaged him, because he couldn't allow those plans to succeed. Not now. Not when he was so close.

The door to the makeup trailer banged open, and Max emerged, ready for his fucking close-up.

"All set, Logan." Max posed in the open trailer door wearing the exact grim expression Logan had worn for the last two days. "Let's hit the trail."

A PA armed with a high-powered flashlight led the way down the narrow path, Max mincing in her wake as he tried not to get mud all over his boots. Logan brought up the rear, and at just after ten, they made it to the Witch's Castle.

The rest of the crew was already there, milling around the site, and Logan had to hand it to them—they were careful. They didn't muck up the trails or disturb the foliage or underbrush. He gave Julie a lot of the credit for that. She patrolled the place like a Prussian field marshal directing her troops.

She wasn't so busy, though, that she couldn't take time out to give Logan a look that made his balls glad she carried a clipboard and not a pair of pruning shears.

The crew had set up their equipment oriented toward the Witch's Castle, arguably the most scenic and haunted-looking backdrop. Excellent. If they were focused on the ruins, they'd be out of range of the ghost war barrier when it rose. They'd be safe. They might not get much usable footage—who knew what the eldritch light from the barrier would do to those night-vision cameras?—but they'd be out of the way. Fewer opportunities for any of them to fuck this up.

"No, I told you. The building is not the place you want to focus."

At the sound of that voice, determined, unafraid, and clearly un-fired, the hair on the back of Logan's neck rose, along with his rebellious dick. *Goddamn it!* Sure enough, when Scott rounded the corner of the Castle, Riley was dogging his heels, carrying a ventilated metal ball trailing smoke that reeked of mint and thyme and some less pleasant smells Logan couldn't identify.

"Why's Rye-Lee here?" Max bumped Logan's shoulder with his own. "I thought we got him reassigned to craft services."

Logan moved out of shoulder-bump range. "Guess not."

"What's he doing? Bombing for insects?" Max peered up into the foliage. "Must work. Haven't seen a single mosquito since we got here."

"That's because the bats eat them."

Max's eyes bugged out. "Bats?" He pulled his hat lower on his forehead, negating all the time he'd spent getting its angle right in the makeup trailer. "Next time, we're sticking to ghosts who had the sense to die inside a house."

Logan loitered near the camera setup as Riley cornered Scott in front of the shallow stone steps that led to the roofless upper story of the Castle. "Scott. This is all wrong."

"It's a better shot." Scott didn't bother to glance Riley's way. "The spot by the bank is blocked by that damn tree and the noise from the creek interferes with the mic."

"The ghosts don't haunt the Castle. It didn't exist during their lifetimes. They—"

"I don't have time for this shit." Scott pointed at Riley's nose. "You and I both know there aren't any ghosts."

Riley's mouth fell open. "But—"

"This whole fucking show is one big gimmick, with a little scam thrown in for shits and grins."

Logan groaned. *No, you idiot. Don't challenge his kung fu.* He left Max perched in a folding canvas chair with *Stone* stenciled on the back, and strode across the clearing before Scott had a chance to detonate the Riley stubborn-bomb.

Riley shut his mouth, and his jaw took on a familiar mulish cast. *Too late.* "Maybe that's why you've never had a true sighting. You pick your episodes by what looks good, not what the we—*research* supports."

"Research?" Scott guffawed, obviously not realizing he'd just lit a second fuse. "Research supports fuck-all, unless it gives us a decent backstory. Smoke and mirrors. That's all this shit is. That's all it's ever been." He turned away. "Zack. Max. I want to stage a walk-through of the ruins. The two of you, with me now."

He walked off. Riley's chest heaved, his breath forming a misty cloud in front of his face. *Surprised matching clouds don't shoot out his ears.*

Logan closed the final distance between them, angling his back toward the curious crew, unable to resist crowding close enough to feel the heat radiating from Riley's skin, although the smoke from the damn censer blocked Riley's own scent and made Logan's eyes water.

"What are you doing here? Without your files, I thought—"

Riley took a giant, deliberate step away, his expression not softening in the slightest. "You really think I didn't have online backups? I may be stupid enough to fall for your line more than once, but I'm not *that* stupid."

"I know you're not stupid, but this isn't safe. Riley, believe me. You need to get far away from here."

"No. *You* need to believe *me*." Riley's voice was low and fierce. "The answer to this is in the ritual." Riley inhaled sharply, and for an instant, his eyes widened. "Oh, right. I almost forgot. You're on Team Max now. You don't think I know what I'm doing."

"Hey!" Max's shout from the upper level of the Witch's Castle startled them both, and they broke away from each other. "Who the hell is that?"

A chill zinged down Logan's spine. It couldn't be a ghost; the war wasn't due to rise until midnight.

He took two strides and shoved Riley behind him. The ragged figure who shambled out from behind the Castle wasn't a ghost, though.

It was Danny Ball, aka Danford fucking Balch.

When Logan took off to converge on the grimy stranger along with Scott and Max, Riley glared at his retreating back and wished for a couple of spare lightning bolts from Zeus. Or maybe Odin. He wasn't fussy as long as it got the job done and zapped Logan off the set.

Failing that, he'd have to channel Anansi the Spider and rely on cunning, with a little annoying limpet persistence thrown in. He ran across the clearing, the mud slippery under his high-tops, and joined the group now looming over the cowering man.

"What are you doing here?" Scott shouted. "Answer me."

"Come on, Scott." Max tugged at Scott's arm. "It's obvious. He's got to be the saboteur."

"Use your fucking brain for a change, Max. How could a smelly homeless guy break into two different suites at that hotel? Don't you think someone would have noticed?"

Max nodded owlishly. "Maybe this is only his temporal disguise."

Scott rolled his eyes. "Jesus Christ. Don't tell me you buy your own line of bullshit."

Logan took the shivering man by one arm and hauled him to his feet. "I'll take care of this. Isn't that what you hired me for?"

"Yeah." Max brightened immediately. "Yeah, it is."

When Logan turned, Riley drew his shoulders back and met his gaze. At first, he thought Logan would relent, finally accept that Riley had as much a right to be here as Logan did. Instead, his expression grew cold, his gaze implacable.

"Christ, somebody keep Wiley out of my sight. I've got enough to do tonight without him panting at my feet." He turned and dragged the stranger away.

Riley flinched, the pain as acute as if he'd taken a blow to the body and not to the heart. He wrapped his arms across his chest, anchoring his freezing hands in his armpits, and wished for a convenient rock to crawl under.

Next to him, Max's mouth sagged open. "Man, I can dig the Teflon attitude, but that was just mean." He shoved his hands in his jacket pockets. "How am I supposed to use that? The fans'll never go for it."

Riley blinked, the pain fading. If the world's most narcissistic fake ghost hunter thought Logan's behavior was out-of-character, then this was nothing more than another stupid attempt to drive Riley away under some misguided notion of protecting him.

Oddly enough, warmth washed through his chest. *He still cares, the big idiot. He just refuses to believe he needs help too.*

He circled the Witch's Castle, searching for Logan, and spotted him leading the intruder up the path toward the spot where Riley's research indicated the main skirmish in the ghost war would occur.

Wait. If the man didn't belong on the scene, Logan, with his damned inconvenient knight-errant complex, would have hustled him off-site without a blink. If he was keeping him here, inside the perimeter, that must mean...

"Holy shit," he breathed. "Danford Balch."

Riley ran after them, dodging a couple of grips, and nearly collided with Logan's back when they stopped under the tree next to the creek.

The ragged man hunkered down in the mud and wiped the back of his hand under his nose, smearing snot across his cheek.

"Jesus." Logan fumbled in his jacket pocket. He pulled out a wad of tissues, and his pocket knife, a crumpled piece of paper, and one glove came along for the ride. "Here, Balch. Try not to be completely disgusting."

Riley ran a trembling hand through his hair. "It's really him? Danford Balch?"

"Shut up," Logan growled. "You want Max or Julie sticking their noses in?"

"Right. Sorry." Riley knelt and collected the stuff that had spilled from Logan's pocket.

Balch wiped his nose and scrubbed the side of his face with the tissue until it shredded, leaving bits of white in his stubble. He nodded at the creek.

"This was my homestead, my legacy, land for my children— but I found out none of them got a single acre. She gave it all to *him*. And he cared so little about it, about my children, that he gave it all away."

"'Him'? You mean your wife's second husband?"

He snorted, spreading more mucus in his mustache. "Her third. I was her second. That woman didn't stand still for long."

Logan crossed his arms and glared down at Balch. "Why are you here? You ran pretty fast the other night."

Balch peered up at them from under matted hair. "Same reason I'm always here. For a chance to see my Anna." His gaze skittered among the *HttM* crew littering the site. "But that don't seem likely, not with all these folks in the way."

"That's what I'm afraid of," Logan muttered.

"Here." Riley handed off Logan's knife and glove, but the paper fluttered away. He chased it down and caught it before it took a header into the creek. He tried to smooth it out, brushing at the splotches of mud that dotted it. "Sorry, I don't think…" He stared at the paper and his stomach dropped. "It's—it's a map. To the Vaughn Street Hotel." Max's room number and the room number of the equipment suite were scrawled across the top of the page. He raised his head, the paper crumpling as he clenched his fist. "You lied. You were the vandal after all."

CHAPTER TWENTY-ONE

Logan carded his fingers through his hair. He didn't need this. Not another fight with Riley. Not now. "I told you, no. Besides, why would I need a map to your hotel? I know where it is."

"Why bother to deny it now, Logan? What can you hope to gain?"

"Riley." He grabbed Riley's shoulders, forced him to meet his gaze. "That's just a random scrap I used the night I went to find Balch." He unfurled Riley's fingers, removed the paper, and showed him the addresses of the shelters. "See. Here are my notes." He flipped the paper. "This? This isn't my writing. It's Bert's."

"Bert? Your boss? Why would he—"

"Now who the hell is *that*?" Scott's annoyed bellow didn't drown out Balch's rattling breath. "Julie, goddamn it, you said this was a closed set."

Logan caught the flicker of movement as another man, tall and gaunt, emerged from the trees on the hillside above the Castle. When he stepped into the wan moonlight, Logan swore under his breath.

"Bert," he growled. "Christ. *Bert*. How fucking stupid could I be? *Stump*town Spirits. Right in front of me the whole time. Cuthbert fucking Stump." He pushed Riley behind him. "It was you. You trashed the cameras. Trashed Max's room."

"That was before." His burning gaze passed over the ragged man who huddled at Logan's feet and focused on Riley, his lips drawing back in a rictus excuse for a grin. "No man can escape his destiny."

A babble of confused voices, random shouts from Max, Scott, Zack, and Julie, filled the air, but he dismissed them as irrelevant. "You escaped yours, though, didn't you, Cuthbert, and left my grandfather twisting in the wind."

"He was a blame fool. Not my fault he didn't have the sense God gave a goose."

"He helped you, you bastard. Gave you a place to sleep. Food. Clothing. Money. And you destroyed his life."

"I had my own way to make, same as any man. Your grandfather? He made his own bed. I paid my debt to his blood, though. Looked out for you, gave you a job. You got no cause for complaint."

Logan lurched forward, fists clenched, the urge to coldcock Bert stronger than he could resist, but Riley grabbed his arm and pulled him back.

"Wait. Logan, I know how you must feel, but don't you see? This must be it. The engine that drives the ritual: Cuthbert's quest for vengeance." His voice was low, urgent. "We could do it, Logan. We could unravel this whole mess. End it. Here. Tonight."

"I thought you said it wouldn't end unless the need was resolved."

"This may be as close as we'll ever get. All the original players are here. We can do the banishment ritual."

"Will that release Trent?"

"I don't know, but—"

"Then no."

"Logan. Do you want to leave Cuthbert loose in the world for another half century?"

He pried Riley's fingers loose from his sleeve. "The world will have to take its chances. I've got another debt to pay."

Riley caught Logan's hand, his eyes wide. "Look."

A sulfurous glow had appeared, hovering at ankle level just beyond Bert—no, *Cuthbert*, damn it all to hell—snaking back into the trees up the hill. "Shit." Logan glanced behind him. The crew and Scott were still wrangling equipment at the far side of the clearing. "What time is it?"

"Maybe eleven, eleven thirty."

"It's too soon. It shouldn't start until midnight."

"Maybe the presence of a Balch and a Stump activated it. I don't know. We were always just guessing." Riley's voice vibrated with tension. "God, Logan, anything could happen."

Logan glanced down at Danford, still huddled at his feet. But as the sullen yellow light crept along the ground, picking up speed, bisecting the clearing, Logan realized Danford wasn't his biggest problem.

Fear washed through his gut like ice mixed with fire. *Anything could happen.* He wasn't the only one at risk: Riley, Julie, the crew... He wouldn't wish this on anyone, not even Max Stone.

The cameramen and support crew were still safely outside the ghost war perimeter, along with Scott, but Julie and Max were on the inside, only a couple of yards from Riley.

"Run, you idiots!" Logan shouted, grabbing Riley's arm and hauling ass toward the diminishing gap.

Max didn't need to be told twice. He bolted, losing his stupid hat in his rush. Julie remained frozen in place, clipboard clutched to her chest in gloved hands as if it could protect her.

"Riley?" she whispered. "It's real, isn't it?"

Riley pulled out of Logan's grip, his breath erratic. "Why is everyone so surprised? I told you it was real. I showed you the evidence. Just because every other episode was bogus"—he gulped air—"only means you weren't looking in the right places."

Logan snatched Julie's sleeve and made a grab for Riley, who evaded him. "The two of you can debate later. But now, you need to get the fuck out of here before the barrier closes." He managed to get Julie's feet moving, but she kept slowing down, staring at Cuthbert, at Danford. "Come *on*, Julie. You heard what Riley said. All bets are off."

She dug her heels into the spongy ground. "Are you kidding? A real, honest-to-god manifestation could make this stupid job worthwhile. I'm not going anywhere."

"Fuck this." Logan picked her up and slung her over his shoulder, her clipboard falling to the ground with a muffled thump. "Come on, Riley."

He sprinted for the knot of wide-eyed crew members as fast as he could while carrying a buck fifty of pissed-off woman. Out of the corner of his eye, he caught the glowing snake of the barrier approaching from the woods on his left now too, cutting straight through one of the walls of the Witch's Castle, accelerating, reducing the safety margin by the second.

He skidded on the muddy path and staggered outside the danger zone, into the tangle of equipment and cable, and set the furious Julie on her feet between two burly grips.

"Hold her."

Amazingly, they obeyed. *Score one for tattoo bodyguard guy.*

She struggled in their grasp. "Logan Conner, you *suck*, you—you dick-spawned shit-bucket!"

"Save the compliments for later." He heaved a relieved sigh and turned, searching the crowd for Riley. Julie's gasp, hand covering her mouth, clued him in. He spun around.

In the center of the now nearly complete barrier, Cuthbert held Riley with one arm twisted behind his back. The greenish light glinted on the knife in Bert's other hand, at the angle of Riley's jaw.

"Bert. No!"

Bert bared his teeth and brandished the knife. "Never could see what was right in front of your nose, boy."

Riley didn't struggle—smart man—but he probably didn't have much choice. Logan knew from watching Bert heave cases of liquor around that his stringy body held muscles out of proportion to a man his age.

His age. Christ. Logan had known Bert since childhood, so he knew the guy was old, but *this* old? Nobody over a hundred and fifty should be in that good of shape. Danford sure wasn't. Hell, nobody over a hundred and fifty should even be *alive*—or passing for living. Who knew what tricks Cuthbert had up his undead sleeve? Logan didn't intend to leave Riley to face them alone.

He raced back toward the rapidly closing gap, pushing Scott out of his way, and in a final burst of speed, leaped into the circle. His knee buckled, and he went down just as a curtain of eldritch fire sprang up, enclosing them inside the war zone.

Riley cursed all the time he'd spent in the library instead of the gym. If he'd worked out more, he'd stand half a chance of escaping the SOB who had him as helpless as if he were a goddamned ventriloquist's dummy. Why had he ever imagined he could control this situation when he couldn't even keep himself out of trouble?

Green mist boiled out of the barrier, separating into roughly person-sized globs, but no recognizable figures.

Scott's voice carried through the ringing in Riley's ears. "Shit. The readings are off the charts. This is the biggest manifestation we've ever seen."

It's the only one you've ever seen.

Bert's rusty chuckle sent gooseflesh creeping up Riley's back. "Let's give 'em something better to look at, eh, boy?"

He jerked Riley's arm up, his bony fingers less yielding than handcuffs, and slashed the base of Riley's palm. Fire shot from Riley's hand to his shoulder, and he caught a scream behind his teeth as his blood pattered to the ground—and a whole half-transparent cast faded into focus: figures in midcentury garb complete with horses, wagons, firearms.

Despite the pain, and his proximity to a madman, Riley's folklore-centric brain registered the data. *I was correct. It's a ritual and blood is the trigger. I prepared for the right thing.* No matter what happened to him now, he had faith that the protections he'd woven around the site with his ridiculous censer and pine broom, around Logan with the charm bag, would at least shield the people he loved.

He heard a cry from Julie, and Scott ordering Zack to get this on film. On the bank of the creek, Balch whimpered, his gaze locked on the specter of a girl with her hand tucked in the elbow of a strapping young man.

Bert shoved Riley in the back, and he stumbled forward, his throbbing hand clutched to his chest, and fell to his knees on the muddy ground. He scrambled up, regardless of the pain in hand and knees, and staggered to Logan's side.

He held out his uninjured hand, and Logan took it to lever himself up, wincing when he put weight on his left leg.

He grasped Riley's wrist, angling his hand until the gash gleamed in the barrier's glow. "Christ. I never thought he'd hurt you."

"Still think leaving him loose is a good idea?"

"No. But it can't change my mind."

"Logan." Riley kept his voice low, but infused all the urgency into it that he could. "We may never get this chance again. The blood on the ground. Balch and Stump both inside the barrier. You and I, two people who know what's going on and have the will to stop it."

Logan cupped the back of Riley's head with one hand, his fingers threading through Riley's hair. "Babe, the stuff you figured out... it's amazing, but you said it before. We're just guessing. We know for sure that a player can get displaced, but only in this time window. I can't take the risk on untried hoodoo."

"Once this episode airs, how many other people do you think will try this? Sacrificing yourself might not even save Trent. We have the chance to save everyone."

"Then you do it. You tell them to stay the fuck away from this place." He jerked his chin at a spot beyond Riley's shoulder and turned him gently in that direction. "Show them the evidence—you've got it all on film."

"Don't do it, Logan. Please." Riley clutched the lapels of Logan's jacket, smearing blood on the leather. "For once in your life, don't be the fweaking hewo."

A smile tugged at Logan's mouth, and he ran his thumb over Riley's lower lip, just as he'd done in that long ago picture. "I ever tell you how much I love the way you talk?"

Riley half sobbed and plastered himself against Logan's chest. Logan's arms closed around him, and from their circle, he watched the sad little scene play out on the bank of the creek, with Bert observing from atop a stump at the edge of the clearing. Danford had retreated to huddle against the mossy stones of the only Witch's Castle wall inside the barrier, his hands over his head.

The answer rang inside Riley's head like a brass gong. *Danford.* If Cuthbert wanted vengeance, the only way for him to truly get it was if Danford was back where he belonged. And if Danford returned to the war, surely Trent would be displaced, and Logan would be free of guilt at last.

As little as Riley wanted to give Cuthbert any satisfaction, at least when the asshole got what he wanted, the ghost war would disperse for good.

Riley pulled away from Logan and scuttled to Danford's side. "Danford. You always claimed you were in the right. This is your chance. Prove you have some shred of decency left. Take your place again and put this all to rest."

"I can't," Danford gibbered. "You don't know what it was like. The censure of my friends, who should have taken my part. I only wanted my daughter, my first born. The Stumps didn't deserve her." He jerked his chin at the clot of apparitions across the uneven ground. "You know what Cuthbert called her? A common little bitch. My Anna, my angel."

"But you killed his son." Riley hunkered down next to Danford, willing him to listen to reason. "That's all in the past, and you can't change it. But you can we—*redeem* yourself. Accept the consequences of your actions. Give Stump his vengeance and save an innocent man."

The ghost Danford broke from the crowd, his misty face suffused with half-resigned horror. *God, that must be Trent, playing Balch's role.* He glanced at Logan, who was staring at the Trent-Danford, his jaw tight and his fists clenched at his sides. As the script demanded, Trent-Danford stormed past them, his spectral hand brushing an icy trail on the back of Riley's neck.

The present-day Danford tracked his spirit double, rocking back and forth, his hands tearing clumps from the sparse fur lining of his parka hood. "No. No. No. I can't. Don't ask me to."

Cuthbert's voice rang out in tones of a fire-and-brimstone preacher. "If you think he's man enough to pay for his crimes, you're a bigger fool than I thought."

Logan drew Riley to his feet. "Bert's right. Balch is a coward. He won't step up. He's proved that for the last century and a half."

"But…" Riley tried to break away and winced, cradling his left hand.

Ah Christ. He was still bleeding from where that bastard had cut him. Logan gentled his hold on Riley's arm. Nothing could happen until Trent-as-Balch returned with the shotgun, so he had a little time left in this world. *I'm spending it caring for Riley.*

"Come here. Least I can do is bandage you up before I go."

Riley resisted for a moment, then gave in, and Logan drew him as far from the spirits as he could.

"Sit." He lowered Riley onto a fallen log, making sure he had a clear view of the spot Trent-Balch would reappear.

"I'm okay, Logan. We don't have time for this."

"I'm taking the time." *For the last time.* He dug in the pockets of his fake jacket, searching for Charmaine's bandana. When he pulled it out, something piggybacked it and fell to the ground.

"Shit." Riley lunged for it but Logan blocked him and urged him back onto the log, dropping a kiss on his forehead.

"I'll get it. You stay put." He checked for Trent-Balch again. Still nothing, but it had to be close. Minutes at most. His last minutes with Riley.

The object next to his boot was a little cloth bag, barely as big as the palm of his hand, a bit worse for wear after its dive into the mud. Logan caught a whiff of mint. Was this some costume sachet shit, to keep Max's spare costumes daisy fresh? The bag was lumpy, though. Something else was in there other than deodorizing herbs. He tugged at the drawstring.

"Don't open it." Riley's voice held a note of panic.

What the hell? He wasn't afraid of Cuthbert, but he's afraid of this?

So of course Logan ripped the damn thing apart. A faded green confetti of herbs fluttered to the ground, along with a large blue stone.

And a platinum wedding band.

Logan's heart tried to trip over itself. He picked up the ring and held it out. "What are you trying to do?"

Riley jumped up from the log, cradling his injured hand against his stomach. "Protect you, you big jerk. What do you think?"

"I think…" The blurred ghostly Trent-Balch returned, carrying his shotgun and the present-day Balch cringed, seeming to shrink inside the soiled folds of his parka. "I think we're out of time."

"No! Please, Logan, don't."

Logan evaded Riley, gritted his teeth and *willed. My battle. My debt. My choice.* He grabbed for the shotgun.

And got nothing but air. Trent-Balch continued on his way.

"What the fuck?" He caught up with him and tried again. Failed again. Logan had seconds at most before the place in the story where Trent had made his fateful choice. "Riley. Are you doing this?"

"No. You destroyed the charm bag. The anchor is gone."

"Anchor?"

Riley edged closer and reached for him. "The anchor to keep you here."

He stared at Riley's wide eyes, his trembling mouth, his hand resting over Logan's heart. *You. You're my anchor. You're the only reason I'd stay.* If he expected to make this work, he had to cut that anchor loose. He pulled the chain with the other ring out of his pocket.

He took Riley's hand, set the chain and both rings in his palm, and closed his fingers. "You keep this. Keep them both." Logan covered Riley's hand with his own. "I've got to do this."

"You don't." Riley threw the rings down. "Please, please don't. Please stay." He wrapped his hands behind Logan's neck and pulled him down into a kiss, his passion and heat startling in the double-chill of October midnight and paranormal proximity. Logan moaned into Riley's mouth, desperate for this last taste, a memory to take with him, to keep him warm, to help him remember being alive.

Christ, Riley was so much stronger than he was, always had been. He'd faced those drunken frat boys with his folklore smackdown. Owned up to being gay unapologetically. Hell, he'd have kissed Logan anywhere and everywhere, openly, if Logan hadn't been such a chickenshit, his dad's endless railing about keeping his public nose clean still rocketing around in his brain.

Whatever his dad said, though, loving Riley had been the best thing in his life. He ought to be brave enough to admit that before he left it behind.

Reluctantly, he disengaged from the kiss and rested his forehead against Riley's. "You're the hero, babe. *My* hero.

Always were." He kissed Riley again. Soft. Tender. Lingering. "I love you."

Then he pulled away and strode forward to stand between the spirit of Balch and the last place Trent had stood in this world. This time, when Balch held out the shotgun, Logan took it.

CHAPTER TWENTY-TWO

"Logan!" Riley lurched forward—too late. The instant Logan's hand closed around the stock of the shotgun, the ghost flickered and reformed with Logan's features superimposed on Balch's phantom face. In Logan's place, a young man in a PSU hoodie appeared and collapsed on the ground, curling into a fetal ball, and shielding his head with both arms. Danford let out a stifled sob.

Balch—no, Logan—moved toward the knot of townsfolk by the wagon's tailgate. By his stuttered pace, it was obvious he was fighting what the story demanded of him, but equally obvious that he couldn't stop the inevitable. Riley raced forward, passing him, hearing a faint protest as if Logan was calling to him from down a deep well.

He whirled and stood in front of Logan. "You can stop this, Logan, remember? Force of will. Belief. That's what it takes."

A hand like a steel band gripped Riley's wrist, and he looked away from Logan to meet the cold eyes of Cuthbert Stump.

"Vengeance is the most forceful will of all," Cuthbert crowed and yanked Riley into the thicket of ghosts. Cold jolted him each time he touched one. He resisted, tried to pull away, but Cuthbert's strength easily overcame his own.

They stopped next to the ghost of a young man loading a sack of flour into a wagon.

Riley faced Cuthbert with a bravado that was totally fake. "I'm not afraid of you. If I don't want to join the battle, then there's nothing you can do."

"Doesn't matter what you want. I want it enough for both of us. 'Sides, you belong here. Smelled it on you the first time I saw you. Blood of my blood, blood of his. This here's your place. Easy for you to slip in. All it takes is a little shove."

Riley tugged against that steely grip to no avail. "What are you talking about?"

"Don't you worry." Cuthbert's breath gusted over Riley's face, cold as January and stinking of the grave. "I'm right behind you."

He shoved.

Riley's nerves buzzed, his skin tingled, then went numb, as if he'd passed through a shower of static and ice. Suddenly, the scene wasn't ghostly at all. It was real. Solid. Forest Park had faded to a pale overlay and instead he was in a frontier street, rutted and muddy, a bag of flour just leaving his hands to land on a stack of other supplies.

Damn it. I'm in the ghost war? How? Who...?

He glanced around wildly. If he squinted hard, he could still see the clearing, the Witch's Castle looming against the hillside. Where he had stood, a young man in pioneer garb kneeled in the mud, bewildered alarm on his face.

In the next instant, the young man was joined by another man, older, dressed in a dark bulky sweater and rough work pants, who staggered several steps before crumpling to the ground.

A yank on his elbow forced Riley around. Cuthbert's angular face sneered from under a flat-brimmed hat. A young girl, maybe in her mid-teens cowered next to Riley, her eyes fixed on a spot over his shoulder.

Holy shit. She must be Anna Balch. And if she was Anna, that made him—

As if something had taken control of his body, Riley was forced to turn in the direction of Anna's terrified gaze and saw Logan-as-Balch advancing toward him, an all-too-real shotgun tucked under his arm.

God. That young man in the park must be Mortimer Stump, reanimated within twenty feet of the man who killed him.

Which meant Riley had taken his place and was sixteen paces from having his face blown away by Danford Balch.

Only Danford wasn't Danford. He was Logan and Riley was about to be murdered by his own lover.

Not just tonight, but forever.

Beyond Logan, Riley could still make out the shadowy form of the real Danford Balch in his tattered coat, watching with a combination of fear and shame. Logan's face was twisted with his effort to stop, but Riley knew it wouldn't help. Logan had taken the role willingly and he couldn't escape.

Cuthbert's laugh rang out in the street. "I know you can hear me, Balch. Don't you recognize him?" Cuthbert gripped Riley-Mortimer's shoulder in a viselike grip. "He fits right here. Blood of my blood." The grip tightened further, and Riley whimpered. "Too bad it's tainted by the blood of your whore daughter."

In the shadowy park, Balch's horrified gaze flicked from Anna to Riley.

"She whelped, your bitch of a daughter. Didn't you know? While you cowered in the woods, she birthed a son. When we sold her off to Eli Morrel out in Hillsboro, she took the brat with her. Changed his name." He shook Riley's shoulder again. "He's the last of the line. The line that mixes your filthy blood with mine. And tonight?" His fingers closed like a vise on Riley's shoulder. "That line ends."

Balch's scream was audible through a century and a half of time. Baring his teeth in a grimace, he staggered forward, hands outstretched and fingers curled into claws.

But Riley's attention shifted back to Logan-Danford, who raised the shotgun, his eyes his own, tortured behind the mask of the role he'd taken on. Riley strained to move, but between the bounds of his own role and Cuthbert's grip on his shoulder, he couldn't duck or dodge. He could do nothing but face Logan and wait for the end.

"I'm sorry," Logan mouthed, even as his finger tightened on the trigger.

Riley nodded. "I know," he whispered. "It's all right. I love you." He closed his eyes.

The shotgun blast ripped the air, deafening Riley, but he felt nothing. The accounts said Mortimer died instantly. Is this what they meant? No pain? Riley's hand crept to his chest, and he opened his eyes.

Balch—with no overlay of Logan's features—stood at the end of the wagon, townsfolk converging on him from all sides, his shotgun smoking in the chill air. Beyond him, behind the curtain of time, Logan crouched, a discarded bundle of matted fur and stained nylon on the ground in front of him.

Balch gestured at a spot near Riley's feet with the barrel of his gun. Riley looked down. Cuthbert Stump lay moaning in the mud, his chest an open wound.

"I told them it was an accident, Stump," Balch said, as the crowd hemmed him in and a burly man in a blacksmith's apron yanked the shotgun out of his hands. "I was aiming for you."

Cuthbert took one last gurgling breath, and in a flash brighter than a carbon arc spotlight, the entire tableau disappeared.

CHAPTER TWENTY-THREE

"Riley!" Logan had shouted, he was sure, but he couldn't hear himself, as if his ears were stuffed with cotton. He couldn't see a damn thing either, but the vision of Riley's face, superimposed over Mortimer's, was burned into his brain. *No, goddamn it, no!* Kneeling in the mud, he pressed his fists to his belly as he fought the urge to howl.

Christ, he'd done it again. Pulled a man he cared about into a nightmare. This time, though, Logan wasn't sure he could survive the loss. Trent had been his best friend, a fuck buddy who might have turned into more given time. But he loved Riley to the bottom of his wretched worthless soul.

"Help me. Help me. Jesus God, someone please help me." A voice he hadn't heard in seven years bled through the ringing in his ears. *Trent. Thank God.*

Although his vision still consisted of alternating black and white blotches, Logan crawled toward the pitiful whimper, feeling his way along the ground, until he ran into a jeans-clad thigh.

"Trent? It's me."

"Logan?" Trent's body shuddered, and his hands scrabbled on the leather sleeves of Logan's jacket. "It's really you? What —"

"Never mind. Let's get you out of here."

"God, please, yes. But I can't—I can't see. Why can't I see?"

"Don't know, man. I'm having trouble with that myself. Piss-poor rescuer I turned out to be, eh?" Trent wrapped his arms around Logan's waist and sobbed against his chest. Logan rocked him, heedless of the mud and the weeds that caught at his clothes and skin. Rain began to patter on the ground, on his face, in fat, sullen drops. "Shhh. It's okay. You're okay now."

Logan, however, might never be okay again.

He kissed the top of Trent's head and stroked his hair, as the other man's sobs gradually subsided.

Footsteps pounded past. "Someone get the medic." Julie's voice. "Riley!"

Riley?

"Yeah. Give me a minute. My eyes are wonky."

At the sound of that voice, relief flooded Logan's chest and his head swam. Riley was here? Alive? Christ, he needed to see. He squinted, struggling to focus his still-blotchy vision, and tried to get up, but Trent wouldn't release him.

"What the hell just happened?" Scott's voice cut through Trent's fading sobs. "Where'd that light come from? Where'd it go? Where'd that other guy go? Who the hell is that with Conner?" Scott's footsteps thumped and squished past him. "Where's Max?"

"Not sure about Max. At the trailhead maybe?" Riley's voice was tired, dispirited. "But we kind of staged a supernatural search and recovery."

"No fucking shit?" Scott let out a whoop they could probably hear at the St. Johns Bridge. "Give me the deets. Are these the guys from the story?"

"Yeah. The men who disappeared were the temporal avatars of Danford Balch, Cuthbert Stump, and Mortimer Stump. They vanished when Danford Balch's quest to kill the right person succeeded. Come on. I'll fill you in." Their footsteps retreated, squelching in the mud.

Why did Riley sound so defeated? He'd fucking done it! He'd deactivated the ghost war. Trent was free. Logan was free. Riley wasn't dead. What could be the problem?

Surely any minute now, as soon as Riley finished debriefing Scott, he'd appear next to Logan and put one of those warm hands on his neck the way he always did when Logan was having a bad day.

But when his vision finally cleared enough to see anything, the first person he saw was Julie, glaring at him with that I'd-as-soon-cut-your-balls-off-as-look-at-you expression.

He groaned. The downside of surviving the night was all the shit he'd have to clean up. He'd betrayed Riley again. Twice. Three times if he counted getting him trapped in the ghost war as the fucking murder victim. Plus, he'd ejected Julie from the story of a lifetime.

He wasn't sorry about that. Who knew what could have happened? She could have ended up as Anna Stump, and they'd have had to wait another seven years to rescue her.

But Riley. Yeah, he was sorry about everything he'd done that had hurt Riley, starting with that heartless scene he'd staged back in Eugene, all those months ago.

He scanned the clearing, which was now filled with the thankfully solid forms of the milling crew. Max was notably absent, and Riley— No, there he was, approaching a man in workman's clothes. *Holy shit.* That must be Joseph Geddes, his grandfather's downfall and Cuthbert's ticket out of time. Poor guy was going to need some serious therapy and job retraining.

Trent snuffled against his neck. *Another guy with therapy in his future.*

"Trent? Hey, man, let's get you up. I'm gonna turn you over to someone who'll take care of you, okay? Get you something hot to drink."

Trent moaned as Logan helped him to his feet. "Can you make it alcoholic? Because Jesus, I need to get seriously wasted."

"Yeah, sure. Whatever. I just... I've got to..." Logan practically thrust Trent at a passing grip. "Take him to the medic, would you, man?" He'd make it up to Trent later, but first, he needed to prove to Riley that he was boyfriend material.

Fuck that. *Husband* material.

Starting right fucking now.

After his vision had cleared from the ghost war implosion, the light of epiphany had nearly blinded Riley a second time. Clearly Logan had no trouble with public displays of affection when the affection-ee was the correct person, because while Riley had given Scott the rundown of what happened inside the ghost war, Logan had sat there, cuddling with Trent in full view of the crew. Damn it, practically on camera.

Riley had obviously never been the correct person. Time he faced that fact and moved on.

So he turned his back on Logan and Trent, and hunkered down next to the shivering man in workman's clothes. "Mr. Geddes?" The man looked up, eyes wide and terrified. "You are Joseph Geddes, aren't you?"

"You know my—" His voice rasped worse than a lifelong smoker's. Guess sixty or seventy years of not using it would do that to a guy. "I don't... Where...?" He rolled to his hands and knees, retching into the weeds.

Riley beckoned to the show medic, who was already sprinting toward them. "Alonzo, this is Mr. Geddes. He'll need some serious TLC. He's been... away for quite a while."

Alonzo nodded and knelt by Geddes, who'd already stopped heaving, but had resumed shivering.

Riley turned away. Logan still had his arms around Trent. So much for the stupid expectations that Logan's last-minute declaration of love had raised. It had clearly been nothing but battlefield adrenaline. Riley's own adrenaline-crash had left him feeling as hollow and transparent as one of the Stumptown spirits.

He trudged across the clearing, his shoes and the hem of his jeans soaked and caked with filth. Metal glinted at his feet. *The chain. The rings.* He picked them up, along with a generous helping of Forest Park, and shoved them in his pocket before anyone else saw them and asked inconvenient questions.

"Hey." Logan appeared at his side, his voice low. Neutral. No doubt he didn't want to muddy the relationship waters in front of Trent. "You okay?"

Riley nodded, afraid to look at him in case Julie's assertions about his stupid open face were true. "Yeah. Fine." He swallowed and his shoulders shook momentarily. "We were wrong. It was Balch's war all along."

"We were right enough. You did it, Riley. You fucking did it. You saved Trent."

He nodded numbly. "I'm glad you found your friend. I've got to go."

Logan murmured something that sounded like "fuck sensitive," and he grabbed Riley by the shoulder and spun him around.

"Damn straight you've got to go. You've got to go with me." Logan caught Riley's head with both hands, lacing his fingers through Riley's hair, and kissed him, hot and hard.

Riley squeaked into Logan's mouth. *What? But— Oh, screw it.* He wrapped his arms around Logan's waist and participated fully in the tongue war.

A chorus of whistles erupted around them, along with a smattering of applause.

Logan pulled away and smiled down at him. "Sorry." He swiped his thumb across Riley's lips.

Riley blinked. God, he was probably a dead ringer for that stupid cartoon of himself Julie had drawn, with his smile curved up above his eyes. "I'm not." He tucked his hands under Logan's jacket, the better to feel his warmth. "You mean it? You're back for good?"

"Yep. You and me, babe. No matter where you go, I'll be there."

Scott strode over. "You guys. I can't even— Oh my fucking God. You should see the footage Zack got through that crazy curtain. Only problem is, I'm not sure anyone will buy it as anything but FX."

Riley reluctantly withdrew his hands from under Logan's jacket, but grabbed his hand instead. "Yeah. I expect the light played hell with the camera."

"Fuck it. We'll work with it. The thing is, I've got a whole new idea for a paranormal investigation show. But this time, the real stuff. Like you said, Riley: research, that's the ticket. It won't be a series. Specials. Only when we've got a rock-awesome lead like this one." Scott scrubbed his hands across his head, causing his hair to stick up until he looked like a manic bearded Einstein. "Holy fucking shit."

Riley blinked. Had Scott actually used his name? "I don't think Max'll go for that, Scott. He didn't like the experience much." The last time Riley had seen him, Max had been racing up the trail like a scared *wabbit*.

"Fuck Max." Scott glanced at their interlaced fingers. "No offense. I want to star the two of you. Gay guys kick ghost butt. *Queer as Folk* meets *The Haunting*. High concept all the way."

Logan laughed. "Not for me, man. I've got an architecture degree to finish." He kissed Riley's temple. "What Riley wants is up to him."

"I'm on board for the research, Scott, but I don't know about the on-camera stuff. I'm not weally—"

"Later." Logan pulled Riley past the cluster of crew.

Scott kept pace with them. "I'm not shitting you."

"*Later*, Scott." Logan lengthened his stride until Riley had to trot to keep up.

Julie jogged up on Scott's other side. "Nice idea, Scott, but I've already got Riley locked for my next project. Right, Riley?"

"Well..." He glanced at Logan, who mouthed, *Later,* and happiness burbled under his sternum like warm champagne. "Later, Jules."

Julie winked at him and linked her arm with Scott's and led him off. "I'm sure we can work something out, Scott. Let's do lunch. We'll talk."

Breathless after Logan had hauled him up the trail at a near-sprint for a couple of minutes, Riley tugged on his hand. "So. We're building up quite a list of things to do later. What do you have in mind for now?"

Logan stopped and faced him on the path. "Is anybody watching us?"

Above them, the support crew appeared around a bend of the Wildwood Trail, obviously lured away from craft services by the supernatural light show. Behind them, the tramp and squelch of feet in the mud signaled the first of the camera guys slogging their equipment up the path. The two of them were caught in the middle.

"We're kind of center stage. In about thirty seconds, everyone will be watching."

"Excellent." Logan dropped to his knees on the muddy trail.

"*Logan.*" Heat washed up Riley's neck, and he glanced around wildly. "Public displays of affection are one thing, but I don't think you should blow me in the middle of my workplace."

"I'm not blowing you." His eyes sparkled in the intermittent moonlight. "At least not yet, although that's another thing on the agenda for later." He took Riley's hands, despite their less than pristine state. "I'm proposing."

Riley's heart did a double backflip, and his breath stalled somewhere below his throat. "You're what?" he croaked.

"Proposing. I used to have some rings on me, but—"

Riley fumbled them out of his jeans pocket and slapped them into Logan's hand. "I picked them up after we, well, you know."

"Good job, hero." A grin flickered and faded on Logan's face. He peered down the path at the camera crew. "Yo, Zack. You still got that handheld?"

Zack hefted the camera. "Always."

"Then fire it up." At the tender look on Logan's face, Riley's knees nearly buckled. "I want to remember this moment forever, or maybe longer, and I'm taking no chances."

"Aaaand," Zack called, "action!"

"Riley Morrel." Logan's voice was husky, and he cleared his throat. "Sorry. Take two. Be sure you get my good side, Zack." He placed one hand over his heart, rings in his other palm. "Riley Morrel, rock-awesome folklorist and kick-ass ghostbuster, will you do me the very great honor of marrying me?"

Riley laughed, joy rocketing from his feet to the top of his head. "Of course I will." He reached for the rings, but Logan closed them in his fist, his expression earnest.

"You need to be sure, Riley."

"Me? I've been sure since that first ride on your Ducati. What about you?"

"I've got no doubts. This is it. You. Me. Married. Till death do us part. Although..." Logan nodded down the trail where Julie and Scott were advancing on them, then up the trail, where Max approached like an attention-seeking missile. "Considering your job, and what the two of us endured tonight, death doesn't seem like much of an obstacle either." He kissed Riley's grimy knuckles. "So. You and me. Get it?"

Riley laughed. "Got it."

"Good." Logan tugged him down, wrapped both arms around him, and kissed him. Long, hot, *perfect*.

"And that," Logan murmured against Riley's lips, "is a wrap."

WHAT'S NEXT?
FOLLOW TRENT'S JOURNEY IN

WOLF'S CLOTHING

Running from the past.

Trent Pielmeyer is *so done* with legend tripping. Hauntings? Nope. Cryptid sightings? Hard pass. Dimensional portals? Not just no but oh, *hell* no. Because after seven years' captivity in a whacked-out alternate reality, he's been there and done that and done that and done that. No more supernatural shenanigans for him. Ever. Full stop.

Wrestling with the past.

When Christophe Clavret spots Trent in a Portland bar, he detects a kindred spirit—another man attempting to outrun the darkness of his own soul. But despite their sizzling chemistry, Trent's hatred of the uncanny makes Christophe hesitant to confide the truth: he's a werewolf, one of a dwindling line, the victim of a genetic curse extending back to feudal Europe.

Overtaken by the past.

But sinister forces are at work, threatening more than their inescapable attraction. If Christophe can't win Trent's trust, and if Trent can't overcome his fear of the paranormal, the price might be not only Trent's freedom but Christophe's very humanity.

Or it could cost both their lives.

Wolf's Clothing is an age gap, hurt/comfort, opposites attract supernatural suspense romance featuring old rivalries, disapproving families, awkward reunions, disbelieving investigators, and, of course, an HEA.

WOLF'S CLOTHING

How could so many people fit in a bar no bigger than his dad's study? Granted, his dad's study was big, but shit. Trent clutched the edge of the bar counter, willing his heartbeat to settle. The last time he'd been in a crowd this large, the others had all been dead for a century and a half.

It hadn't turned out well.

The bartender stopped in front of him. "No one under twenty-one allowed."

Trent pulled out his wallet and tossed his Oregon license onto the bar. Thank God he'd still had it in his pocket when he'd tumbled out of the ghost war. Although he hadn't seen more than nineteen birthdays, according to this, he was twenty-six. Chronologically old enough to drink. Emotionally? God, did he ever need it.

The bartender checked his birthdate. "Guess you're older than you look. What'll it be?"

"You have Woodford Reserve?"

"Yep."

"Make it a double. Neat."

"Coming up."

Trent rested his elbows on the bar and bowed his head. *Breathe in through your nose; out through your mouth. Concentrate. Calm.* He'd gotten through the third round of Deborah's stupid meditation exercises—not exactly easy when the decibel level in the bar rivaled that of a punk-rock concert—when the stool next to him scraped on the floor. He opened his eyes. *Nice thighs.* His new neighbor sported dress slacks in a smooth gray wool. His father tried to force him into similar high-end suits on a regular basis whenever the family appeared in public, which was one of the reasons that Trent insisted on wearing his thrift-store wardrobe.

Not that he didn't appreciate high-end clothes, but it was the principle of the thing.

The bartender tossed a beer mat in front of Trent. *Stumptown Spirits* was printed on it in spiky letters, along with a logo of a ghost with staring red eyes drinking a beer. Trent shuddered and turned it over.

"Not a fan of nonrepresentational art?" His new neighbor's voice matched his pants—smooth, high-class, with a definite European flavor. French? Maybe, but it was slight.

The bartender set Trent's bourbon on the overturned beer mat without a blink. Trent shrugged and took a sip. "Don't like being watched." He stole a glance at the stranger in the mirror behind the bar.

He wasn't as sneaky as he'd hoped, because—*busted*—the guy met his gaze and a smile quirked his mouth.

Jesus *fuck*. Gorgeous. His chin-length hair was on the reddish side of brown, his close-trimmed beard a shade redder. His eyes were the same color as the liquor in Trent's glass, and his features were chiseled, something about them calling to mind the illustrations in Trent's nearly forgotten medieval history book. *Ascetic*? Was that the word? Like the face of a monk or a saint in mid-martyrdom.

Trent forced himself to stop staring. *What the hell are you doing, asshole? First Bishop, and now a random stranger? You're here to reconnect with Logan, to get your own life back on track. Eyes on the prize and tell your dick to keep its opinions to itself.*

"I'd offer to buy you a drink, but you appear to have one already. May I join you?"

"It's a free country."

The guy made a sound that would have been a snort from anyone less classy. "For some, perhaps." He caught the bartender's eye and pointed to Trent's glass before turning back. "Christophe Clavret."

Oh, what the hell. "Trent." They shook hands. Christophe's grip was firm, lingering long enough for Trent to recognize it as an invitation. In the old days, before he'd sort of hooked up with Logan, he'd have been totally down with the implied offer. Those days were behind him though. Weren't they? He ought to have grown out of them, but sometimes he didn't seem to have grown at all.

Christophe accepted his drink from the bartender and slid his credit card across the bar. Amex Black. *Cool.* Trent could let the guy pay for his drink without guilt.

With a sideways glance, Christophe turned his beer mat over to match Trent's.

Nice touch.

If Trent had been interested in a pickup, Christophe would have scored major points. But this wasn't a pickup. Trent was only killing time until Logan showed. So why did the idea of facing Logan suddenly fill his belly with lead, while sparring with Christophe sent a buzz through his veins like in his acting days, in those heady moments just before he'd stepped onstage?

Must be because one thing mattered and the other was just for fun. He'd always been better at blowing things off. He'd never taken anything seriously except acting, legend tripping, and Logan—and look where that had gotten him.

Was that the problem? Logan was part of the ordeal, snarled up in the Witch's Castle nightmare along with Trent. *He's still the only person who'll ever understand you. Stop fucking around.*

He swiveled on his barstool to face Christophe. "Let's get things straight. You're hot. I know it. You know it."

Christophe grinned. "Indeed? How gratifying."

"Doesn't mean we're gonna hook up."

A trick of the light made Christophe's eyes appear to flash molten gold. "Why is that?"

"I'm . . . well . . . kind of here to meet someone."

"You sound uncertain."

"Nothing's certain."

"Except death and taxes, no?"

"Don't be too sure about that." Trent had learned recently that death could be negotiable, and his father made it his life's work to prove taxes weren't a certainty either.

Christophe grinned. "You, my friend, are a man with issues."

"That a problem?"

"Not in the least." He leaned closer, his voice lowering to a suggestive growl. "I love a man with issues. Happy people are so boring. Who was it who said, 'All happy families are alike'? Tolstoy?"

"Don't ask me. I was a theater major."

"Ah. Then we can rest assured it wasn't Shakespeare. You are an actor, then?"

Trent's stomach clenched. "Not anymore."

"A student?"

"Nope. I more or less dropped out years ago."

"Years ago? You must have been a mere child."

"I was nineteen."

"How old are you now?"

Trent glanced at Christophe from under his lashes and took a deliberate sip of his bourbon. "Nineteen."

Christophe blinked, his eyebrows lifting. "I don't—"

"Or twenty-six. Maybe two hundred and five. Depends on who you ask." And whose skin he was in at the moment.

Christophe turned and leaned an elbow on the bar, his knee brushing Trent's leg. "What if I ask you?"

"Then I'd say I'm old enough to know a wolf in sheep's clothing when I see one."

AUTHOR'S NOTE

As is the habit of authors, I've taken some liberties with history for the purposes of my story.

Danford Balch was indeed the first man legally hanged in the new state of Oregon, on October 17, 1859, for the murder of his son-in-law, Mortimer Stump. Accounts of the crime include Cuthbert Stump's insulting remarks about his new daughter-in-law, and Danford's subsequent incarceration, escape, and recapture.

While it's a matter of public record that Anna Balch Stump married Eli Morrel of Hillsboro about a year after her first husband's death, there's no evidence that she and Mortimer conceived a child in their week-long marriage.

Personalities and motivations are strictly my own invention and are not intended to be a reflection on the nature of historical persons.

A MESSAGE FROM E.J.

Dear Reader,

Thank you so much for reading *Camera Shy*, my first plunge back into contemporary romantic comedy in (jeez, really?) two years. I'm so happy you've taken this journey with me! I'd be immensely grateful if you'd take a moment to leave a review at the retailer and any other site you use for reviews. Believe me, reviews make an *enormous* difference to the health and well-being of books (and not incidentally, to their associated authors!).

Did I mention I don't spend a lot of time in the real(ish) world? My backlist is heavily weighted toward paranormal rom com, but contemporary rom com, supernatural suspense, and (just once) historical, are sprinkled in there too. Pop on over to my website, https://ejrussell.com, for all the deets on my books and audio.

For exclusive content, ARC giveaways, not to mention gratuitous dance videos and cat pictures, join me in Reality Optional, my Facebook fan group (https://facebook.com/groups/reality.optional). My newsletter is the place to get the latest dish on new releases, sales, and more. I promise I only send one out when I've got...well...news. You can subscribe here: https://ejrussell.com/newsletter.

All my best,
—E

ALSO BY E.J.

Paranormal Romance
Mythmatched Universe
Fae Out of Water Trilogy
Cutie and the Beast
The Druid Next Door
Bad Boy's Bard

Supernatural Selection Trilogy
Single White Incubus
Vampire With Benefits
Demon on the Down-Low

Other Mythmatched Romances
Howling on Hold
Possession in Session
Witch Under Wraps
Cursed is the Worst
The Skinny on Djinni

Mythmatched Companion Stories
Rusty's Really Bad Day (free to newsletter subscribers)
Second First Date (free to newsletter subscribers)

Quest Investigations Mysteries
Five Dead Herrings
The Hound of the Burgervilles
The Lady Under the Lake

Death on Denial

Art Medium Series
The Artist's Touch
Tested in Fire
Art Medium: The Complete Collection (omnibus edition)

Legend Tripping Series
Stumptown Spirits
Wolf's Clothing

Enchanted Occasions Series
Best Beast
Nudging Fate
Devouring Flame

Royal Powers Series (shared world)
Duking It Out
Duke the Hall
King's Ex

Magic Emporium Series (shared world)
Purgatory Playhouse

Monster Till Midnight

Historical Romance
Silent Sin

Contemporary Romance
Camera Shy
The Thomas Flair
Mystic Man
For a Good Time, Call… (A Bluewater Bay novel, with Anne Tenino)

ABOUT THE AUTHOR

E.J. Russell (she/her), author of the award-winning Mythmatched paranormal romance series, writes LGBTQ+ romance and mystery in a rainbow of flavors. Count on high snark, low angst, and happy endings.

Reality? Eh, not so much.

She's married to Curmudgeonly Husband, a man who cares even less about sports than she does. Luckily, C.H. also loves to cook, or all three of their children (Lovely Daughter and Darling Sons A and B) would have survived on nothing but Cheerios, beef jerky, and Satsuma mandarins (the extent of E.J.'s culinary skill set).

E.J. also writes traditional cozy mystery as Nelle Heran. She lives in rural Oregon, enjoys visits from her wonderful adult children, and indulges in good books, red wine, and the occasional hyperbole.

News & Social Media:
Website: https://ejrussell.com
Newsletter: https://ejrussell.com/newsletter

ACKNOWLEDGEMENTS

Many thanks to Natasha Snow for the rockin' cover; to NOLAKim PA for keeping me organized and reminding me to peek out of my writer cave occasionally; to Carol-Ann Galloway for wrestling with this manuscript originally and to Meg DesCamp for bashing at it in its second life; to my family for endless support; and of course to you, my readers, for accompanying me on this wild journey.

Without all of you, I wouldn't be able to continue to do what I love.